CANINES & COCKTAILS

CANINES & COCKTAILS

Novellas of dogs & drinks by

DELILAH S. DAWSON

KEVIN HEARNE

CHUCK WENDIG

Horned Lark Press

This is a work of fiction. All of the characters, organizations, and events portrayed in these stories are either products of the author's imagination or are used fictitiously.

A Horned Lark Press Book
Published by Horned Lark Press
2482 Yonge St. #1087
Toronto, ON M4P 2H5

www.hornedlarkpress.com

First Edition
ISBN: 978-1-7382792-0-3

Printed in a Secret Volcano Lair by Antifascist Capybaras

BY DELILAH S. DAWSON

The Violence

Bloom

Midnight at the Houdini

Mine

Camp Scare

Servants of the Storm

THE SHADOW SERIES, WRITTEN AS LILA BOWEN

Wake of Vultures

Conspiracy of Ravens

Malice of Crows

Treason of Hawks

THE HIT SERIES

Hit

Strike

THE BLUD SERIES

Wicked as They Come

Wicked as She Wants

Wicked After Midnight

Wicked Ever After

STAR WARS

Inquisitor: Rise of the Red Blade

Galaxy's Edge: Black Spire

Phasma

The Skywalker Saga

THE MINECRAFT MOB SQUAD SERIES

Minecraft: Mob Squad

Minecraft: Never Say Nether

Minecraft: Don't Fear the Creeper

Disney Mirrorverse: Pure of Heart

CREATOR-OWNED COMICS

Ladycastle

Sparrowhawk

Star Pig

www.delilahsdawson.com

BY KEVIN HEARNE

THE SEVEN KENNINGS

A Plague of Giants

A Blight of Blackwings

A Curse of Krakens

THE IRON DRUID CHRONICLES

Hounded	*Hunted*
Hexed	*Shattered*
Hammered	*Staked*
Tricked	*Besieged*
Trapped	*Scourged*

THE IRON DRUID CHRONICLES NOVELLAS

Two Ravens and One Crow	*A Prelude to War*
Grimoire of the Lamb	*First Dangle and Other Stories*

OBERON'S MEATY MYSTERIES

The Purloined Poodle

The Squirrel on the Train

The Buzz Kill

The Chartreuse Chanteuse

www.kevinhearne.com

BY CHUCK WENDIG

Black River Orchard

The Book of Accidents

Zer0es

Invasive

Dust & Grim

You Can Do Anything, Magic Skeleton

WANDERERS DUOLOGY

Wanderers

Wayward

MIRIAM BLACK

Blackbirds

Mockingbird

The Cormorant

Thunderbird

The Raptor & The Wren

Vultures

THE HEARTLAND TRILOGY

Under the Empyrean Sky

Blightborn

The Harvest

www.terribleminds.com

THE CHARTREUSE CHANTEUSE

CHANTEUSE

BY KEVIN HEARNE

CHAPTER 1

The Quick and the Dead and the Sausage

Do any other animals display the utility of cows? They are beef and the source of many delicious recipes. And the range of products produced from cow squirts is a whole thing called Dairy. (Atticus says I should say *milk* instead of *cow squirts* because humans might find it a bit icky, but he also won't explain why, so I am sticking to cow squirts until I get an explanation.) Cows are also leather for jackets and footballs and upholstery and those chewy rawhide strips Atticus won't give me because he says I make a mess, but he doesn't understand that the mess is part of what makes them so dang good. Cows are amazing.

If you thought I was going somewhere with that, I wasn't. Sometimes I just think about food and it makes me happy, so that's reason enough to share. I don't need a plot.

Except Atticus says I need a plot.

Luckily, I have one of those, but it doesn't let me think about food as much as I'd like, so I am going to share some food stuff (but not foodstuffs) every so often to keep myself happy. Because what happened was very sad. There were these sausages, you see, perfectly good sausages, and no one ate them. Plus, there were some dead people. I'll let you decide which was more important. I know my answer.

The sadness began in the main chunk of Australia, rather than the part where we live now, which is Tasmania. Atticus had taken Starbuck and me up there and we found a demon in a fire and some monsters in the mountains and got hardly any food. I mean, sure, we got some nice pets from people and we got promises that we'd get some great sausages later from some visiting Scottish people, but we didn't get anything crammed into our meat holes. (Atticus says I should just say "we didn't eat anything" but he won't explain that either, so I am going to insist that my meat hole needs to be filled with foot-longs until he tells me why it's wrong.)

After our adventures, we boarded an overnight ferry from Melbourne to Tasmania and Atticus's new girlfriend, Rose Badgely, picked us up at the terminal or dock or whatever it's called. This was on a Friday morning, which is important because it was that Friday night that everything got sad. But Rose was very happy to see us, because we'd been gone for seventeen years or whatever, some unit of time I can't grasp except that it was long enough for her to miss us. She almost tackled Atticus when she hugged him and she made lots of kissy noises and that got Starbuck excited and he started to hump her leg and I thought that was pretty funny. Eventually she knelt down and gave me a hug around the neck and kissed my check and made high-pitched happy squeaks like she always does when she gives us love, and she got Starbuck to calm down and accept attention with only some minor twitching, aided by a stern mental warning from Atticus.

"What happened to you?" she asked me, noticing some bald spots where some of my fur had singed off.

"That fire in the Blue Mountains," Atticus said.

"Connor, you said you were going to help put it out, not send the dogs into it!" She calls him Connor because that's the name he uses with other humans nowadays, but I still call him Atticus.

"We did help. And Oberon's going to be fine. His coat will be all sleek and shiny again in no time."

<It better,> I told him through our mental link. <Poodles are okay with stylized grooming, but this patchy stuff looks like I have mange or something.>

We piled into her tiny car, which was not designed for the comfort of large Irish wolfhounds like myself, but I liked it because you could smell the ghosts of old fast-food meal deals consumed on stakeouts. Did I mention that Rose is a detective? She's actually a detective inspector, which is sort of like saying *canine dog* or *feline cat*, but humans like their formal titles. Atticus said the detective part was what she did, and the inspector part was her rank, like captain, but why they used *inspector* when *captain* was sitting right there wasn't a thing that he knew, so I chalked it up to English being weird. As a rule, she liked to be called Inspector instead of Detective.

During the drive, Starbuck and I enjoyed the smells coming in through the open windows for a while, but we curled up for a nap eventually and woke up when we got to Rose's house in Launceston. She was excited because Atticus had agreed to join her at an open-air concert that night at some public park, and *we* got excited when she said she'd prepare a picnic basket.

Open-air concerts are great. You get to roll around in some grass, which is the best; you get all these people saying how beautiful you are and then they want to pet you, which is the bester; and then you get snacks, which is the bestest. I should probably say something about the music part of concerts, so I will say, uh…I don't care. I mean, I do like music—Danny Elfman is still my favorite soundtrack composer; that work he did recently for *Wednesday* was fantastic—but crooning humans usually don't sing about anything interesting. The best song I've heard so far is "My Bologna" by Weird Al Yankovic and yet, somehow, humans are not properly obsessed with it. Atticus told me that this is because the majority of humans like to listen to songs about mating habits.

"Most songs," he said, "are in fact about mating habits. Even the ones that don't seem like they are. It's kind of a game to figure out how the words actually mean something else."

<Are you saying "My Bologna" is code for something else?>

"No, that one is a rare exception. I think. I might have to revisit the lyrics. But I think it's confined to the joys of eating bologna."

The artist that they were going to listen to was apparently not to Rose's usual taste, as far as music went, but Rose was a friend of a woman named Harry—short for Harriet—who was also a friend of the artist. So it was more of a support-your-friend thing than an I-like-this-music thing.

The artist in question had a stage name that Atticus had to confirm that he heard correctly: Koochie Koo. But Harry told us, once we got to the park and settled down on a checkered blanket, that Koochie Koo's real name was Shiloh Timmins, and she hailed from Virginia in the United States. She and Harry had become pen pals when they were little kids and had kept in touch until the present.

"We met in person about three years ago, when I visited the States," Harry said. Her voice was a bit higher-pitched than

Rose's, but she still had that same Australian accent. "But this is the first time Shiloh's been to Tasmania. She scheduled this appearance specially so we could meet up again."

I liked Harry instantly. She gave great belly rubs and smelled like lavender and plums. She had dark brown skin like Rose, wore dangly silver earrings that tinkled and a diamond on one side of her nose, but no bracelets that might get caught in my fur. It was obvious she was the kind of human that other humans would fly around the world to hang out with, and I hoped she would come visit Rose more often.

The belly rub ended when Koochie Koo was announced because Rose and Harry started clapping and saying "Woooo!" which is one of many ways that humans signify their approval of other humans. Atticus told us privately that Koochie Koo sang old human music from a century ago, which is like ten months or something. And since they didn't have electric guitars a century ago, the band was a motley assortment of tootling hornblowers.

<Horns sound like poots,> Starbuck said, since the baritone saxophones and trombones were prominent at first. <Or unhappy geese.>

I agreed with him. Koochie Koo was a white lady who wore a sheer green dress that only came down to her knees and a headband with a big green stone on it, and it was definitely a decorative thing instead of a dang-I-need-this-for-my-shaggymane thing, because her honey-colored hair was kinda pasted to her skull and rippled in waves.

<How did she get her hair to look like that, Atticus?> I asked, because I hadn't seen a human do that since Gwen Stefani and I'd always assumed Gwen just did it with her superpowers. (I know she has superpowers because of that one song where she turned her shit into bananas.) He replied mentally to me in his Irish accent, which he started doing five billion years ago, soon after we came to Tasmania, so he could feel like himself again. He always spoke aloud in his American accent though since his passport was from the United States. If he didn't sound American, people would ask questions he didn't want to answer.

She probably used mousse, he said, and that was the strangest thing I'd ever heard.

<How could she use a moose for that? Did the moose slobber on her hair and create those waves with its tongue? And what the heck is a moose doing in Australia?>

He explained that mousse was a creamy hairstyling product that sounded like the animal but absolutely wasn't. But mousse could also be a creamy dessert you found sometimes on restaurant menus, so I just filed that under reason five thousand why English makes no sense.

Anyway, Koochie Koo's voice was warm and low and syrupy instead of high and screechy, so Starbuck and I appreciated that about her even if she didn't sing about anything good.

We rolled around in the grass. People petted us. And most importantly, we got snacks!

First, there were succulent chunks of dry-cured sausage. Next, a dollop of soft goat cheese, which I probably should have tried to savor but look, it's hard to savor dollops. And to top it off, we got some of those rawhide strips that we were allowed to tear up in the grass but absolutely not take home. Starbuck and I laid into them with vigor because there was a time limit.

I thought when the singing was over, we'd go home, but that's not what happened. There was a lot of clapping, some grunting as people levered themselves up on old weak haunches, and then we headed across the street with Harry to a hotel that had a bar and bistro on the ground floor with outdoor seating. We were going to meet Koochie Koo there and the humans were going to have a cocktail, while Starbuck and I were going to get a shot of whipped cream.

<Fluffy cow squirts! Yes food!> Starbuck said.

The humans kinda scrunched a bunch of small tables together on the patio, and Atticus told the server, a tanned and toned woman, that he'd be taking care of the bill. He ordered an old-fashioned for himself with some kind of Australian small-batch whisky and whipped cream in a bowl for me and Starbuck, while Rose ordered a gin and tonic. Normally, I wouldn't pay attention to what humans drink, but it turned out to be important. Harry ordered a cocktail called a Paper

Plane, and Koochie Koo—I guess I should call her Shiloh— ordered something called the Last Word. Another super-big, mega-turbo important detail was that Atticus ordered a huge board of charcuterie and cheese for the table, and get this: he asked for *extra sausage*. That particular pair of words is in my top three of all time, right up there with *long nap* and *consenting poodle*.

Shiloh brought two people with her, the band leader and her boyfriend. The band leader was a Cuban-American fellow named Guillermo Trujillo, and he had one of those super thin mustaches and goatees that looked like they're painted on. He ordered three shots of tequila: A silver, a reposado, and an añejo, and I hoped they would adjust his attitude, because he was scowling about something and radiated some negative energy, sort of like the opposite of Bob Ross.

<Is he…a bad cat person?> Starbuck wondered.

<I don't know yet. We'd better stay away from him.>

Shiloh's American boyfriend, Peter Lassiter, was a scruffy white guy who was into craft beer and thought IPAs were a really good idea, but he smiled at us and said we were awesome, so I cut him some slack on the whole hophead thing. But I wasn't going to trust any snacks from him without thoroughly investigating them first, because he thought an infusion of bitter flowers was delicious. He probably liked cauliflower, too.

Once everyone was seated, Starbuck and I began "snack farming," which is a clever procedure where we put our heads underneath hands to get some pets, which is rewarding in itself, but also makes humans want to feed us later because we're so adorable.

<The part where we make them pet us is like planting the seed,> I explained to Starbuck, <and maybe it's like watering them, too. Then you just wait, and eventually, you harvest sausage! It's the best kind of farming.>

<Yes food! You know what, Oberon?>

<What?>

<It's good to be a good dog.>

I agreed as we made our rounds. We avoided the potential cat person but got lots of love from everyone else. The drinks got dropped off first, but it wasn't long after that before the *food* arrived! I may have whacked somebody upside the head with my tail by accident, and it might have been Harry, and she might have been a tiny bit annoyed with me because she almost spilled her Paper Plane, but what am I supposed to do when I see a server coming our way with a huge board of meat and cheese, *not* wag my tail? Please.

The bowls full of whipped cream were frothy and delicious but didn't last very long, and I was still hungry. And I could smell the sausage and the cheese on that big board they brought out. It smelled like three varieties of each. But the humans— get this!—the humans were more interested in their drinks.

They took pictures of them. Even Peter took a picture of his beer bottle because it was an Australian IPA he'd never tried before. In Shiloh's case, though, I think she was justified in taking a picture. Her drink's color matched her dress, and it was sort of artful, which I pointed out to Starbuck.

<What? What's art?>

<Shiloh, her moose hair, and the Last Word. That's art. Peter and a skunky beer is sad.>

<What about the bad cat person?>

I shifted my gaze to Guillermo. He was frowning at Shiloh and holding a shot glass of clear liquid, which I think humans call silver tequila even though it's not silver. If I remember correctly, tequilas that have color to them are older, and younger tequilas are clear, but maybe they're called silver so their feelings aren't hurt.

<Hey, Atticus?>

What is it, Oberon?

<Why are young tequilas called silver but old men are silver foxes? And why are neither of them silver and how did the men become foxes?>

What? Oberon, I don't— Well, okay, look at this way: In both cases, it's just marketing. Silver is more attractive than more accurate words would be.

<Is the fox thing marketing too?>

Definitely.

Guillermo tossed the tequila down his throat but didn't make any gasping noises or squint or anything after he did so. He just turned the shot glass upside down on the table next to the others, but he didn't look any happier. He was still scowling in Shiloh's direction. Maybe he would lighten up after the second drink. Or maybe he was not very nice. Or hey, maybe he was beleaguered by PFAs in his pancreas. (I don't know what that means, but Atticus said it one time about a customer in his old tea shop who lost his mind for no reason, so from context I think it means the human has something wrong with them on the inside but they can't afford to see a doctor so they randomly lash out at someone when what they're really mad at is capitalism. Guillermo hadn't lashed out yet, but it looked like he was thinking about it.)

It was after Guillermo had downed his shot and everyone had taken sips and selfies with their drinks that things got interesting, because that's when they started in on the food.

It wasn't just beef and pork. They had kangaroo on there, too. They talked about it. And ate it in front of us.

<When?> Starbuck asked me. <When is the sausage harvest? We farmed! We are farmers! We need a harvest!> He was quivering and dancing on his little paws in anticipation.

"Would it be all right if I gave the dogs a little something?" Peter asked Atticus, and he grew greatly in our esteem.

<Yes Peter! Yes food!> Starbuck shouted in my head, and we went right over to him and wagged our tails and oops, he noticed. His eyes got big the way they do when humans are surprised.

"Whoa, did they understand me?"

"They're very smart," Atticus replied, "so I imagine they cued in on something. Go ahead and give them a little bit of whatever you want." Privately, he said to us, *Don't give away the game here, fellas. You can't act like you understand everything you hear.*

<Sorry,> I said.

<Not sorry,> Starbuck added, because he got a piece of kangaroo from Peter and enjoyed the first harvest of our snack farming.

I remembered to give what Peter offered a good sniff before I ate it, but he didn't try to trick me with cauliflower or mustard, so I got my delicious smackerel of kangaroo and decided he was a good guy. We watched carefully who ate what after that and estimated how much food there was left to feed us. Or I did, anyway—Starbuck wasn't tall enough to see the charcuterie board. Atticus had a rolled-up slice of Genoa salami; Rose had a schmear of soft cheese and fig jam on a tiny piece of crunchy bread; Shiloh enjoyed a wedge of hard Spanish cheese that she said paired nicely with the acid citrus of her drink; Guillermo laid a slice of pepperoni and a pickle on top of bread, absolutely ruined it with mustard, then put the whole thing in his mouth, chasing it with his second shot of tequila; and Harry wrapped a kangaroo slice around a different hard cheese and just went after it, no bread or condiments or anything. Strangely, Peter didn't eat anything—he just fed us. Maybe he was able to subsist on hoppy beer.

That might sound like a food tangent but it's not. It's vital plot information, because as Atticus was telling Shiloh that she was quite the chanteuse—which he told me was a fancy word for singer—a hundred tiny shifts in body language came over her and she frowned, set down her nearly empty drink with a trembling hand, and tried to stand up from her chair.

"I don't…feel well," she said, and pressed her hands the sides of her face. "My jaw hurts."

"Shiloh?" Harry said, her voice uncertain.

"What's wrong, babe?" Peter asked. "Was it the cheese?"

She didn't answer. She collapsed into her chair and began convulsing violently, so much that she fell over backwards and crashed to the ground, where she continued to thrash about. I don't think it was the cheese, because I'd heard of (and smelled) lactose intolerance before, and this was way beyond that.

The humans all made noises of alarm, even the ones nearby at other tables, and Rose did a completely awesome thing: She pulled out her phone and called triple zero, the equivalent of 911 in Australia. She did that without telling someone else to do it, which is what police always did in shows and movies if they were around when someone got hurt.

Fact: If you are a main character in a police show, at some point in Season 1 you will be off-duty and shout, "Call 911!" because a civilian chokes on a biscuit or gets shot or something, and at another point you will be on duty and say to a superior officer "with all due respect" before pointing out politely that they are making terrible decisions, and the superior officer will never appreciate the feedback and overrule the main character, who will be proven right later in the show. So far, I'd never heard Rose say either of those things, and it was one of many reasons that I believed Atticus was very lucky to be with her. (That might have been a tangent, but it wasn't about food, so…I deserve food.)

While she was doing that, Atticus did his best to help, along with Peter and Harry. Peter was asking Shiloh what was wrong when she was obviously unable to talk. Harry kept saying, "What's happening?" over and over again, increasingly distressed with each repetition. Atticus knew what it was.

"Strychnine poisoning," he said, and caught Rose's eye. "Tell them to be prepared for strychnine poisoning." Rose nodded to indicate she'd heard him as she spoke to emergency services.

"What's strychnine? How do you know?" Harry asked.

"I've seen it before. It's an alkaloid with no antidote, but you can treat the symptoms and maybe survive it. It hits the jaw muscles first."

"Isn't it rat poison?" Peter said.

"Yes. But it can take out humans, too. Especially in large doses, and based on how quickly the symptoms attacked and how severe they are, I think she got one."

That exchange probably sounded a lot smoother than it was. Atticus and Peter and Harry were trying to get hold of

Shiloh's limbs or shield themselves from getting kicked or thwacked, because these were severe convulsions. Not like a seizure, where you have lots of tiny twitches, but more like different muscles wanting to flex to the maximum. Mostly they were just trying to keep Shiloh from hurting herself more, but there wasn't much else they could do.

As a Druid, Atticus might have been able to help if we were back in the park and he could be in touch with the earth, asking the elemental to help him break down the poison and let her stabilize. But we were on the patio of the bar, and the nearest bare earth was across the street. Atticus used to be able to do some healing on his own because he had a binding tattooed onto the back of his right hand that gave him that ability, but he lost that whole arm a while back, so there was nothing he could do.

Shiloh Timmins, that pretty singing lady in green who was so artful and kind, arched her back in agony and died before the ambulance could get there.

And so did this other random guy.

CHAPTER 2

The Profound Inadequacy of Police Procedure

One of the things that amazes me about cow squirts is that you can churn them into butter, and that can be used to make sauces and gravies for beef. That just blows my mind pretty much every day. Can you believe cows? They give you squirts to make a sauce for their own meat! How considerate is that? Name another animal that's so kind to carnivores, being big and slow and delicious and willing to help you make gravy. You can't.

And I had to talk about that for a minute because the restaurant was a little like jumping into a ball pit, and each ball was an unhappy human being very loud about how unhappy they were. Harry was just wrecked that her friend had come around the world to visit her and then died in tremendous pain. Peter was also understandably upset that his girlfriend had perished in front of him. And we were coming to understand that someone else had been poisoned in the same way, and was currently also on the floor convulsing. At which point Detective Inspector Rose Badgely raised her shield high in the air and called out as loud as she could that she was taking charge, this was a murder investigation, nobody could leave and we couldn't touch anything on the table.

<Hold on, Atticus, why can't we touch anything on the table? That would include the sausage, you see, so I'm worried.>

It's all evidence now, Oberon. Nobody can eat it.

<What? That doesn't make sense! Shiloh never ate any of the sausage, and everyone who did is just fine!>

<No food makes no sense!> Starbuck agreed.

It's just police procedure, Atticus said. *You have to secure the scene and analyze everything for clues.*

<But Atticus, I know what she ate. I know what everyone ate. She didn't eat the sausage, so the sausage can't be evidence. It's *sausage*, Atticus, and its purpose is to be eaten! You have to let the sausage fulfill its purpose!>

Sorry, guys, but once a crime's been committed like this, investigative protocols determine what we can and cannot do.

<Unacceptable!> I turned to my little Boston buddy and caught his eye so he would know I was serious. <Starbuck, whoever did this basically stole our sausage harvest from us.

We can't let them get away with it. They must pay for their malicious snack thievery!>

<That's right!>

And for murder, Atticus said.

<Oh yeah! And murder too. If we solve the murder, Starbuck, then we also bring justice to the snack thief.>

<Let's do it!> The Boston leapt around in circles a few times then abruptly stopped, frozen by a question. <How do we do it?>

<We probably need to start with what happened. How do you think she was poisoned, Atticus?>

Most likely her drink. Strychnine is bitter, but the Last Word contains so many sweet and herbaceous notes that it might have been well disguised. A few milliliters would have sufficed.

<What's the Last Word made of?>

Gin, maraschino liqueur, Chartreuse, and lime juice, all in equal proportions.

<And what is Chartreuse?>

It's a bright green herbaceous liqueur with many botanicals used in its distillation. It's also the name for a particular shade of bright green—sort of like the emerald she has in her headband.

<Aha! So what we must do is deduce who gave the deadly juice to the moussed chartreuse chanteuse!>

Oberon, what the fuck?

<We must fight crime and rhyme all the time!> my Boston terrier buddy added.

Aw, no. Now you've corrupted Starbuck.

<I say nay! He's elevated and illuminated, underrated when he should be celebrated.>

<That's a fact, Jack! Give us a snack pack!>

You guys are rhyming like Fezzik and Inigo and I'm reduced to the role of Vizzini.

<Oh no, I think you should pick a different role, Atticus, because Vizzini died from poison. We don't need any more dead poisoned humans here, especially you.>

I agree; thank you.

<Do you think you can convince Rose that the sausage is innocent and she can let us have it?>

Maybe. We will have to work quickly. But if you solve this case, I promise you will get sausage, even if it's not the sausage on the table.

<Yes food!> Starbuck leapt in circles again and I told him to be patient a minute because Rose was giving lots of instructions to people like TOUCH NOTHING and DON'T MOVE while she went to go see about the other person who'd been poisoned.

As soon as she left, however, Atticus moved, motioning to us to follow him.

"Where are you going, Connor?" Harry asked, her face streaked with tears.

"To the bar," he replied. "The drinks came from there, so we should take a look."

The bar was a long slick slab of polished gray stone in the front, and the top was a polished hardwood of some kind, protected with a resin coating. The back bar was a lot of bottles on tiny stone shelves, almost like they were slate roof tiles cut down to serve as displays, and there was all this recessed lighting that lit up the bottles and made it look fancy. It was large enough, and the place busy enough, that there were two bartenders back there, both of the goth persuasion, sheathed in black outfits and wearing studded bracers on their forearms that made them look super badass. Both had dyed hair. The one on the right was a bit taller and had dyed her hair chartreuse, and I thought that was too perfect, too matchy-matchy. She couldn't have done it, right? But the one on the left had dyed her hair a kind of bluish-purple, and she had arched eyebrows above some thick-rimmed glasses, plus a bunch of tattoos on her neck going right up to her jaw, and I have to admit she looked like a criminal mastermind. Or maybe a vampire librarian. Except she was a Tasmanian bartender, and that didn't bode well for discovering a motive. Why would she want to poison an American chanteuse? Maybe she was into death metal, emphasis on the *death*?

Atticus flashed a high-wattage grin at the green-haired bartender and did his charm thing. "Hi, just wanted to ask if you made the Last Word for our table over there?"

"Yeah?" she said uncertainly.

"Well, it looks like it was poisoned, so I'm not suggesting you did anything wrong, but I am suggesting you set aside the ingredients for that drink and not use them to make any others."

"What?" the purple-haired bartender said, even as the green-haired one said, "Oh my God. Is that the murder investigation the lady shouted about? A poisoned drink?"

"The Last Word, specifically. Which you made," he said, pointing at the green-haired one.

"Oh, no. I didn't know anything was poisoned!"

"I'm sure you didn't. But that's why we need to set aside the ingredients to make sure no one else gets hurt."

A red-faced, jowly man burst through the kitchen doors to the right and caught the tail end of that.

"What's that? You say someone was poisoned?" He looked a bit like what a bulldog might if you shaved one down and left it in the sun too long.

"Yes. At least one person, possibly two, with a cocktail from your bar."

The man took in the two different clusters of people gathered around prone forms on the ground and said, "Shiiiiit."

"Police are already here—Detective Inspector Rose Badgely is with that second group. I assume you're the manager."

"Yeah," the man said, but he didn't stick around to introduce himself. He said dogs shouldn't be inside the restaurant as he moved purposely over to the second group because there was quite a bit of shouting and movement there, whereas our group was mostly crying at that point. Starbuck and I decided not to hear that part about where we shouldn't be.

Atticus gestured to the other table where the manager was headed. "Did someone at that table also order the Last Word?" he asked the bartenders, and they both shook their heads. "Well, how about a drink that uses one or more of the same ingredients as the Last Word?"

"Ffffffuck," the purple-haired bartender said. "I made a D.A.C. for someone a few minutes ago."

"What's in that?" Atticus asked. "I'm not familiar with that one."

"Full name is Detroit Athletic Club, which is where the Last Word originated. The bartender who created the D.A.C. was riffing on the Last Word, so he honored it in the name—which is more than you needed to know, right? Sorry. It's made with Irish whiskey, sweet vermouth, falernum, and green Chartreuse."

"So, the Chartreuse is the common ingredient. I'd suggest you don't make any more drinks with that bottle and set it aside for testing."

<Did you just identify the murder weapon, Atticus? That was fast!>

Maybe.

The green-haired bartender picked a green bottle from the wide selection with a fancy black-and-gold label on it and set it on the bar. She looked very sad and scared and wiped at a tear at the corner of her eye.

"Did that lady die? I really killed someone?"

"She died, yes. But unless you poisoned the drink yourself, you didn't kill her. You were just doing your job, and the real killer was counting on that."

I think Atticus was trying to be reassuring there but it didn't calm her down at all. She became even more upset, and the purple-haired bartender got upset too as it became clear that the other person had died as well. Our tanned server came over to the bar, worried about the fact that she'd served up a deadly cocktail to someone. (I never did catch her name but she smiled at me, so we can conclude that she recognizes a handsome hound when she sees one.)

<You'd better stay here and keep an eye on the murder weapon, Atticus,> I said.

That was my plan. But where are you going?

At that point, three members of the staff emerged from the kitchen to see what was going on, two of them in white cook's aprons. I almost got distracted by the smells of meat and grease wafting out of there, and I saw some stains on those aprons I wouldn't mind investigating, but I firmly held on to my objective. <I'm going over to the other group where Rose is. We have murders to solve and sausage to earn.>

Starbuck couldn't resist going over to give the cooks a quick sniff, however, and one of them looked down at us and said, "What are these dogs doing in here?"

<Starbuck, come on, we're going to help Rose.>

<Coming! Yes food!> he said.

Sirens could be heard wailing as they closed in on the restaurant, and as we trotted past interior tables toward the patio, we met the red-faced manager who was waving both hands at the staff to get their attention.

"Shut it all down. No more orders for the night. And what the hell, get these bloody dogs out of here! Christ, what do ya feed that big one, a whole ostrich?"

CHAPTER 3

The Other Dead Human

The second person to die from a cocktail was a tanned white man whose drink was a bit orangey-brown, I think. I am not very good at human ages. There are five: Eagle Bait, Child, Always on the Phone, Often in Crisis, and Might Croak Any Minute. This guy was Often in Crisis. He had thick dark hair and a full bushy beard with no gray hairs in it at all, but he had some fine crinkly lines around his eyes that disqualified him from the Always on the Phone category. He was wearing a linen suit, one of those light summery ones, and Atticus said it was a custom job, because it was a pale lavender or periwinkle or something like that, which is not a mass-produced sort of thing, and he had on a white shirt underneath, the buttons undone, no tie, but a white pocket square. He was wearing some boat shoes and no socks, which might mean he either had a boat or just wanted people to think he did.

The people surrounding this man really wanted to get away from there, but Rose was insisting that they stay because she had an investigation to conduct and until they were cleared, they needed to comply.

One thing I noticed was that this man didn't have anyone shedding a tear over his passing the way Shiloh did. It reminded me of this weird human saying that goes "I wouldn't want to be caught dead with that guy," or caught with those jeans or pajamas or whatever, except that these people didn't want to be caught alive with this man. Or with anyone else. The situation rapidly deteriorated to where the people were pointing fingers at each other, saying *that* woman always wished he would die, *that* guy fantasized about murder as a problem-solving strategy, and that *other* guy hated him for saying in public that he had a tiny dingus.

<I still don't know who the victim is because no one's said his name,> I told Atticus, <but there seems to be no shortage of motives over here.>

You're not leaping to conclusions, I hope. We can't assume no one had a motive to murder Shiloh. I don't know if you noticed it or not, but the band leader seemed to be displeased with her.

<I did notice that! So did Starbuck!>

<Yeah! Bad cat person!>

<I'm just noticing the vibe here, Atticus. No assumptions. Apart from assuming we will eventually solve this and enjoy a victory feast.>

The ambulance arrived, shortly followed by more police. The medical folks pronounced the victims dead and covered them up with sheets while the police, under direction of Rose, started taking statements from people so they could eventually go home. She assigned a sergeant to interview our party because there would be a conflict of interest if she was interviewing her friend Harry, but Starbuck and I stayed with her, and people thought it was strange.

The woman who others claimed had often wished the deceased would die pointed at us and said, "Why are those dogs standing there watching us?"

<Because we're very polite to humans,> I said, which was really for Starbuck's benefit since no one else could hear me. <If we weren't told how to behave by our Druid, we'd be sniffing your ass right now to see if you're guilty.>

<Haha! Yeah! Why don't we do that?> Starbuck asked.

<Human asses aren't like ours, little buddy. They *all* smell guilty. They know what they did.>

When Rose turned around and saw us, her eyebrows shot up. "What are you two doing here?" She stabbed a finger at the ground. "Sit."

We sat immediately, and Rose nodded once in satisfaction.

"Don't mind them. They're with me. Now, what's your name, ma'am?" Rose flipped open a little notebook and clicked a ballpoint open.

"Darla Hutchens." She had yellow hair and was a bit flushed, and she smelled of vanilla and honeysuckle shampoo, cheap deodorant, and nervous sweat, as well as a bit of cigarette smoke. I didn't think she was a smoker herself, though—more like she'd spent time with someone who was.

"What's your relationship to the deceased?"

Darla crinkled her nose in distaste. "Not much of a relationship to speak of."

"How did you know him?"

"He bought some property next to my parents' farm."

"Ah. So you're a farmer, or he is?"

"No, no. My parents are farmers. And he's only a farmer if you count server farms as farming. He's…a techbro."

Darla managed to say that without condemnation, but the little shudder of disgust afterward signaled her opinion of him.

"And what's his name?"

"Godwin Taggart, but he wanted people to call him Win." Darla looked like she was being asked to remember a time she ate some bad seafood and suffered days of explosive diarrhea.

"So why are you here?"

"I'm in commercial real estate. I was trying to get him to sell the land next to my parents' farm and buy another place for his new server farm."

"Oh. Why is that?"

"Server farms are resource hogs. Not just electricity but water. It would have made things difficult for my parents."

"I see. Do you have a business card?"

"Oh. Yeah, just a sec."

Once Rose had it, she said, "So Mr. Taggart's death makes your parents' lives easier?"

The blood drained from Darla's face. "No. I mean yeah, but no."

"Which is it?"

"It's both, yeah? No. I mean, technically, yes."

It was time to report to Atticus. <The victim is a *tech*bro whose death *tech*nically helps a suspect. If she is arrested and walks on a *tech*nicality, we'll have a trifecta of tech.>

You might be focusing on the wrong thing, Oberon. I mean, I like your observation, but that's not getting you any closer to sausage.

<Oh. That's a good point.> Atticus was always very good at redirecting me and keeping me on task.

"Someone here said you wished he was dead," Rose was saying when I tuned back in.

"Yeah, I mean, I did say that in front of an obviously indiscreet person," she said, glaring at a brown-skinned man with some interesting tattoos on his face, "which I now regret, but I wouldn't have acted on that."

<I think she did it,> Starbuck told me.

<Why?>

<Because of the detective shows. On the shows, women like to use poison. Man was killed with poison. She is woman. So she did it.>

<Maybe. But Harry's a woman. The bartenders are women, and I think one of the kitchen staff was a woman. We can't assume it's Darla yet, or that this guy was the target.>

Rose turned her attention to the man that Darla said was indiscreet. "And you, sir? What's your name and relationship to the deceased?"

"Gary Morton. I'm—I was—Mr. Taggart's personal assistant."

"Oh? Was he a good boss?"

Gary shrugged. "His checks didn't bounce."

"Did you have any reason to wish Mr. Taggart dead?"

"Of course not. I'd be out of a job. I am, in fact."

"But Ms. Hutchens suggested you often wish people to come to harm."

"Not seriously, though. That was, like, hyperbole. I'll admit I've been in a scrape or two, and you might see me punch someone's nuts someday, but I'd never go beyond that. No weapons, and certainly no poison."

"Why were you all here tonight?"

"Well, there was this Koochie Koo concert across the street

in the park, and we were here to see that because Kurt here likes her." He hooked a thumb to indicate the third member of their party, a pale, shrinking, bespectacled man that would most likely fall over if Starbuck tried to hump him.

"I see." Rose shifted her gaze to Kurt, who visibly quailed in her regard. "Your full name, sir?"

"Kurt Helford."

"Are you aware that Koochie Koo is dead? She's the other victim over there."

"No. She is, really? She's dead?"

"Yes."

"I didn't see her there. It was so crowded. That's…terrible." He seemed to crumple in on himself like soggy origami, half-collapsing into a chair. "She was amazing."

"Yes. She was amazing and it's terrible. Isn't it terrible that Mr. Taggart's dead, too?"

"Sure," Kurt said, but it was the sort of thing you say just to humor someone instead of saying how you really feel.

"What's your relationship to Mr. Taggart?"

"I'm a code contractor. He needed me for a new project and wanted me happy for now. So this concert and dinner was his way of wining and dining me."

"And did Mr. Taggart publicly humiliate you through body shaming?"

A little bit of fire lit up Kurt's eyes. "Yes. That's one way of putting it. Typical bully behavior. But if I killed everyone who's ever bullied me, I'd leave a string of corpses from here to Alice Springs."

"Not worried about everyone who ever bullied you, Mr. Helford. Just wondering if you decided to kill this particular bully."

"Of course not. Taggart was an asshole, but he at least recognized my value and paid me well, and he threw me little perks like this concert once in a while. God, Koochie Koo was beautiful tonight. Can't believe she's gone. What a disaster." He buried his face in his hands, but Rose wasn't finished.

"What was this project that Mr. Taggart had you working on? Was it something that someone might want to kill him for?"

Kurt emerged from his facepalm to shake his head. "It was ATP protocols for a social media startup. Nobody would care. I barely care, and I was paid to."

Rose got a card from him as well and asked which drink on their table belonged to Win Taggart. They pointed to his half-empty coupe glass, which still had some orange-brown liquid in it. Rose had an officer put on some gloves and secure it, and said they needed to get Shiloh's drink too.

"I need to go talk to the restaurant staff for a while, but I will have some more questions for you after that, and then you can go home. I'll be as quick as I can. Don't leave."

Rose left an officer there to kind of watch over things and turned to the bar, telling us to follow her. She went straight to the red-faced manager, who complained about us being inside again.

"We can't have those dogs in here," he said, pointing a finger at us and shaking his head. "We just can't."

CHAPTER 4

The Unsavory Smell of Fear

nlike humans described in a founding document of the United States, sausages are not created equal and endowed with certain unalienable rights. Some sausages are significantly lesser than others—I'm looking at you, Vienna sausages, and also you, supposedly gourmet sausages that contain things like orange and ginger. Sausages like that are practically meat crimes.

Sadly, humans have not crafted many laws regarding meat, except that it be stored and prepared in such a way that it doesn't kill them if they eat it. That's, like, a *bare minimum* of thought put into a hugely important part of our lives. Orange and ginger sausages should be illegal, but humans don't have the political courage to make it so. Or they don't understand how terrible it tastes. It might be both. But I think all sausages *should* have the right to be eaten by somebody. Like those sausages on the charcuterie board that were perfectly good and going to waste as evidence.

I didn't want you to think I'd lost sight of what's important, see. And Rose didn't lose sight of what's important either, because she shut down that red-faced manager guy right away.

"We're going to pretend the dogs are not here. They're very well trained and might help with the investigation. So might this gentleman at the bar." She indicated Atticus and said to him, "Find anything, Connor?"

"Yes. This bottle of Chartreuse is likely poisoned. It was used to make the Last Word for Shiloh and a drink called Detroit Athletic Club for the other victim. No other drinks were made with Chartreuse tonight. This young woman is Lauren," he said, waving at the green-haired bartender, "and this young woman is Mallory," referring to the purple-haired one.

She said thanks to Connor, g'day to the bartenders, and told them her name. Then she asked for the manager's.

"Bart Simmons."

"Great. Mr. Simmons, do you have cameras trained on the bar area?"

"Well, nah, not the entire bar. Just on the registers."

"So your cameras wouldn't show us who handled that bottle of Chartreuse throughout the day, based on where it's kept?"

"Right. You'd only see it when they pulled it from the backbar and brought it to the front to make a drink."

"We're going to want to see that footage, but just as a basic matter of operation, who'd be back there throughout the day?"

"Well—them, of course," he said, nodding at the bartenders, "me, the dishwasher, and maybe the servers go back there sometimes, even the cooks."

"Why would they go back there?"

"The cooks wouldn't during business hours, but they come in early to prep, and they're allowed to grab a soda or whatever. The dishwasher brings out racks of clean glasses."

"What about vendors dropping off deliveries of alcohol?"

"Oh, yeah. But we didn't have any of those today."

"And would any of the patrons of this establishment have the opportunity to go back there?"

"Nah. There's somebody back there at all times once the doors open."

<Oh! So the people with Shiloh and Win Taggart are all innocent!> I said.

Maybe, Atticus replied. *That information makes it less likely they were involved, but it's not impossible.*

<So it's most likely one of the employees who poisoned the Chartreuse?>

Most likely.

That explained why Rose was so keen to start asking questions of the staff; I thought she'd spent very little time interrogating the people closest to the victims and wondered why. But that's why she's the detective inspector and I'm the most adorable hound in the world, yes I am.

Rose turned to the bartenders. "Were you both working here yesterday too?" When they said yes, she followed up: "Did you make any drinks yesterday using this bottle of Chartreuse?"

"I didn't," Lauren piped up. "It was a game night and we had a lot of footy fans in here, so it was mostly beers. A few old fashioneds, a few rounds of shots, but that's it."

"I used it," Mallory admitted. "I made the Last Word for somebody."

"But they left the restaurant alive?"

"Yes."

"So, that means the bottle was poisoned today—or it's a new bottle that you opened that was already poisoned."

Lauren shook her head immediately. "No, we've had that bottle for at least a week, if not more."

"Okay. That narrows things down, then. If this bottle is indeed poisoned—we have to confirm that—then it was poisoned sometime after Mallory made the Last Word last night and shortly before you made the drinks tonight. Mr. Simmons, if you'd show me your camera footage now, we can narrow things down further."

"Right. The office is through the kitchen."

"Lead the way."

Atticus spoke up as she started to move. "Detective Inspector," he said, which was super formal of him, but maybe it was because Rose was acting in her professional role and it wouldn't be proper to call her the things he did when they practiced human mating habits. "Would it be all right if my hounds had a good sniff around? They were very helpful in that previous case."

He was talking about how Starbuck and I helped solve the murder of a man named William Howe who looked like he was attacked by bees but had actually been shot in the back.[1] That was the case where he'd met Rose, in fact, and they started dating after the case was closed.

"Sure, Mr. Molloy. It couldn't hurt."

"Hold on, I don't think the dogs should be back there," the manager said. "They're not trained police dogs, are they?"

"They're not police dogs, but they are trained, and they've been helpful in a previous murder investigation."

"Helpful how?"

---

1 In The Buzz Kill, available in ebook and audio as part of the Death & Honey anthology, or in print at the end of the trade paperback edition of Scourged.

"Identifying and tracking suspects."

"Tracking I understand, but identifying? How?"

"By sense of smell. They can place someone at the scene of a crime."

"That's not admissible in court, is it?"

"Doesn't have to be. Once they give me a clue, I confirm it in other ways. Now let's look at your security footage, shall we?" She gestured to the kitchen doors, neatly cutting off that topic, and she winked at Atticus once the manager's back was turned.

I'm going to say some commands out loud for the benefit of the others, but I want you guys to note the scents of all humans behind the bar and how recent they are. We'll see if we can eliminate any of the staff based on that.

<Got it,> I said, and Starbuck added that he understood.

"Okay if they come back and say hello?" Atticus asked Lauren and Mallory. "They're super friendly."

Lauren nodded and smiled, but Mallory looked uncertain. "I probably smell like my cats. Are they going to get upset about that?"

"Nah. They'll be fine. Can we put the bottle back where it was so they can focus on the area around there?"

"Sure."

Lauren took the bottle and placed it back on the shelf, and then Atticus led us around to the side and then pointed at the bartenders. "Go say hello."

Lauren was very nice and seemed relieved to be petting me. She needed some kind of release because she was very nervous and sad and had some tears leaking out of her eyes. Mallory was also nice, but she did have a telltale scent about her.

<Cat person,> Starbuck declared. <But not a bad cat person.>

Okay, I'm going to say "scout" and point, then you guys sniff all around the space near where someone would stand to grab the Chartreuse bottle, and catalogue those scents.

<Ready,> I told him.

"Oberon. Starbuck. Scout." He pointed down at the floor beneath the bottle, and it was great performance art. We went over there to snuffle around, and Lauren and Mallory were very impressed at how well trained we were and complimented Atticus. I think it's funny when people think we're regular dogs who don't have a Druid for their human.

We smelled that the bartenders had been there, of course, and the bulldog man, Bart Simmons, but there were others. Two men and two women, if I had it right. One of the women was our server.

<Do you recognize any of these other people I'm smelling?> I asked Starbuck.

<Yes. Kitchen people. But one is weaker. Did not stand right here, or stood here a longer time ago.>

I told Atticus we had a lead on two people in the kitchen who stood there besides the bartenders, our server, and the manager.

Okay, good job. We'll stay out here for the moment because we would probably be over the line going into the food prep area. Best to let Rose call them out here for you to confirm. Would you be okay with comforting Harry while we wait?

<Sure.>

"Good job," Atticus said out loud. "Oberon, Starbuck, go see Harry."

That was our cue to trot out of there and return to the spot where Shiloh Timmins had died. Harry and Peter were both crying, and I went up to Harry and Starbuck went over to Peter and we both got petted and cried on. Harry may have deposited thirty to fifty percent of her body's snot in my fur, but I had thwacked her upside the head earlier with my tail and baths can take care of boogers, so it was fine. Guillermo, I noticed, was dry-eyed, and if anything, looked more cross than he had before. It was like he'd just had his food stolen by a seagull, which happens to humans quite a lot because they don't understand that seagulls are the squirrels of the sky. I wondered why he looked so mad.

Maybe it was because he was being questioned by another member of the Launceston police. I'd met her before; she was a sergeant that often worked with Rose, and she had a bright head covering underneath her police cap, which was a thing she wore for religious reasons. She was very gentle when she gave scritches and she smelled like chai.

<Atticus, do you remember the name of this nice lady interviewing Guillermo?>

He glanced briefly in our direction, then turned back to the bar as his reply came to me mentally.

That's Sergeant Naseer.

<She's asking Guillermo why he looks so angry and he's saying it's because this gig was lower-paying than their regular concerts and the band hadn't wanted to do it, and now the rest of the tour was going to be cancelled and they wouldn't get paid for any of it.>

Wow, what a mercenary heart. Sounds like he won't be sending flowers to Shiloh's memorial service. Whoops, hold on, Rose is back.

I saw him talk with Rose for a few seconds before he turned back to us and called our names. I felt bad about leaving Harry, because she wasn't done crying by a long shot, but my Druid needed me, and we wanted to solve Shiloh's murder.

"Bye," she whimpered as I slid out from underneath her hands, and I hoped I would remember to go plop down in front of her as much as I could when I wasn't doing something for the investigation.

Rose was telling Bart Simmons to bring the kitchen staff out for questioning as we came up. He looked unhappy about that, but then again, I hadn't seen him look happy about anything yet. This wasn't going to be a happy day for him, and he might not have any happy days for a while, because if it turned out that someone on his staff fatally poisoned a couple of customers, he was bound to get some negative reviews on Yelp along the lines of "Drinks so bad that two people literally died. I was lucky to escape with my life. One star." Of course, if he was the one behind it, then he'd really be unhappy when Rose caught him.

Rose, for her part, was unhappy with him because all the security footage was gone. Someone had deliberately sabotaged the system, and it might have been Bart. So, that meant that Starbuck and I were now her best shot at establishing who had poisoned the bottle with strychnine.

When the three people reemerged from the kitchen, Rose took down their names.

There were two cooks: An Indonesian man named Djoko Ningrum and a Thai woman named Intira Madeua. There was also a dishwasher, a white guy named Jerry Fielder, who had a white undershirt on and jeans hanging low on his hips so that we could see the elastic band of his designer underwear. He was sweating pretty heavily from all the steam in his area of the kitchen, and I could tell before I even got close that he was one of the scents I'd found by the Chartreuse.

Remember the lineup we did in the police station on the previous case? Atticus said. *Sniff each one in turn and then bark once if they were by the Chartreuse.*

Rose said we would come give them a quick sniff hello if they'd stay still for that, and the humans looked a bit confused but didn't seem to mind. Atticus gave us a command to make it seem like we were following his training.

"Oberon. Starbuck. Spot the scent."

Going left to right, Djoko Ningrum was first, a tall fellow with long fingers. I recognized his scent, but it was the faint one.

I looked around at Atticus and gave him an open-mouthed doggie smile and explained mentally, <This guy has been behind the bar before but hasn't been by the Chartreuse for days.>

"Okay, next."

Intira Madeua was in the middle and she had probably been there today. Starbuck and I barked once, but it was at the same time and it startled her. She yelped and said, "Jesus, what the fuck, mate?" and Rose rushed to reassure her.

"It's okay; they won't bite."

"What was that, though? What's 'spot the scent' mean?"

Go ahead to the next one, Atticus prodded us, and we quickly sniffed at Jerry Fielder. Because of his job, he had a lot of extra food scents, like rotten ones, and a whiff of the trash can about him because he had to empty the bins. He also had sprayed some discount cologne on himself to disguise his smoking habit, or maybe the fact that he really needed a shower, because the body odor was strong. Starbuck and I barked again, and he jumped too.

"What the hell? Call off your dogs, mate."

Atticus had us retreat behind him and sit down, but we didn't go back to comfort Harry and Peter, because we wanted to hear Rose do her thing. She started with the tall dude.

"Mr. Ningrum, did you know Shiloh Timmins, publicly known as Koochie Koo, or a man named Win Taggart?"

"No," he replied. "But if you're going to grill me, I want a lawyer."

"Not necessary. I'm finished. You can return to the kitchen. Thank you."

"Oh." He'd been expecting a bit more resistance there and deflated when there suddenly wasn't a fight.

"Mr. Fielder, you can return to the kitchen briefly until I'm done with Ms. Madeua."

He shrugged. "All right," he said, and spun on his heel before sauntering into the kitchen.

"Wait, why does he get to go?"

"I'll bring him back shortly. Ms. Madeua, did you know either of the deceased?"

"No. Can I go now too?"

"Soon. I have just a few more questions."

"Why do I get more questions?"

Rose ignored that and asked, "What time did you arrive at work today?"

She crossed her arms across her apron. "Three o'clock, the usual."

"And did you remain in the kitchen the entire time, or did you come out here to the dining area at some point?"

"I stayed back in the kitchen."

"You never went behind the bar to grab a drink?"

"Oh. Well, yeah. Before the customers came in."

"What time was that, approximately?"

She shrugged. "I dunno. Three-thirtyish, maybe."

"Did anyone see you? Were the bartenders here?"

"No, they come in at four."

"So you were alone behind the bar at three-thirty, and nobody saw you, is that correct?"

"Well, I don't know. That sounds like a trick question."

"It's actually a yes-or-no question, not a trick at all."

"What if I don't answer?"

"I would wonder what you're trying to hide when I'm simply asking about when you came out to get a drink."

"Maybe I don't have anything to hide; I just don't trust that cops care about justice. You just want to put someone in jail so you look effective, and it doesn't matter to you if they're innocent or guilty. I'm not going to help you put me away."

Rose let that hang in the air for a few millennia before she quietly responded. "You're correct that I want to put someone in jail, because someone murdered two people today. I want that someone—and no one else—to pay for what they did, and make sure they can't hurt anyone else. Now, you've already said you came out here for a drink at half three. If no one saw you, that means you were alone and able to slip some poison into a bottle of liquor that killed two people."

"What? Hey, no. See, you're trying to blame me!"

"I'm trying to establish a timeline and confirm facts. I've placed you at the scene, but that doesn't mean you did anything wrong. Did anyone see you behind the bar who can confirm that all you did was get a drink? I'm asking this question because if there was a witness who saw you get a drink and leave—nothing else—then you're cleared."

"Djoko saw me leave my station and come back with water."

"But he didn't see you in the bar area?"

"No, he was in the kitchen."

"Did anyone see you in the bar area?"

Intira started to smell differently. I don't mean she peed or anything, just that I could smell her fear and stress. Atticus says human brains produce a chemical called cortisol when they're stressed, but he's not sure if that's what I smell or not. I don't know how to describe the smell exactly but will simply say it's not my favorite.

"Look, I don't like what you're trying to do here," Intira said.

"I'm trying to do my job."

"You're trying to make it sound like I did it, but I didn't."

"Fine. Provide me a witness who can say you didn't poison the bottle."

"What if someone else was out here getting a drink? Jerry came out here before the bartenders arrived. Bart too."

Everyone looked at Bart, including us, and since he already didn't like us, he saw that.

"Of course I did. I'm the manager, so I have to be everywhere." His finger stabbed in our direction. "And do we really need those dogs in here? They're creepy, just looked at me when everyone else did."

Rose ignored him and focused on Intira. "I'll be talking to them as well. But if I can eliminate you as a suspect, that would be good, yeah? So, tell me who saw you get a drink."

She was practically quivering as she said, "No one."

I told Starbuck, <I don't think she did it.>

<No. She too scared. Killer would be a bad cat person, not care.>

Our server said she'd been behind the bar quite a bit but only when the bartenders were also there, and they saw every move she made. She never touched the liquor bottles.

Bart "the Bulldog" Simmons explained that though he didn't have witnesses while he was doing his work in the bar before opening, he wouldn't ever do something like this because it would hurt his bottom line.

"As manager, I get a bonus based on profits, and poisoning customers is going to hurt our profits considerably, heh heh."

If that was a joke, no one laughed but him.

Atticus told us, *That bonus is probably a few thousand dollars. He could be motivated to ignore that. I don't trust him because he doesn't like dogs.*

The unexpected resistance came from Jerry Fielder, the dishwasher. When Rose questioned him—or tried to—he kept saying "lawyer" and nothing else.

"Why do you need a lawyer, Mr. Fielder?" she asked him.

"Lawyer," he replied.

So she arranged to have him taken to the station, where she could question him with a lawyer present, but she didn't make arrangements to save the sausage. I went back to visit Harry so she could cry on me some more, and I watched the forensics people bag up the perfectly edible, nontoxic, delicious sausage that no one would ever eat.

Starbuck and I whimpered in despair. It was a very sad night for everyone.

CHAPTER 5

The Much Better Smell of Carnitas

That was a very long day and we went home without Rose, because she needed to interview Jerry Fielder at the police station and write reports and everything, and that was unfortunately an aspect to the investigation that Starbuck and I couldn't help with. Which I worried about, because she's good at her job.

<What if she solves the case without us, Atticus? Does that mean we get no sausage? We had sausage taken from us for evidence, and now we might get our prize sausage withdrawn on a technicality?>

<No techbros! Bad techbros!> Starbuck said. I think he didn't really know what he was saying there, but I couldn't disagree.

"I have a plan to make it up to you," he said in the kitchen, reaching into a storage cupboard where Rose kept the crockpot.

<Whoa, hey, a slow cooker!>

Starbuck knew what that meant and he spun around in tight circles as he shouted, <Tender meat! Tender meat!>

<What are you making?>

"Carnitas. We'll set the crockpot on low and let it do its thing while we sleep. And when we wake up, the house will smell glorious and you'll have carnitas for breakfast."

<You make excellent plans, Atticus! We're probably going to drool in our sleep.>

Great gelatinous gods of gravy, it smelled good *before* we went to sleep! But we did because Atticus said we needed a rest and he was correct; Starbuck and I arranged ourselves on our big doggie bed in the living room and had no trouble sliding into dreams of poodles bounding through meadows of clover. Oh, what tightly curled delights poodles are!

We woke up when Rose came home, and I don't know exactly what time it was except it was the time of night where there's only bats and cats and rats outside, plus a few ghosts. She gave us quick pets and said we were good dogs, yes we were, before shuffling off to her bedroom to sneak into bed with Atticus.

We woke again when there were birds chirping outside and Atticus emerged from the bedroom to start coffee. And the carnitas smelled *glorious,* just like he promised.

Have you ever had slow-cooked pork shoulder drenched in spices first thing in the morning? If not, you should totally try it. With eggs and avocado and tortillas and beans and a green chile sauce. Actually, I don't need any of that stuff, but Atticus always makes those things for himself to go with carnitas because of that thing where humans like to eat other things besides meat.

Rose came out when the coffee was ready. It was a smell that summoned her forth without fail, but she commented on the lovely aroma of carnitas as well. She'd not had much Mexican food before she started dating Atticus, but he had gotten really good at making it because of those years we lived in Arizona and of course a bunch of years he'd lived in Mexico before I was around. He was, to be honest, a really good chef because of all his years living all over the world and picking up tricks and recipes here and there.

He made up pretty plates with a bunch of human food on it for Rose and himself, but Starbuck and I got deluxe bowls of our regular kibble. The kibble's not bad, you know—it fills the void—but he mixed in some carnitas with it and, most importantly, drizzled it with spoonfuls of decadent juices and drippings and ohhh, praise be to the gravy gods!

As Starbuck and I were chowing down, Atticus and Rose were using forks and slurping coffee for a bit before he asked her how things went last night.

"Harry's a wreck. She's not going to have an easy time getting over this."

"Of course," Atticus said. "It's terrible. Was Shiloh the target?"

"Haven't absolutely ruled it out, but it seems less likely. Win Taggart was the more likely target. Turns out he'd been to that bar on multiple occasions and always ordered a D.A.C., which meant someone knew the pattern and could have planned around his appearance. It's far less likely that they could have planned for Shiloh. How many Tasmanians would know that she would order the Last Word? And how could they know that she'd go to that bar after her gig?"

"Unless it was Harry or Peter."

"Exactly. But they had no opportunity, and no motive that I could figure out. Harry is utterly destroyed. If she's acting right now, then she can kick Meryl Streep's ass. Unless something new points me back in her direction, I think Shiloh was collateral damage. Unlucky in the extreme."

"So, did someone on the kitchen staff have it out for Win Taggart?"

"Not that I can tell. That's what's so frustrating. That and the dishwasher. He's a liar."

"Oh, yeah?"

"Came in with a lawyer—a decent one, too—and said he never went out to the bar area, even though Intira said he did."

"That's bold."

"It is. And he was smug about it too. My gut says he did it. But we have only one witness who says he went out there, no video, no corroboration. It's his word against Intira's. I can't even make a convincing case to arrest him, much less convict him. And on top of that, I can't figure out why he'd want to do it. There's no connection between him and Win Taggart that I can see."

"Not to be a snob or unappreciative of hardworking folks, but just as a matter of practicality, how does a dishwasher afford a decent lawyer?"

"That's something I have Sergeant Naseer looking into."

"Good. I should probably ask: Did you confirm that the Chartreuse was poisoned?"

"Oh, yeah. Definitely. Somebody dosed it really well. Thanks for narrowing that down so quickly."

"My pleasure. So you have a group of people with possible motives to kill Win Taggart and another group of people with opportunity, and as far as you know, they don't have any relationship to each other."

"Right."

I stopped eating and looked at Starbuck, and he stopped because I stopped and he knows you don't stop eating gravy-soaked breakfast unless it's serious.

<What is it, Oberon? Did you hear a squirrel outside? No squirrel!>

<No, I just thought of a connection between the two groups. Atticus, there's a connection!>

He didn't make any sign that he heard me, he just kept eating, but in my head he asked, *Between who?*

<Between Jerry Fielder and the lady with the parents who are farmers. What was her name again?>

<Darla Hutchens!> Starbuck said. <She's the one who did it. I told you that. I said so.>

What's the connection?

<Jerry Fielder is a smoker, and I caught a whiff of his smoke in Darla Hutchens' clothes. Which means that she and Jerry met sometime yesterday before the deaths, and he smoked around her!>

Oberon, are you sure? She could have picked up that smell from anywhere.

<It was the same smoke, Atticus!>

Why didn't you tell me this earlier?

<I didn't make the connection until now. I smelled Darla first and noted Jerry's smoking later. And at the time, we weren't trying to connect the kitchen staff with the friends of the victims. We were trying to figure out who had been by the Chartreuse.>

You are absolutely sure the smoke from Jerry's particular cigarettes was on Darla Hutchens' clothes?

<Absolutely.>

This is a problem.

<Why?>

I can't smell stuff like that. I never even met Darla last night because I was either at our table or at the bar. So, I can't present this information to Rose and pretend it came from me. I would have to say you told me.

<Oh! Three kinds of cat shit, I didn't think about that. Uh. Never mind, then.>

No. You know what? It's time.

<Oh, no, not that again! Atticus, you know I'm not good with time. I mean, I'm good with lunchtime and dinnertime, but unless you tell me what you mean, I'm going to be confused.>

It's time to tell Rose the truth.

<About what? The aliens watching us from their outpost on one of Jupiter's moons? You know, I sometimes wish Mulder and Scully were real just so you could tell them. They would ruin their underwear if they knew about that.>

I mean the truth about being a Druid. The truth about you.

<Wait, what? Great big bears, Atticus, you never said there would be a time for that!>

I've been thinking about it for a while. This doesn't feel like a fling to me. It's real, so I want to be real with her.

<Did you think about how being real with her might mean she tells us to get out for real?>

I have. That's going to hurt if it happens. But it will hurt both of us more, the longer I keep pretending to be someone I'm not. I am going to take the immortal advice of Van Halen and jump.

<Maybe you should think it over some more. Please?>

He didn't answer me. He took another slurp of coffee and got up to get the carafe, which he used to refill both their mugs. He took their plates to the sink to be washed a bit later, and returned to sit across the dining table from Rose, who was zoning out a bit, staring at her coffee mug. She looked up when Atticus spoke.

"Rose, I have something I need to tell you. A lot of somethings, really, and I've been waiting for a good time, and this seems like one."

That's when I engaged in conduct unbecoming of an Irish wolfhound.

CHAPTER 6

The Big Reveal

I yelped and whined, which is not something I do very often, and Rose whipped her head around, worried that I was hurt. She's a very sweet human and I loved her and I also loved living in her house in Tasmania where there were wombats to play with and weird birds singing songs and interesting trees to pee on. And because of that, I was panicking.

<Atticus, you don't have to do this! Just say "Never mind!" Because if she kicks us out, we'll be sleeping outside instead of curled up on a pillow with a chew toy!>

I appreciate your concern, but the chance you might lose a cozy sleeping arrangement is nothing like the burden of living a lie. I have to see if we can live genuinely together.

<There won't be a refrigerator full of food, Atticus! That means a longer wait time between snacks!>

I think I may have pampered you too much.

That, plus Starbuck saying, <Oberon, are you a hound or a Chihuahua?> helped me calm down.

"What in the world?" Rose said. "I've never seen him act like that."

"He doesn't want me to tell you. He thinks you'll kick us out. And maybe you will."

"I guess this isn't going to be a fun conversation, if I'm going to be doing any kicking."

"Probably not. But I care about you too much to keep pretending. I'm aware, and very grateful, that you like what you know of me so far, and I am hopeful you'll continue to like me after you know the rest."

She crossed her arms in front of her, which is a human body-language thing that's generally not positive. I felt my tail drop down between my hind legs. "You have a criminal history?" she asked.

"I have a lot of history, period, but let's not characterize that yet. Let's start small. You know that Oberon and Starbuck are very smart."

"Yes. You've trained them exceptionally well."

"That's the thing. They're not trained. They understand English."

Rose snorted. "What do you mean? They can talk?"

"Not with their mouths. They don't have human vocal cords or the skull structure to make the sounds we do. But they understand everything we're saying."

"Right now?"

"Right now, and from the moment you met them. All along."

Rose blinked a few times and looked at us. "So how do they talk to you?"

"That's a different and bigger thing, so if you don't mind, let's finish with the first thing: They understand us, and I'd like you to accept that as a starting point. You can ask them to do something that's not a typical training command and they'll respond."

"I just say a normal sentence and they'll do it?"

"If they can, yes."

"All right. I'll play along. Oberon, I would like you to circle the couch in the living room and when you get back to me, I want you to place your right paw on top of my left leg." That was too easy, but I did exactly as she said, and her eyes got big when I put my paw on her leg. "What. The. Shit."

Atticus was satisfied that I'd proven myself, so he said, "Starbuck is still acquiring language and abstract concepts are tough, but he's been learning quickly and can do anything concrete."

"Okay." Rose blinked rapidly, trying to process this and think of something a bit more complicated. "Starbuck, please go into my bedroom closet. I think the sock drawer is still open a little bit. Get a pair of socks out of there and bring them to me."

My little buddy trotted off immediately and was back in less than thirty aeons with a pair of socks with unicorns on them.

"Oh my God," Rose said. "So, it's true. Yesterday, Peter Lassiter asked if he could give them a little something and they went right over to him. And when Intira Madeua said that Bart Simmons had been behind the bar, they looked over at Bart at the same time we did. They understand us."

"Yes."

"How?"

"Okay. Here we go. This is going to sound impossible, but let's rip off the bandage and say I have a telepathic connection to them. They can hear my thoughts and I hear theirs. So, that's how they talk to me. Mind to mind."

She blinked even faster than before. "I…I don't know what to do with that."

"I'm pretty sure I can prove it to you. Think of an occasion where you were alone with them and I wasn't around. Maybe you went for a walk or visited the dog park. If something memorable happened or was said, they can tell me and I'll repeat it."

"Well…all right, then. I tend to talk to them while we walk, making comments about the neighbors. Maybe they can remember something I said?"

That was easy. We told Atticus a couple of things and he said, "Starbuck says you hate that one house with the teal front door, it was a terrible decision and you judge them for it, and Oberon says you think the man two doors down is having an affair. Whoa, really?"

"Oh, yeah, he's sketchy as hell— Wait. They just told you that? In your head?"

"Yep."

Rose stood up and began to pace. "Is this some kind of Dr. Doolittle stuff? You can talk to animals?"

"Just Oberon and Starbuck, and one other Irish wolfhound that isn't here. With other animals, I can communicate but it's not in English. More like pictures and emotions."

"Again, I have to ask: How?"

"Whew. Okay. I guess we're moving on to the next thing? You're good with the dogs understanding English and speaking to me mind to mind?"

"I don't know if I'm good with it, but I accept that it's happening. Either that or you are working one hell of a con on me. Is there another shoe that's going to drop?"

"Think of the closet of Imelda Marcos."

Rose's jaw dropped. "*That* many shoes?"

<How many shoes did she have, Atticus?> I asked.

All of them. To Rose he replied, "That might be a slight exaggeration. It's just a lot. And as we go through it, I hope you'll see that I couldn't have laid all this on you at the beginning. When we were working on the murder of William Howe, if I'd told you then that I could talk to the dogs, would you have believed me?"

"No. No, I— Oh my God. I remember thinking they were the smartest dogs I'd ever seen—"

"They definitely are."

"Yeah, but I mean, I just assumed you were an extraordinary trainer."

"Ah! That's good—that realization you're having. It was there the whole time, but you just didn't have the ability to see what was really happening. Keep that in mind, okay?"

Rose crossed her arms. "Fine. Drop another shoe on me."

<I didn't see him drop *any* shoes,> Starbuck said in confusion.

<They are using figurative language. No actual shoes will be dropped.>

"You know how atoms will form bonds to make up molecules, and these molecules will form proteins and all kinds of other bonds to make up life as we know it?"

"Of course."

"We're learning more about these bonds all the time. They've been there all along, regardless of our ability to perceive them. And we're also learning more about the nature of consciousness, how it's an electrical wave form produced by biochemistry, and how even trees have a sort of intelligence and the ability to communicate via more chemistry. When things die or catch fire or whatever, it's just a breakdown of those bonds and they get transformed into something else. Well, there are currently three people on Earth who can see bonds of all kinds and manipulate them. I'm one of those three people. And what I did was bind my consciousness to Oberon's and Starbuck's so that they would gradually learn language and be able to speak to me mind-to-mind."

Rose exhaled a breath she'd been holding and sat down. "That is a damn big shoe. Why are you one of only three?"

"I've been bound to the Earth. These tattoos on my right side that you've been so curious about were produced by thorns from a living bush, and it was a three-month ritual that bound me to Gaia and gave me the power to bind and unbind things. I am a Druid, Rose. Not the modern kind. The really old kind that never wrote anything down, so there's a lot of misinformation about them today. A Druid's magic is simply the Earth's magic—magic in the sense that human science is still figuring it out. But all of it is binding and unbinding."

"That is a lot."

"I know, yeah. And there's more, but maybe you'd like to see me bind something tangible right now, so that it's not just the invisible binding of my mind to the dogs' minds?"

"Like what?"

Atticus stood from the dining table and turned to the kitchen. "How about that wooden spoon you have in the little container next to the stove? I'll temporarily form a bond between it and my palm, and it will fly to my hand. Or you can pick something else to reassure yourself I'm not running a con on you. But I can only bind natural things to other natural things. Synthetic materials are immune to my abilities."

Rose's eyes narrowed. "Okay. Hold on." She left the dining area and walked into the kitchen, and that was simply walking from hardwood to tile because she had an open floor plan, no walls between the main living areas. She opened a drawer and pulled out a pair of wooden salad tongs. "You wouldn't have been able to arrange this beforehand, so bind this to your palm."

"While you're still holding them?"

"Yes."

"Okay, but when the binding takes effect, it's going to move pretty quickly, so let go or you might get yanked."

"I will."

Atticus began speaking in Old Irish to perform the binding, and when it worked, Rose was startled and thrown off balance a bit, but she did let go and the tongs flew to his hand. She froze, staring at the evidence. Atticus kept his hand where it was so that it was visible the entire time but circled his body around it.

"I'm going to bind them now to the front door." He spoke some more stuff I couldn't understand, and the tongs flew across the dining area and living room to the door, *thwack*ed upon contact, and stuck there like they'd been superglued in place.

Rose let out another heavy breath. She was getting upset and maybe a little scared. "What was that language you spoke?"

"Old Irish."

"*Old* as in nobody speaks it anymore?"

"Just a few people. Some scholars in Ireland and the other two Druids."

"Where are they?"

"One's in Arizona and one's in Taiwan."

"I would never have guessed either place. Nor here. Why *are* you here?"

"When you met me, I told you I was surveying Tasmanian devil populations for research on the face cancer that was killing them all off. The truth was, I was healing them with Gaia's help. The population's resistant now and they won't be going extinct."

"I read about that. The papers said they evolved resistance."

"Because I made them resistant, but sure."

"So you...look after the Earth? Your job with the Gaia Stewardship is really your Druid stuff?"

"Exactly. I love the work, but it would be better if there were more of us doing it. Three of us trying to mitigate the damage wrought by billions is not enough."

"Was your trip to the mainland—that whole thing with the fire in the Blue Mountains—something you had to do as a Druid, then?"

"Very much so. Occasionally, there are emergencies and I have to respond."

Rose started circling the kitchen island, thinking, and Atticus didn't say anything, but I couldn't stand it.

<What's happening, Atticus? Is she going to kick us out?>

Too early to tell. She's thinking about it and doing pretty well so far. But there are still a lot of shoes to drop.

<Where are all these shoes?> Starbuck asked. <And why are you dropping them?>

Oh. Sorry, Starbuck. Rose referred to a human expression that I believe originated in New York. People living in tenements would often hear their neighbors living above them drop their shoes on the floor, one at a time. You hear one shoe, then you expect the next shoe to follow. So it came to mean that if one bad thing happened, you expected another bad thing to follow. We are using it here to mean that these truths I'm telling Rose are the shoes. I have a lot of truths, so we are talking about a lot of shoes.

<Language is hard.>

You're doing great.

Rose stopped her pacing and looked at Atticus. "Is there more?"

"Yes. If you're ready to hear it."

"I have a specific question to ask."

"Okay. Are you wondering how old I am?"

"Guess you saw that coming. You spoke Old Irish and you said you're the old kind of Druid."

"Right. So this is maybe the hardest one to accept. And again, it's not something I felt I could tell you right away, but I want you to know everything now. Forget what my ID says; forget that I look like I'm in my twenties. I'm more than two thousand years old."

Rose boggled. "Shut the front door."

Starbuck turned around to check and said, <Door's already closed.>

<She's using an idiom again,> I explained. <She's expressing disbelief.>

<Auughh! Why don't humans just say what they mean?>

"It's true," Atticus said.

"Are you immortal?"

"No, I can die. Just not of old age."

"How is that possible?"

"I periodically drink a tea that refreshes stem cells and slows the cellular decay that ages us. Keeps me young. And just being able to say that represents a major advance in human knowledge, by the way. Until recently, I had no choice but to say it was a magic tea. Or Immortali-Tea, because I like puns."

"Where do you get this tea? I assume it's not for sale at Coles or IGA."

"I make it myself. Secret recipe and all that."

Rose threw up her hands and chuckled. "What the hell are you doing here, then?"

"I'm still human, Rose. Living for millennia hasn't made me better than anyone except when it comes to long-term investing. Old as I am, I still fuck up. I make bad decisions sometimes. I wouldn't even say I make them less often than the average person. I don't know if that's sad or reassuring. I have an excellent memory and know a lot of languages and have street smarts from back before there were streets. But I'm still fallible and vulnerable and have a profound need to make connections with others—it's a key to living a long time. Plenty of recent science suggests that people who keep and make friends as they age tend to live longer and happier lives. You and I have connected, and I want it to continue, if you can forgive me for leaving out a large part of my bio."

"Ha! Yeah. If you're really that old, you have a gigantic biography. You must have more exes than anyone."

"Pretty much."

"You must have had families?"

"Yes. All of them wonderful while they lasted."

"While they lasted? You mean you outlived them all? That's tragic."

"Yes. But all relationships end tragically, without exception. Ours will too, one way or another. That's not a reason to avoid them. You have to embrace what joy you find in the short time you're allowed to do so, and if you don't mind me saying so, Rose, you are an absolute joy."

Her eyes narrowed. "What's your angle here?"

"I'm angling to be open and truthful with you. Because I think there's more joy to be had between us if I don't have to hide who I really am."

"Huh. So what else are you hiding?"

"More shoes, eh? You're okay with my age?"

"I don't know about that yet, but I want the full story."

"Okay. Here's the last one: All the gods and monsters are real. They have been all along, but people aren't seeing it."

"All the gods?"

"Yes. But I should distinguish between the gods and the religions. The gods exist because of collective faith, but large parts of the religions are horseshit. The creation stories can't all be real, for example. And the ones that say there's only one true god are spectacularly wrong about that."

"Have you met some of these gods?" When Atticus nodded, she asked him which ones.

"Off the top of my head—the pagan Irish, of course, and most of the Norse, Inari from the Shinto faith, Ganesha from the Hindu pantheon, lots of the Greco-Romans."

"You mean, like Zeus? What's he like?"

"Eternally horny and not in a good way."

"Jesus?"

"A genuinely nice guy who keeps a file on people who do evil shit in his name."

"That has to be a pretty thick file."

"The thickest."

"You mentioned the Norse. Have you met Thor?"

"A few times. He used to be a huge dick, but he's better now."

"What happened?"

"Well, he died but then remanifested, and when he did that, it was sort of like a reboot; all the accumulated bitterness he'd gathered from being the subject of an apocalyptic prophecy was gone."

"How'd he die?"

"A vampire with a grudge struck him with an enchanted blade that necrotized his flesh."

"A vampire." Rose's tone had gone flat. I was pretty sure she'd reached her breaking point.

"Yes. Their numbers are strictly regulated. And so are werewolves."

"Right. Anything else?"

Atticus summoned the salad tongs from the door to his hand, then he stepped forward and placed them on the kitchen island.

"Lots of little things when you're ready, but those are the biggies. I'm a very old Druid bound to Gaia, my dogs can understand English, gods and monsters are real, and there's no one else I wish to be with except you."

He reached out to her and she stepped back, so Atticus stopped.

"I'm sorry," she said, "but I need some time to think about this."

"Okay, that's fine. Is there something you need proven? It looks like maybe the gods-and-monsters one was tough."

"It's all tough. Because you're either lying to me now or you've been lying all along up to now."

"It's the second one, for which I apologize. Telling you all this from the start was not an option—it has never worked out the few times I've tried it. My choices were to keep lying or to wait just long enough to where you might be able to believe and forgive or, if not, cut me loose without too much heartbreak and wasted time."

"How many times have you had this talk?"

"I haven't kept track, but I'd say fewer than twenty, spread out over two thousand years."

"And how many times have the women to whom you've told all this decided to stay with you? You have to know that."

"Four."

"Only four?"

"Yes. Long odds. But worth it. Because the years I spent with those four were the best of my very long life."

"And what happened to the ones who cut you loose?"

"I hope they lived happily ever after, but I don't know, because I left them in peace and never saw them again."

"And the ones you stayed with—you never gave them this magic tea? You just let them grow old and die?"

"No, I gave them some if they asked. But long life isn't for everyone. The tragedy of outliving everyone you know is truly heartbreaking. So, most of them stopped taking the tea and made the decision to grow old, and we said goodbye."

"Most of them?"

Atticus nodded. "One met a violent end. I couldn't prevent it. That was nearly a thousand years ago."

The most awkward of silences stretched between them as Rose stared at Atticus. It kept going and going until Starbuck turned to me and said, <Do we…finish breakfast?>

<I'm too scared to make a sound,> I said. Rose was the one to break the silence.

"Okay, look, Connor, I appreciate what you said, but I need some time with this, and need you to leave right now. Maybe spend the night somewhere else."

"Understood. Give it a think, and please call if you have any questions. Oh—I almost forgot. This conversation was going to happen soon regardless, but it was prompted this morning because I needed to share an observation that Oberon made: Darla Hutchens' clothing smelled faintly of smoke, the same kind of cigarettes that Jerry Fielder smokes. It's likely that she and Jerry met earlier in the day, long enough for him to smoke around her. So it might be worthwhile looking for a connection between them. Darla had the motive, and Jerry had the opportunity."

Rose caught my eyes. "Oberon? Is that true?" I moved my head up and down and barked once. "Interesting. Thank you. Wait, what am I— I'm talking to a dog."

"Okay," Atticus said, and he strode across the living room and opened the front door for us. "Talk to you later. Come on, Oberon and Starbuck. Let's give Rose some space."

<That's it? We're out? We're gone?> I asked Atticus. With a last mournful look at our unfinished breakfast bowls of carnitas and kibble, we trotted out and down the front steps and Atticus closed the door behind us.

For the moment, yes.

<Is she going to let us come back?> Atticus didn't answer until we were on the street, heading in the general direction of the local park.

I don't know. She has to accept a paradigm shift and *forgive me, and it's a pretty big thing to ask of someone. Odds are against it. But I like her too much to keep pretending to be normal.*

<I like her too,> Starbuck said. <But I don't know why a pair of dimes would shit or why she has to accept it.>

<They wouldn't, buddy. He said *paradigm shift*. But yeah, Rose is great,> I agreed.

Someone was coming toward us on the street—I couldn't tell if it was a man or a woman from a distance—but I could tell that their feet weren't actually touching the ground.

<Atticus, I'm pretty sure that's a faery coming toward us right now.>

Starbuck and I growled, because that usually meant trouble.

CHAPTER 7

The New Old Way

Normally, Atticus can handle any faery that feels like messing with him. He's the Iron Druid, after all, and his touch is fatal to beings of magic. But too many of them had tried to kill Atticus for Starbuck and me to overlook that, so we were disposed to growl at the Fae until we knew everything was gravy. In this case, it turned out to be Coriander, Brighid's Herald Extraordinary, and while he sometimes brought bad news, he wasn't bad news by himself.

One of the things I like about Coriander is that he usually has a glamour on when he floats around in front of humans. He always looks like a very pretty man or a super handsome woman, but his outfits are usually some sort of vintage. In this case, he looked like Joan Jett if she had been a blonde. His clothes were all black leather with lots of chrome buckles and studs on things, and he had such heavy black makeup around the eyes, it was almost a superhero mask. It was the sort of getup that screamed he thought his parents were hopelessly corrupt and they thought he was a criminal and had quite likely disowned him.

"Hello, Coriander," Atticus said. "This is a surprise. Is there something up?"

"Good morning. There is indeed something up, but nothing worrisome. For once, I have good news."

"Do tell."

"Brighid herself has constructed a new Old Way in the hills nearby, which should allow you some more freedom of movement since you are no longer able to use the network of bound trees."

Coriander was referring to the loss of Atticus's arm there, because the tattoos on his forearm were the bindings that allowed him to shift planes. "Oh, no kidding? That was very thoughtful of her."

"Then you should like what follows. She has also made one near Taipei and Flagstaff, allowing you access to Granuaile and Owen. She plans to have eighty-seven more made for a total of ninety but would like your input on where these should be placed. She wondered if perhaps you had a list of projects you wished to work on, now that the Tasmanian devils are largely stabilized, and if the location of those projects might inform the location of new Old Ways."

<Why are they new and old at the same time?> Starbuck asked me. <Shouldn't they just be one or the other?>

Atticus heard and answered his question. *They are called Old Ways because they used to be the way we connected Earth to Tír na nÓg before we started binding trees for our travel. So we are talking about a new passage to Tír na nÓg here but constructed in the way we used to make them in the very old days.*

To Coriander he said, "I'll give it some thought."

The herald asked if he might show us the Old Way now, and Atticus readily agreed. Now we had a destination besides the park!

<Where are we going to go, Atticus?>

Instead of answering, he asked Coriander a question. "Do you know if Owen and Granuaile are free at the moment?"

"Owen is. Granuaile is dealing with a situation."[2]

"Oh? Anything I should worry about?"

"She'll call if she needs you. She's been doing very well on her own."

"Well, I can't go to Flagstaff. Greta basically banished me from her territory."

---

2 This situation will be revealed in the third book of the Ink & Sigil series, *Candle & Crow*.

"I'm aware. But I thought we might arrange for Owen and his charges to come visit you. And their squirrel-chasing companions."

<You know what that means, Starbuck?> I said.

<Yes! Puppies! Big puppies!>

<And knocking Owen down. We have to do it at least once so he can access deep wells of rage and call us creative names.>

<Sounds fun!>

I was a little disappointed that we wouldn't get to see Orlaith, the beautiful wolfhound who belonged to Granuaile and gave birth to our puppies, but it would be a blast to see the puppies again, since I'd hardly seen them at all and didn't even know their names yet. My vague plan was to play with them a lot and then nap super hard. Plans like that are great because they don't need to be specific to work out perfectly.

Negotiating an Old Way is basically walking in a weird pattern so that you slip between planes and arrive in Tír na nÓg, the Irish land of eternal youth. From there you walk a bit and take a different Old Way that slips you back somewhere different on Earth. In this case, we left Launceston and arrived in Tír na nÓg, which smelled of grass and orange blossoms, and turned right around to wait for Owen to join us on our hilltop in Launceston, but the purpose had been served: Atticus knew how to use the Old Way now, so he could take us anywhere in the future.

Owen arrived soon after, trailed by his small grove of Druid apprentices who just all happened to be the children of werewolves—normal human children, I mean, whose parents got turned into werewolves after they were born. They wanted their kids to be bound to the Earth because once that happened, they'd be immune to lycanthropy.

Since there were six apprentices and Orlaith had six puppies, it was perfect: they would become the hounds of a new generation of Druids.

With all those squealing human kids and barking puppies making noise—great big bears, I could feel a case of the zoomies coming on, and I'm sure Starbuck did too. Yeah—front paws down, butts in the air, tails wagging? It was happening.

<Zoom now!> I shouted.

<Copy that, Grey Leader!>

And we were off, six puppies and a Boston terrier chasing me through the eucalyptus and startling a sleeping wallaby into frantic flight. The humans laughed at us, and once I tumbled down and let the puppies dogpile me, the kids made happy noises and joined in.

In general terms, humans don't understand how fun dogpiles can be. They're extremely fulfilling. But these apprentices knew what was up. We had a great time.

Because happy dogpiles don't come along every day. They're a special thing that happens when you collectively realize how awesome it is to be on the same patch of the planet together at the same time.

And I was very happy because my pups were happy, and I got to learn their names given to them by their miniature Druids-to-be.

The biggest of them all was named Oso, which was Spanish for Bear, and he belonged to Luiz. Khalid was with the boy named Mehdi, and the smallest of the litter was named Pico, who belonged to Ozcar. Amita named her puppy Sakari; Tuya loved her hound, Orghana; and the oldest apprentice, Thandi, also had the firstborn and therefore oldest puppy, Malika.

The hounds weren't bound to their humans' minds yet and didn't know much language, though they understood some basic words. Apparently, the kids needed an elemental's help to connect to their puppies' minds, and they weren't able to maintain a connection for long before they got headaches, since their brains were still developing. They got one single minute per day, supervised by Owen, and that was good, because there was love exchanged and maybe the pups learned a new word. By the time the humans were finished with their training and bound to the Earth, the pups would be full-grown and fluent and ready to run with them wherever they went as Druids.

We played for a good while, and Atticus even got some wombats to come over and join in, then we all took a nap, just like I planned, while Atticus and Owen talked about Druid things and picked out some spots where they'd like to have the Fae construct new Old Ways.

When we woke up, it was because of a phone ringing and Owen cursing the damned nuisances always ruining a quiet time. It was Rose calling Atticus, and he made his apologies. But it was around noon and way past bedtime for the kids and pups, who were in a different time zone than us, and Owen said they should head back to Flagstaff. I was sorry to see them go, and sorry that I never got around to knocking Owen down, but so glad we had the chance to play and nap together. Maybe soon we could arrange for the kids and pups to visit at the same time as Granuaile and Orlaith. A family reunion would be the best.

As soon as they faded out of sight, Atticus said into the phone, "Okay, be there as soon as we can," and ended the call.

"Your tip paid off, Oberon," he said aloud. There were no other humans around to hear.

<It did?>

"Uh-huh. Rose followed up almost as soon as we left, and the connection became clear. Come on, let's get moving; we have some ground to cover." He started moving pretty fast down the hill—not all out, but certainly not a casual jog either—and we kept pace as he filled us in. "Sergeant Naseer was looking into Jerry Fielder's finances. He was having issues because dishwashing didn't pay him well enough to indulge his taste for designer clothes and fast cars. He went into serious debt to get them anyway."

<Oh, so he decided to do a little sidecrime?>

"Exactly."

<No sidecrime!> Starbuck said. <We capture criming man! We pee on criming man! Then we feast!>

<Those are excellent action items,> I told him. <But Atticus, how did she connect Jerry Fielder to Darla Hutchens?>

"She didn't give me all the details, but the short answer is city traffic cams. She looked for both Darla's and Jerry's cars in yesterday's footage, and apparently that worked. We can get the details from Rose when we see her."

<So you're forgiven? We're going home?>

"Not yet. We're going to Trevallyn State Park on the southwest side of town. Rose is going to meet us there."

<Why are we going there?>

"Because Sergeant Naseer has already arrested Darla Hutchens without a problem. Jerry Fielder, however, fled into the bush, and Rose is hoping you can track him down quickly."

<When we catch him, I pee first!> Starbuck said.

<Why?>

<Because I said Darla did it and I was right.>

<But Jerry was the actual murderer and I connected him to Darla!>

"You can pee on him in stereo," Atticus said, which surprised me because he normally doesn't let us pee on people.

We can slobber on whoever we want but not pee, and that is a weird rule if you think about it because science humans would probably say there is more bacteria in our mouths than there is in our pee. Atticus continued: "You both helped tremendously and will help some more. I helped too, you know. I found the murder weapon."

<Oh, that's right! Are you going to pee on him with us?>

"No, no, I would never do that. I was making the point that it was a team effort. Sergeant Naseer did a lot of work, and so did Rose."

<She wasted sausage, Atticus.>

"She had to follow procedure. You need to forgive her for that."

<I already have. But I will never forget.>

CHAPTER 8

Operation: Sidecrime

Once we made it to a main thoroughfare, we caught a ride from a taxi driver who was worried I was going to cause damage to his car, which was not in excellent condition to begin with. It was like someone with a spiderwebbed windshield worrying about me cracking the glass. Or a guy with a tiny crust of bread on his plate worrying I would eat his sandwich. The damage had already been done. But we got to Duck Reach Power Station Carpark in fifteen minutes—I know because Atticus mentioned it—and found Rose with no trouble, because it wasn't a huge area. The huge area was the Trevallyn State Park to the north and west of it. The South Esk River formed the boundaries of the park to the south, east, and west. On the west side was the Trevallyn Dam, and on the east side was the Cataract Gorge Reserve. We were on the southeastern side of the park.

"Thanks for getting here so fast, Connor," Rose said.

"Of course."

"Thought he was off his nut coming here at first, but it was pretty smart. He ran up the stairs and crossed the suspension bridge to the power station, and kept going. So Jerry Fielder is in the bush somewhere out there," she said as she waved in the general direction of the park, "and we have units setting up blocks at the exits, as you no doubt saw coming in, but there's plenty of room for him to squeeze through and cross the river if he keeps to the bush. We don't have the manpower yet to get him. Wondered if you and the dogs would be able to track him more quickly."

"We can certainly try," Atticus said. "I'm assuming that there's only one way to go until he gets to the other side of the bridge?"

"Yes, he probably stuck with it until the viewing platform above the power station, but after that, he could have gone in almost any direction, and I didn't think going after a murderer alone in the bush was a good idea."

As we started moving to the bridge together along a dirt track from the carpark, I said, <Ask her about how she connected Darla to Jerry. If I'm gonna be a law dog, I need to know the proof.>

Atticus relayed my message and Rose said, "Launceston only has a few major traffic arteries. We knew where Jerry lived and what he drove, and the same for Darla. So we scrolled through the traffic-cam footage from yesterday until we found their cars going through one of the intersections, and we were able to trace them pretty well. We saw them turn onto Charles Street from Frederick Street and thought we lost them at first—there's a Coles grocery store near there, and they didn't show up on their cameras at all. But there's also a Caltex gas station across the road. They'd parked on the street just past it, not realizing that security cameras have a very wide angle by design. We have footage showing Darla giving Jerry a thick envelope of cash, which he takes out and counts, and also a little vial full of clear liquid. He put the cash and vial away, and then, get this, Oberon—he took out a cigarette and smoked it while they chatted a little bit. Probably Darla telling him to poison the Chartreuse because Win Taggart always orders a D.A.C.—we're pretty sure we can pick that up through lip-reading."

I did a little *roo-roof* noise to let her know I appreciated that, but spoke mentally to Atticus and Starbuck.

<Victory is mine! And yours, and Starbuck's, and Rose's, and—let me try that again: Victory is ours!>

"He feels validated," Atticus said. "So you have proof she gave him some money, but how are you going to prove it was for the murder?"

"Sergeant Naseer did a lot of the financial work. A pattern of identical withdrawals over five days from Darla's accounts slowly filled that envelope. That's all premeditation. And Jerry has been depositing cash far in excess of his dishwasher's wages for a long time. He's got a lot of side hustles going on— and that's probably how he got on Darla's radar. She asked around, you know, who could do some dirty deeds for cash, and Jerry was the name she got. We're going to delve in to what else Jerry's been up to when we catch him. You know he drives a souped-up Ford FPV F6?"

"You're saying that like it's fast or expensive or both."

"It is. It's an Aussie car that isn't in production anymore, but guys like Jerry love them. Looks like a sedan, drives like a racer. It was parked next to mine. Did you see it?"

"Oh, the yellow one?"

Rose confirmed that, but I'd seen it too. <It wasn't just yellow, Atticus; it was obnoxiously yellow, a garishly gauche getaway car. I deserve a snack for alliteration and adverbs.>

Maybe. Starbuck, can you earn a snack too?

<Uh…killer cares for criminally uncool crime car?>

Well done. You both will get snacks.

<Yes food!>

Jerry's scent was easy to pick up on the trail and likewise across the suspension bridge, then up some metal stairs on the other side that allowed us to climb the side of the gorge quickly but were not very nice to our paws. We paused at the viewing platform and were all winded a bit from the climb, but Atticus would fix that soon, I was sure.

"So, from here, he could have gone anywhere?"

"Yes. There are multiple tracks that branch out from this one soon, and of course, he could ignore them and simply head into the bush."

"Do you know if he has any weapons?"

"He might have a knife, but I don't think he has a gun, or else he would have taken a shot at me."

"Okay. Jerry is going to get tired and slow down," Atticus said as he took off his sandals. "We can catch up if we give ourselves a boost."

"What do you mean?"

"One of the little things I can do as a Druid is temporarily increase my speed with Gaia's help, and I can also replenish our energy so we don't tire. That way, we can run with the dogs."

Rose's mouth dropped open first in surprise, then her eyes widened in realization.

"So much of that last case is making sense now. You ran up that hill, and I just thought you were in extraordinary shape."

"I am. But Gaia gives me some advantages too. Makes me a better champion of the Earth if I'm faster and stronger."

"Stronger?"

"I can boost my strength, too."

"Okay, uh." Rose looked around, saw that we were alone. "It's hard for me to suspend my disbelief here. Do you mind if I try asking the dogs something in English again?"

"No, go ahead." And to us he said privately, *Please do whatever she says.*

"Okay. Oberon and Starbuck, please look over your left shoulder at me as you walk backward in my direction."

That was not a comfortable or easy thing to do, and it was kind of embarrassing to maintain eye contact as we advanced on her ass-first, so as we did it, I said, <Atticus, I'm just now noticing that Rose might be into some weird shit. And I'm not saying that in a judgy way, okay? I mean *weird* as in *different*, not weird as in bad.>

<I don't like this walk,> Starbuck said.

<Starbuck, I will bet you all the sausages that Aerosmith never, ever walked this way.>

<Who is Aerosmith?> he asked, and Atticus laughed.

"What?" Rose's eyes darted between us and said, "Did they say something?"

"They are saying lots of things."

"Oh, I'm sorry, you guys, stop. Okay? Stop. I was trying to think of something Connor couldn't have trained you to do or expect beforehand. It's hard to accept that you really understand everything I say, or that any of this is real, but I guess this part is."

"It's all real," Atticus said. "But I do realize that it's a lot to digest. You guys ready? Go ahead if so. We'll follow."

<Let's catch criming man!> Starbuck said, and together we left the view platform and followed the scent as it led into the park.

"The dogs won't hurt him, right?" Rose said. "If they bite him, things could get really complicated."

"They won't. They'll trip him up and you'll arrest him. Easy peasy."

<Atticus! You just jinxed the whole thing! Now that you said that, it will be anything *but* easy peasy!>

<We had a shot, Oberon,> Starbuck whimpered mournfully. <We could have had it so easy peasy. All we had to do was not talk about it. And then the human—the Druid!—talks about it.>

You guys are such drama hounds, Atticus told us privately.

To be fair, at the beginning it was pretty easy: The trail was strong and easy to follow, and since Jerry Fielder wasn't the type who knew how to leave booby traps behind, we didn't have to take it slow. And the landscape didn't throw up a lot of obstacles either. There were trees of different kinds, but they were mostly the kind with narrow trunks, and the groundcover was dominated by grasses instead of shrubbery. It gave us a decent sight line and we were cruising pretty fast. Like, not a full-out human run that Jerry was probably doing until he figured Rose wasn't right behind him, but a nice pace that we could maintain and he definitely could not.

We pulled ahead of Atticus and Rose at first, but once Atticus did his thing, Rose whooped as they sped up and then kept pace behind us.

Once we reached the top of the mesa—there was more climbing to do to get there from the platform—Jerry actually kept to the loop circuit that ran along the edge of the mesa, moving counterclockwise. But eventually, he must have given some thought to where he was going, along with the very real possibility of being seen by other people out for a hike or bike, and he turned west into the bush.

Starbuck and I had actually been in this area before—we'd been to most wild places in Tasmania as Atticus went around healing devils. We could smell that there were some wombats nearby, and also some potoroos and bettongs, bandicoots and quolls, but most of these were sleeping through the day.

"This is an interesting choice," Rose said about the direction change. "He might be headed for the Hoo Hoo Hut."

<Is she being cute?>

No, I think that's really the name of a place.

"He's either got someone waiting for him there, or he thinks he can find a way down to cross the river on that side," she continued.

"Can't he?"

"I suppose you could, but that's a very steep drop on the west side, and it's full of brush, unlike what we have here."

"Or he's looping around to the south, thinking you won't expect him to try circling back in that direction," Atticus said.

"Maybe so. Though it's steep both ways in that direction, too—especially climbing back out. You'd need rock-climbing gear for that. But this is why we need the dogs. There's too much ground to cover, too many places he can slip through."

I was thinking we'd plow through any kind of bush to get some satisfaction when all the trees suddenly disappeared. There was just grass and electric wires. Humans had bulldozed a path through the trees to give their electrical transmission wires space. And it was right there that Jerry's trail turned sharply right, heading north along the electrical highway.

<He zigged! Or zagged. Which is which again, Atticus?>

If you zig one way, then zag is the other way.

<I can explain, Oberon,> Starbuck said. <Usually we zig, see, but Rose made us zag.>

<Oh! I see, yes. Very different. Right now, we are zigging toward Jerry.>

<Correct! We must not zag. Criming man ahead!>

"Now this makes sense," Rose said behind us. "There's actually a trail along the edge of this space. He could move fast and head north and dive into the bush on either side at any time, and there's no great elevation issues. This will take him right into a neighborhood if he keeps going. Might be his best shot at an escape."

<We can still track him in a neighborhood," I said.

Not if he steals the first car he sees.

<Oh. So, we need to speed up?>

Yes. As fast as you can go without losing the scent. He might take another sharp turn.

So we sped up, and Rose remarked that she couldn't believe they were keeping up with us, because we were actually running now, though we did have to double back a couple of times because of strange deviations in the trail. It would veer into the bush for a short distance and then return to the electric alley, where it continued north. Atticus figured Jerry was doing that to avoid people seeing him on the trail, so they couldn't give away his position to anyone following, like us. Because we did meet some people on the trail and asked if they'd seen someone who looked like Jerry, and they said no, even though they should have seen him.

There was a long stretch of running I won't forget, because it kept going, and we were hauling a huge amount of ass, which Atticus says is not how I should phrase it but whatever, and suddenly I heard Rose laugh behind us, just a quick "Ha ha! Woo!" And when I glanced back, I saw her face lit up with such joy that she was keeping up with a couple of dogs running all out, and Atticus was just so glad that she was having a blast, and she smiled back at him and I knew then it would be okay. Even if we didn't catch up to Jerry, it would be okay, because Atticus and Rose made each other happy, and they finally knew it for sure, the way you know it's going to be a good night when someone throws you a T-bone and you catch it perfectly on the filet side and the juices explode in your meat hole.

T-bones are the best cuts of steak, by the way. There's a strip side, a filet side, and a bone to gnaw on! It's three dining experiences in one, and none of them are cauliflower.

Sorry, I had to talk about steak for a second because steak! It's out there right now! You can have some! But also because we have come to the part where things stopped being easy.

Because we saw Jerry ahead of us, and Atticus told us not to bark but to just run up behind him and make him fall down. The speed binding that he'd given himself and Rose he now gave to us, so we were suddenly very fast dogs.

But Jerry heard us coming. He turned around, saw us, recognized us, shouted at us, and then I think he saw Atticus and Rose following behind, and he lost it. His chest heaving, teeth clenched, he let loose a desperate war cry like someone who knows Conan the Barbarian is going to cut them down but they've decided to die fighting, and then he spun, turning his back to me as I leapt at his chest to basically tackle him, and something clocked me upside the head and I lost my vision for a bit. When it came back, there were spots in it and my ears weren't working right except that Starbuck sounded mad and Jerry sounded madder. Also, I was on the ground on my side and I didn't remember lying down.

Then Atticus was there kneeling next to me, hand on my shoulder, worry in his voice as he said my name, but Jerry was getting up. I guess he'd been on the ground too? When did he fall? What happened?

Atticus said something in Old Irish and Jerry was abruptly flat on his back again and sinking into the ground just a little bit so that he couldn't move. Atticus asked the Earth to hold on to him and Jerry yelled a lot, and Starbuck was barking at him and shouting in my head at the same time.

<Shut up! Super bad criming man! Worst man ever! You should be thrown into a bathtub of ticks!>

And then Rose knelt down next to Atticus and she was making loud noises too and it was just all very loud and my head hurt as my vision popped and spun.

"Okay, let's all calm down," Atticus said. "Jerry's not going anywhere. Let me fix Oberon up and then we can attend to him."

"He's… You did that?"

"The local elemental did it, really. I asked it to hold on to him and not hurt him."

"This is another small thing you can do as a Druid?"

"Yes. But now I need to fix up Oberon."

"Right, that's good. You can do that? I don't need to call a vet?" She had her phone out and looked like she was about to make a call.

"Yeah, don't call anyone yet."

<What's broken that you need to fix, Atticus?> I asked him.

"He tagged you pretty good with a roundhouse kick, buddy. So you probably have a concussion at minimum and maybe more. I'm going to see."

At that point I got pretty sleepy and might have drowsed off just a bit, maybe a blink, but when I opened my eyes again, they worked like they did before, and my head didn't hurt, and my hearing seemed normal. Jerry was still yelling, but everyone else was quiet.

"Feel better?" Atticus asked.

<Yeah! Did you do something?>

"We fixed you up, yes. Can you stand?"

I stood up and felt the tiniest bit dizzy but otherwise okay.

<Did we earn our sausages and snacks?> I asked.

"Absolutely. But there's one more thing you have to do before Rose puts him in cuffs and calls in the collar. Operation: Sidecrime."

He told us hounds what to do in our heads, and I moved into position on one side of Jerry while Starbuck moved to the other side. When Atticus said go, we lifted our legs, aimed, and peed on Jerry Fielder for a very long time, right on his crotch. He called us bad dogs but also used a bunch of other curse words and promised to actually kill us. When we were finished, Atticus leaned over his face.

"You're an absolutely terrible human being, Jerry Fielder. The first two days that I've known you, you murdered two innocent people and kicked my dog. You've really misunderstood the assignment here. You should walk the Earth in kindness, with a deep sense of wonder and a deeper sense of gratitude, and give it the one gift you can give: a well-lived life in return for the countless gifts it gives to you. You had one job, Jerry, and you cocked it up. You probably won't be able to admit that to yourself, but if you do, maybe you can salvage some years down the road and live well." He turned to Rose. "You ready?"

She simply nodded and got out her handcuffs. Atticus had the elemental release Jerry's torso and arms but not his legs, and as soon as he felt the pressure ease up, he sat up, thinking his legs would also be freed, but nope. Rose was able to cuff him that way, though he fought against her and cussed a lot, and once he was secured, she told him all that legal stuff about being under arrest. Atticus freed his legs and they got him to his feet, and the ground smoothed out so that you'd never know the earth had done anything weird there.

Rose called it in: "Suspect in custody."

CHAPTER 9

Starting with Happy

It turned out that we had run so far that we were closer to Cataract Gorge than Rose's car by Duck Reach Power Station, so we walked there with a loudly complaining Jerry, and Rose handed him over with a sigh of relief to a couple of constables. We got a ride back to her car, and once we were all alone, she hugged me around the neck and said what a good boy I was, and how much she appreciated my help, and then she did the same with Starbuck, or tried to, but he got excited and licked her ear and she told him from a distance after that.

"Get in," she told us, and we piled into her tiny vehicle. Once on the road, she said to Atticus, "I'm taking you home. We have a lot to talk about. But...you're a real old-fashioned Druid."

"Yes."

You know what? I was so tired that I zoned out and napped. But I am pretty sure I didn't miss anything important: Rose was taking us home. That was the headline and all I needed to know, because I already knew about Atticus's Druid stuff.

And when we got home, I went straight to the doggie bed in the living room and napped some more because I'd earned it, and Starbuck sprawled on top of me for a tandem napping session. We woke to the sounds and smells of meat frying in a cast iron skillet. Atticus was cooking up a slice of cow cooked in cow squirt sauce!

He maybe ruined it a little bit by making me drink his Immortali-Tea afterward, which makes you feel amazing later but tastes terrible, and he gave Starbuck a swallow of it, too. "These rich foods you love so much aren't good for you, and you need some regeneration after that injury today, so no complaining."

<About the tea? So I can complain about something else?>

"Not if you're going to pretend that something else is my tea."

<Dang it! You're always a step ahead.>

Atticus frowned, looking at my back. "Oberon, what happened to your fur? It's all matted and gunked up with something. Did that happen while you were playing with the puppies?"

<Oh, no. That's all of Harry's snot. She cried on me for a long time. I would like to make an appointment for a bath, please.>

"We'll do that as soon as we can.>

<Is Rose not here?>

"She went back to work because she has a lot of paperwork to do to formally lay charges against Darla Hutchens and Jerry Fielder."

<Oh yeah, I should make sure I understand: Did Darla do it because Win Taggart was going to ruin her parents' farm, and Jerry did it for money?>

"That's right."

<Okay, I get the money motive because that's a popular one with humans, but why would anyone kill someone over a farm?>

"Farms are handed down through generations. A large part of Darla's identity was probably bound up in that farm, and I imagine she would have inherited it herself eventually. Win Taggart's project represented a threat to her and her family's future, and that's what often motivates women to kill. It was also a money thing in a way, just tied up with emotions that Jerry Fielder has probably never felt. She saw an opportunity to remove the threat to her future without pulling the metaphorical trigger, and she took it."

<And she would have got away with it, too, if it weren't for us meddling hounds!>

<We good boys though,> Starbuck said. <Yes we are.>

"You've solved another case," Atticus said. "What are you going to call this one?" I thought about it for a bit, because it was strange. I mean, *Don't Kick Dogs* immediately suggested itself, but maybe it would be better to stay positive and go with *Puppies Are Great*. The puppies didn't have much to do with the case, though.

<That steak was so good, Atticus, the perfect ending. Maybe *Beef in My Meat Hole?*>

"Hmm. I urge you to think about it some more. Your culinary reward was unrelated to the story of the crime, and people might get the wrong idea."

I thought about why the case made me sad and how upset I was at first about the sausage we didn't get to eat, but ultimately that wasn't the real tragedy. It was that Shiloh Timmins, a beautiful person who made other people happy to be alive, was ripped out of the world because she had the bad luck to be living her best life in proximity to murderers. And then Harry and Peter—and no doubt many more humans who loved Shiloh—were hurt so badly by her death. Atticus was right when he told Rose that all relationships are tragic in the end, but maybe especially when they end before they're supposed to. And while I'm sure someone, somewhere was upset about Win Taggart's passing, and *The Techbro is Toast* had a nice ring to it, I thought it best to shine a spotlight on this beautiful person that the world lost.

<We'll call this one *The Chartreuse Chanteuse*,> I said, and Atticus nodded his approval. <Do you think Harry will be okay?>

"I do. She's very sad at the moment, but she will get better."

Atticus said I should go hop in the bathtub because he wanted to pet Snotless Oberon, so I happily complied, and for my bathtime story he told me about the amazing Hildegard of Bingen, who was a nun that basically created modern beer by adding hops—Peter and every hophead should praise her name, for it was she who made IPAs possible! She also composed a lot of music and was a mystic healer who took a holistic approach to wellness and did so many other great things. *She* understood how to live a life, unlike Jerry Fielder. But it did make me worry that I wasn't doing enough stuff.

<Atticus, am I living right? All I do is think about food and poodles and nap."

"Nonsense. You are a loyal friend, you fight crime, and you comfort the grieving. And you always defend humanity against the evil of squirrels."

<No squirrel!> Starbuck said. He was sprawled across the bathroom doorway while I was getting my bath and had remained silent until then.

"Don't worry, Oberon. You're doing it right. You both are."

I shook myself and water flew everywhere, drenching Atticus.

<Am I still doing it right?>

"Nope, not that part. That wasn't right."

<Still! Behold my glory! I am now Snotless Oberon, Protector of Humanity!> I was going to continue in that vein, but we heard the front door open and close, and Rose called out that she was home. Starbuck leapt up and went to go greet her, and I wanted to do the same, but Atticus said no way, I had to get dried off first.

"We're in the bathroom," Atticus called. "I'm drying off Oberon."

"Oh, bathtime, is it? Hey, wait—Starbuck, stop humping my leg! You know better!"

Rose eventually appeared in the doorway, Starbuck at her feet, and she waved to me from there. "Hi, Oberon! I have updates. When we showed Darla the security tape from outside the gas station, she confessed in return for testifying against Jerry that she paid him to poison the Chartreuse. It'll reduce her sentence a little bit but make sure we get Jerry, because he's still lying about going out to the bar area. When we searched his house, we found a camera jammer, so that's how he disabled the manager's video surveillance of the bar. He had some other illegal items and drugs on the premises, too, so we'll get him for that even if his lawyer helps him beat the murder rap. I want to thank you again for telling Connor about the connection between Darla and Jerry. We might have made that connection eventually, but maybe not in time to catch that footage at the gas station. They only keep their security tapes for two days, so you made it possible for us to deliver some swift justice here."

<I am Snotless Oberon, Dispenser of Swift Justice!>

Atticus said, "Oberon is glad he could be of service and very proud of himself."

"As he should be. Okay. Come on out and sit next to me when you're dry, Oberon."

When Atticus was finally finished with me, I was still damp, of course, but at least I wouldn't leave puddles on the floor. I went out to the living room and draped myself across Rose's lap, and she petted my head idly while she spoke with Atticus.

"I accept that you're a Druid and capable of doing some extraordinary things, but I feel like there's still too much that I don't know. I have more questions."

"Of course. Fire away."

"Have you killed anyone?"

"Yes. Wars and whatnot. But also some Fae, demons, assorted vampires and other monsters, a gnarly wizard, and a couple of gods."

"Gods?"

"Yeah. Long stories in themselves. Those bad decisions I mentioned brought me into conflict with them. But the good news is I'm not on anyone's shit list anymore. My debts are paid and I no longer have to hide. I can just serve Gaia and enjoy walking in the world again."

"What debts are you talking about?"

"I was basically marked for death by several deities and had some different deities in my corner. A plea bargain was negotiated and now I'm free."

"What was the bargain?"

Atticus dipped his head to one side. "My right arm, basically. They took that, which removed some of my abilities. I used to be able to shape-shift into four different animals."

"Holy shit."

"Exactly. It was some holy shit. Punishment for my hubris. It was rough going at first, but I'm fine with it now. In fact, I love where I'm at."

"There's so much to unpack there, but you've actually landed on my next question, so I'm going to go after it: You're this guy who's seen and done most everything. I shouldn't be on your radar. Why me?"

"Why you? Because you're brilliant and you're trying to help. Who wouldn't want to be with someone like that? And you're a dog person, which is a prerequisite for hanging out with me. You're kind to people so long as they don't paint their front doors a heinous shade of teal. And, you know. You're beautiful. Capable of making my heart speed up whenever I see you. A little shot of serotonin every time you smile. You make me happy, Rose. That's it. There's no other angle."

This is a thing that humans do sometimes: They don't let themselves feel stuff they're already feeling unless they say it (or hear it) out loud. If they had tails, they would be wagging or not, and there would be no need to ask these questions about feelings. So, as far as biological design goes, great job on the thumbs, but terrible job on the asses.

There was some silence then, and Rose's mouth and chin did some squirming around because her emotions were doing the same. But her eyes filled up at the bottom, and she said quietly, "You make me happy too."

I figured that out *hours* ago. You see how slow humans can be about this sort of thing?

"That's great," Atticus said, letting out a breath and chuckling at the release of some tension. "Why don't we start there and take our time unpacking stuff? If you can forgive me for holding back up till now, I promise I'll tell you everything from now on, and prove to you whatever I can when you need proof."

"Okay. I forgive you, because you're absolutely correct that I would have dismissed it all if you led with it from the start. But you hold nothing back now, understood?"

"Understood."

"Good. Uh—Oberon, sweetie? I know you're comfortable, but you have to let me up. I have to go over there and kiss that man."

I recommend starting with happiness if you can. It can take some work to get there, for sure, and you may have to redefine what happiness means for you. For us it's food and love and no squirrels. I think that works for a lot of people, honestly. As long as you have that, you can handle the rest of life's challenges, and do that thing where you live happily ever after.

THE BARTENDER AND THE BEAST

BY DELILAH S. DAWSON

CHAPTER 1

Cassia King stood over a dead doe, wishing the world wasn't quite so full of assholes. Nobody liked hitting a deer, but everyone who did got out of the car to inspect the damage, and most people had the good sense to do the right thing and get the carcass out of the road. But no. Whoever had hit the doe just left her lying there, risking the lives of every other car on the twisting Georgia mountain road.

"Poor girl," she muttered, grabbing the doe by her slender ankles and dragging her off the asphalt and onto the shoulder.

And that's when she spotted a tiny fawn hiding under the brush, curled up in a nearly invisible ball, too new to know that a quiet tragedy had just occurred.

Cash was angry, she was in a hurry, she was frantic and sleepless, and she didn't have time for this shit.

Of course, that wasn't the fawn's fault.

"Come here, little guy." She approached the baby, boots crunching in the scree, trying to seem as small and harmless as possible.

She was taller than average and had been told she carried herself like an angry Valkyrie, which usually worked in her favor, but today she had to soften up and approach lightly. Luckily, the fawn's nervous system wasn't yet firing, and so it merely watched her, eyes like pools of molten chocolate. When she scooped it up, it barely weighed anything at all, and she held it like a football while she pulled a rank towel out of her gym bag and made a little nest in the passenger-seat floorboard. She thought about keeping the doe for meat but then, after looking down at the fawn again, realized that she would feel guilty as hell with every bite.

Once she was back behind the wheel, Cash immediately called her sister.

And again, for the forty-seventh time, received no answer.

"This is Keelie; leave a message."

Perky, sweet, clueless. That was Cash's baby sister.

And she was in trouble.

That was all Cash knew.

She looked at the clock, looked at her phone map, and probed her mind for the location of the Arcadia Falls humane society where they'd adopted their mutt, Parfait, back when Keelie was a toddler. How long would a detour take? Cash didn't know what was wrong, didn't know what she was rushing toward; she just knew that Keelie had left her a frantic voice mail begging her to come home. For an emergency, whatever that meant.

And so, after five long, angry years, Cash was coming home.

She sent Keelie another text. They were all marked as read, but Keelie wasn't responding. The whole thing was bizarre.

**Almost in town. Found a fawn, taking her to the animal shelter. Where do you need me?

And then, wonder of wonder, those three little dots wavering suggested that her sister was finally answering—and that she wasn't in the hospital or dead in a ditch. After two days of frantic driving, Cash's heart jolted as she waited to see what Keelie would say.

Come to MacGillicuddy's downtown, it said. And then, after a few moments in which Keelie had to be typing and erasing and typing and erasing: *I'm sorry, it really is an emergency.*

Cash frowned. MacGillicuddy's was a family restaurant on the downtown square, and it seemed like a strange place to go during an emergency. Sure, Keelie worked there, but if something truly terrible had happened, wouldn't she be... home? Or at the hospital? Or at Grammy's house? Something funny was up. Keelie had a perfectly functional phone, and she could clearly read messages, so why hadn't she responded when it was obvious her older sister was freaking out and dropping her entire life in Colorado to hurry home? A simple text would've solved everything.

Which meant Keelie was… avoiding her.

Which meant Keelie knew she'd done something wrong.

Worry warred with anger as Cash aimed her Jeep for the humane society, which was an old wooden building out in the middle of nowhere. Maybe thirty minutes later, she pulled up the gravel drive. The fawn hadn't made a single noise the whole time, had barely moved. He—Cash had decided it was a he—just put his little head down and slept. Being born was probably a very exhausting process.

Cash picked up the fawn in his gym-towel nest and carried him into the building to a cacophony of dog noises. A gnarled battle-axe of a woman turned from her ancient desktop to blink at her.

"Found a fawn," Cash said, holding out the evidence.

"If it's not a dog or a cat, I can't help you," the lady told her, turning back to her screen. Cash was amazed that she could be that enraptured by a computer so old that the screen was still black with green words until she realized that she was writing…

Oh, lord. A smutty story. In a huge font.

She tried to ignore that.

"Who could help me, then? I don't want the little guy to die."

The woman scribbled something on a Post-it and handed it to her. Just the name Riley and a phone number. As soon as the old lady's eyes returned to her screen, Cash knew she'd been dismissed in favor of a turgid member.

She took the fawn back out to her Jeep, looked at her phone map, swore under her breath, and drove like a bat out of hell to MacGillicuddy's. Once she'd parked in a back corner of the lot, she texted the number the humane society lady had given her. She followed enough kitten rescuers on Instagram to assume Riley was a tattooed woman in her twenties with a soft spot for fuzzy things.

**Hi, found an abandoned fawn, real new, mother dead. Can you take him? I'm at MacGillicuddy's bar and worried about him.

Thanks, Cash.

Cash knew it wasn't cool to text in full sentences with punctuation, but she didn't really care. She said what she meant to say and would put commas where she meant to pause instead of leaving it up to the reader's imagination, and that was that. Nobody could tell her where to put her goddamn commas, and if they did, they could complain about it to her face.

The answer was nearly immediate.

**At work now but can stop by after 6pm.

That was two hours away. Cash didn't want to take a baby fawn into—whatever Keelie's emergency was—and yet she wasn't going to leave the poor little thing in the car on a warm spring afternoon, even with the windows down. He'd been through enough for one day.

That settled it. She was taking the fawn inside, and if the restaurant had a problem with it, they could solve Keelie's emergency.

Cash checked herself in the mirror, swished with mouthwash and spit it out in the gravel, sprayed on some perfume from her gym bag, touched up her eyeliner, picked up the fawn, and walked inside MacGillicuddy's with as much dignity as she could muster. Ever since she'd left Colorado, she'd been frantic with worry. But now that she was beginning to suspect there was no actual emergency, she felt what she always felt in Arcadia Falls.

Furious.

CHAPTER 2

"**D**ogs on the patio only," the hostess said, barely lifting her eyes from her phone as she pointed at a sign.

No shirt, no shoes, no service

Dogs welcome on the patio.

No raccoons.

Cash wondered what had happened to cause someone to woodburn that deeply specific addition along with the normal house rules.

"It's not a dog," Cash corrected.

The hostess looked up, did a double take, and cocked her head. She was young and trying very hard to look mature, but to Cash, who felt ancient at twenty-five, she looked as wobbly as the baby deer; she was maybe eighteen. "I guess deer on the patio?" The girl looked at the sign and chewed her lip. "But there's water bowls out there."

"I'm Cassia King," Cash said, hoping this would clear things up.

This apparently meant nothing to the hostess, but luckily, Keelie appeared at exactly that moment, shrieking as she galloped over to embrace her taller, older sister in a fairly awkward hug, thanks to the fawn in her arms. Keelie and Cash shared the same coloring—olive skin that wanted to be tan, dark hair, opaque blue eyes—but Keelie was shorter and often described as perky, a more traditional sort of feminine that Cash had never quite been able to figure out. Cash sometimes felt like they were two entirely different dolls, Skipper beside an original GI Joe, as if they'd been made in different factories instead of by random iterations of their parents' genes.

"She's new," Keelie said, tipping her head to the hostess. "Taylor, this is my sister Cash. She's going to be our new bartender."

The girl finally looked up from her phone, taking Cash in. "Oh! Not another gross guy. Thank God. Hi." She smiled and looked down at the fawn, her eyes going soft. "It's real cute."

"The humane society couldn't take it?" Keelie said, frowning.

"Forget the humane society. What about a bartender?"

Keelie blanched. "Don't be mad…"

"I'm always mad, Keelie! What's the emergency? Are you okay? Why didn't you answer my calls or texts? It's been two days! I've been freaking out!" Cash felt like her heart had been squeezed like a peeled tomato in a fist the entire drive from Colorado, and the fact that there clearly wasn't an emergency wasn't making her blood pressure go down at all.

Keelie glanced around nervously before grabbing Cash's arm to drag her outside.

"Okay, so for real, though, don't be mad…"

"Too late."

"It's just… we really need you." Keelie was doing that thing where she begged with her eyes, the sort of look that made boys swoon and promise to give her whatever she required. Cash, on the other hand, was not so easily melted.

"Who needs me and why, and how come that couldn't that be stated in a text?"

Keelie lowered her voice. "It's just… we really need a bartender."

"Are you serious?" Cash barked. "Needing a bartender is not an emergency! I have a job in Colorado! Or—had one! I told my boss I didn't know how long I'd be gone and he fired me! I thought maybe Grammy was in the hospital—"

"No, she's fine. Ornery as ever."

"Or that you were sick or pregnant or—"

"Nope, fit as a fiddle."

"Then how is tending bar possibly an emergency?"

Cash's voice was loud enough that customers from the patio were craning their necks to see what all the fuss was, and Keelie motioned for her to be quiet. "Okay, so I accidentally backed into my boss's truck—"

"Oh, Keelie," Cash moaned.

"And I needed to get in good with her so she wouldn't dock my hours, so I told her my sister was the best bartender in the world. It's a good gig. I swear. I love it here. You're going to love it too."

Cash dragged a hand down her face, remembering how hard it was to stay mad at Keelie. It was like being angry at a baby sloth. Her eyes were just so big and wobbly.

"Did I mention that I like my life in Colorado? That I liked my job? That I like the fact that *it's not here*??"

Keelie's head hung, her shoulders hunching up. She was such a little, helpless-looking thing when she was sad. "I need this," she said, real low. "It *is* an emergency, I swear. We haven't had a bartender in two months, and it's hurting business."

At that, Cash snorted. "Come on. Hiring a bartender isn't hard unless you don't pay shit, in which case I definitely wouldn't take the job myself."

"Pay's good, hours are good, boss is great, when you haven't recently hit her car. Just come inside and meet her, okay? It doesn't have to be forever."

Cash looked out to the sidewalk that led to the town square. Ever since she'd passed the Arcadia Falls sign, she'd felt like an apple was stuck in her throat. "I left for a reason, if you recall. A very good reason."

"And you came back for a very good reason—to help out your sister, who loves you very much and who made up the spare room for you at her house. Your sister who's going to make her famous apple buckle and clean up after you and do all your laundry forever."

A deep sigh.

Cash felt it—the giving in.

Everything in the world conspired to make her tough and hard, and then Keelie came in and melted her. Every time. It had been like this when they were little. Their parents had died, and Grammy had taken over and done a good job, but Cash had always known that Keelie needed her. When she looked at her little sister, she still saw that thirteen-year-old girl standing at the funeral in a too-big dress, looking lost.

Just like she had then, Cash put her arm around Keelie— the arm that wasn't holding the fawn. "I'll help for a while, but this isn't permanent," she warned. "And I'm still mad. I'm just not shouting because I don't want to scare the baby."

"A while is good. Just find us a new bartender, and then you can go, if you want."

If you want.

Like a knife in the gut.

Love was a complicated thing.

Love had driven her away from this place, and love had brought her back, and Cash wasn't quite ready for all the feelings storming around in her heart. She hadn't been in Arcadia Falls for five years, and she suspected nothing had changed. Keelie certainly hadn't. She'd yet again manipulated her older sister into doing exactly what she wanted, and Cash had fallen for it. And just as Keelie had planned, now she had to stay.

"Someone's coming by for the fawn tonight," she said, practical as ever. "Until then, I guess I'm on the patio. Or maybe there's a box I could put him in?"

Keelie waved that away. "Don't worry about the patio. He can come to the bar. The patio thing is for Peach Pit."

"Am I supposed to know what that means?"

Keelie grinned. "She's the bar dog, and she's the best girl. You're going to love her, trust me."

Great. A bar that nobody wanted to tend, and a dog that she'd probably have to clean up after. With a little wave to the hostess, Keelie led Cash through the dining room and toward a big, old-fashioned bar. Internally, Cash sighed with relief. Maybe she didn't want to be there, but at least it was a place she could be comfortable, a place designed by a bartender, or maybe even built by one, with everything in easy reach and plenty of room to move. MacGillicuddy's was a sturdy, well-kept, well-loved sort of place, and working there wouldn't be too terrible. Probably.

Except for whatever kept driving away bartenders.

Keelie led Cash over to the far corner of the room, where a table for two was outfitted for one permanent occupant who required highly cushioned, ergonomic seating. Beside this throne was a fuzzy pink dog bed, and in this dog bed, stubby tail already wagging as she rolled over for belly rubs, was a thick, stocky, bow-legged meatball of a pit bull. Judging by her teats, she'd had plenty of puppies, and judging by her smile, she'd never met a stranger.

"This is Peach," Keelie said. "She's sweet as can be. As long as you're not a raccoon or an asshole. We never know whether other dogs will be friendly, which is why they have to stay on the patio. As you can guess by the scars, wherever she came from, it wasn't good, and other dogs make her nervous." Keelie rubbed Peach's belly, and Peach wriggled with happiness, the tags on her blue tie-dye collar jangling, before righting herself. Her ears had been docked and chewed to pieces, and there were little scars all over her head. She was the exact color of a peach pit, a warm, apricot brown, her eyes a light blue. If this dog had chosen violence, Cash could only imagine the bite force in those smiling jaws.

"Do you think she'll mind the fawn?" she asked.

"I mean, she likes babies…"

Cash got down in a squat and let Peach see the fawn. The little baby blinked at the dog but didn't know enough to be scared, and after a moment of curious sniffing, Peach hopped up, tail wagging furiously, making her whole body shake, and licked the fawn all over, leaving his spotted coat in spit-wet whirls.

"Well, Peach approves," said a new voice.

Cash looked up to find a square-shaped woman in her sixties with her asymmetrical hair dyed an audacious shade of turquoise. She was wearing a bedazzled MacGillicuddy's T-shirt with the neck cut low to show her cleavage and acid-washed jeans so tight, Cash didn't know how she could sit down, plus enough jewelry to drown her if she fell in a pond, with heavy earrings and a necklace covered in charms and crystals. Her eyes twinkled, and Cash liked her immediately.

She stood and held out the hand that wasn't holding the fawn. "Cassia King," she said. "But everyone calls me Cash. And you're the boss?"

The woman shook her hand firmly despite the fact that it was covered in fawn hair. "I am. Farrah MacGillicuddy. Owner and manager. You ready to start this interview?"

Cash gently shoved the fawn into Keelie's arms. She'd gotten Cash into this mess, and she could sort out the baby while Cash applied herself to saving her little sister's butt for the millionth time.

"Not really, considering I came here under extreme duress, but why not?"

Farrah ignored the attitude. "Get behind the bar, then, and let's see you move."

So, it wasn't going to be your standard interview, then. That was okay—Cash wasn't a standard sort of person, and this didn't seem like the standard sort of bar, especially not if they were having this many problems keeping a proper bartender.

After sliding under the counter flap, Cash shucked her leather jacket, went to the sink, rolled up her sleeves, and washed her hands with soap and hot water. Once that was sorted, she put on her practiced smile and went to the few customers seated at the bar to ask how they were doing and if she could get them anything. It was just three people, and they all had the look of functional alcoholics who haunted these stools for hours at a time. After delivering two beers and a Jack and Coke and marking their tabs, Cash checked the bottles, garnishes, ice, and bar supplies, glad to see that everything seemed to be relatively clean and fresh. A waitress brought a ticket, and Cash greeted her warmly and expertly pulled two beers for her. Satisfied that she was caught up on general business, she ambled over to where Farrah sat on one of the stools, watching her like a hawk as she worked. She hadn't noticed it at first, but Peach was lying on her belly just under the counter flap, back legs splooted, likewise watching her every move. The polished wood bar felt good under her hands—homey and sturdy.

"What can I get for you, miss?" she asked Farrah, a bar towel over her shoulder.

This was where the job interview would get interesting.

Farrah slid a laminated half-sheet menu across the bar with her long, lavender glitter nails. "This is our cocktail menu. Make me one of each."

"Is well okay, or do you want the good stuff?"

Farrah's penciled eyebrows rose. "You tell me."

"A good bartender makes everything taste like the good stuff."

That earned her a smile. "Good philosophy."

It wasn't the most interesting menu, but Cash had expected that. There were no photos or drawings, so she used her best judgment. Cash had worked in rough bars and fancy bars and even, horribly, the kind of place where they made her wear a scratchy polyester sports jersey covered in pins, so she had a good idea of what Farrah was looking for, thank goodness.

Then again, the restaurant owner couldn't be that harsh a critic if she was as desperate as Keelie said she was.

As Cash finished each drink, she placed it on a cocktail napkin in front of Farrah and turned to her next task. There was shaking and stirring and muddling, a twist of lemon peel here, two olives on a toothpick there. Once she had finished the last drink on the menu, she noticed Peach was panting and put down a bowl of ice water for her, which the dog gratefully lapped up, her back legs still splayed.

"How'm I doing so far?" she asked as Farrah delicately sipped her old-fashioned.

"Not bad. But I want you to make me one more thing. Make me your very favorite drink, the one you think more people should order but don't."

Interesting.

Very interesting.

Cash reckoned this would be the sort of job where she mostly popped the top off IPAs and poured Chardonnays, but Farrah wanted a bartender who could do more. And that was Cash's favorite kind of work—making art out of liquor. She looked at the line of drinks, noting which ones Farrah had just barely tasted and which ones had kept her sipping. Maybe she was trying to keep it light, but people can't help taking another drink of what appeals to them most, which meant Cash could look at the level of liquid in a glass and tell which ones had made Farrah smack her lips.

Cash smiled.

She knew exactly what to make.

Luckily, the bar was well stocked, even for the unusual. She pulled down green Chartreuse, maraschino, and the good gin, mixed everything without measuring anything, and placed a perfect coupe of filmy yellow-green liquid in front of Farrah, complete with two Luxardo cherries on a bamboo pick.

Cash saw it—saw Farrah's lips twitch, even though she was trying to look stern.

"A Last Word," Farrah said, holding it up to the light. "Why?"

Cash pointed to the drinks in front of her. "You liked the margarita, gimlet, and cosmo best. Didn't drink as much of the brown drinks or the tropical ones. And as a confident woman who knows what she wants, I suspect you always want to have the last word."

Farrah winked and tipped the drink toward her in a salute before sipping. "If you're confident enough, you don't need to have the last word. You let your actions speak for you."

"Touché. I guess I'm not there yet, myself."

Cash knew she was in the moment Farrah tasted it.

"This isn't really a Last Word kind of bar," Farrah warned her.

Cash shrugged. "It can be if I'm pouring. It can be both."

She felt something against her leg and looked down to find Peach Pit leaning against her, looking up at her with adoration in her eyes. She rubbed the dog's silky head, scratching around one of her ruined ears and making her wiggle.

"Well, we need a bartender, and Peach loves you, so you passed the interview. When can you start?"

Cash looked from the dog to the neat lines of bottles behind the bar to her sister, surreptitiously watching them as she took an order across the room. "I know you're desperate, so I can start now, if you don't mind having the fawn around until this evening. But I'll need to know about salary and benefits..." She met Farrah's eyes. "And why you can't hire a bartender."

Farrah met her gaze. "Because the last two died on the premises." Before Cash could ask how, she added, "They were mauled to death."

CHAPTER 3

"**M**auled to death. Are your customers that demanding?"

Farrah didn't blink, definitely didn't laugh. "Mauled to death by bears."

Cash was more amused than shocked.

"Were they dumbasses?" she asked.

"They were indeed." Farrah took another sip. "Dumbasses and creeps. One hired the other, and I went against my gut. I won't make that mistake a third time." She set down the glass and leaned forward, all business. "I can start you at twenty plus tips. We have insurance after six months, but—not gonna lie, it stinks. The fawn's welcome as long as it doesn't mess on the floor, and if it does mess on the floor, you clean it up before I see it or a customer complains. And as to the dead bartenders, this is a mountain town full of bears. Anybody who visits the dumpster after midnight is risking their life."

"So, you're sure it was bears? Because I thought we only had little black bears around here."

Farrah lifted a shoulder, unconcerned. "I only know what the police tell me. But I also know both boys were drunks and likely weren't at full mental capacity when it happened. Are you a drunk?"

Cash met her eyes; this was important. "I drink, but I don't get drunk."

"Why not?"

"Because drunk people do stupid things. I don't do stupid things, and I try to prevent other people from doing stupid things on my watch because stupid is bad for business."

That got a nod of respect. "Good. Folks don't like a bartender who won't drink, but I don't need to find another bartender out back in chunks." Farrah sipped the Last Word again. "Keelie tells me you used to be local. Why'd you move away?"

Cash felt that old familiar sourness of shame move through her, like when the air changes just before a storm, goes still and sick and greenish-gray. "I had a bad breakup. Needed some new scenery. Decided to try different mountains."

"And why'd you come back?"

She looked at Keelie, who quickly hurried away after getting caught watching them. She'd settled the fawn in an old wine box in the corner by Peach's bed. "When my little sister asks me for help, I help."

Another nod of approval. "Good. She's a sweet kid—and apparently a bad driver."

Farrah stood up, swigged the last of her Last Word, and walked to the corner of the bar, where she pulled out a much-stained beer and wine list. "Here's the full menu. Get used to it. Try a sip of the local wines and beers when you can; people are gonna ask for your advice. The Wi-Fi password is taped to the register. Everything you made off the menu will do. If somebody at the bar orders food, just flag down one of the girls. I'm headed home."

Cash nodded, but Farrah stepped closer, her voice dropping. "I'm a straight shooter, Cash, so here's how it is. I like a man behind the bar because this place is mostly estrogen and we need someone who can break up fights, kick out the mean drunks, and take care of my girls. Keelie tells me you're tough—that you carry, and that you're a good shot, and that you know what to do with the bat under the bar. I'm counting on you to get my girls out to their cars and out of my parking lot in one piece every night. Can you do that?"

Cash looked around the bar and nodded. "I can do that."

"Then we're good."

Farrah flapped a wave as she left, and then Cash went to work getting the bar up to her particular standards. It was headed toward dinner now, and she had to be ready for whatever crowd arrived. While Cash worked, Peach watched her from under the counter flap. Whenever Cash looked over at her, the pit would lift up her head and smile, stubby tail wagging. The fawn was still in his box in the corner, and Cash was worried that he might be dehydrated or need something she didn't have to give him, but the rescue girl, Riley, would be there soon. She would know what to do.

As the room filled with customers, a pleasant sort of flow took over. Cash's mind became a series of open tabs, neatly shutting as she accomplished each task. Seemed like everyone was a local, and they all knew exactly what they wanted, including a few minutes to interrogate the new girl. Cash didn't mind; it was part of the job. She might show the world her Resting Bitch Face outside of work, but when she was in her element behind the bar, working, mixing, pouring, it was like the layers of rust came off her smile, and she could wriggle her way into anyone's heart with the same open gladness of the pit bull watching her from the floor. There was a sort of magic to that—to having enough pleasant work that she forgot how angry she was with Keelie for lying to her. Men flirted with her, but she gave them just enough professional friendliness to earn tips but not requests for her number. She'd gotten good at walking that line.

"Doing okay, sis?" Keelie asked for the fifth time. Cash handed her a ticket and took the one she'd left on the counter.

"Doing what I do, Kee." Cash gave her a reassuring smile, and Keelie returned it with an eyebrow up to suggest that they both knew Cash wasn't okay, but it was about more than just today, and it wasn't going to magically fix itself, and there was a grim talk in their future. Keelie was talented about saying things with that eyebrow.

Cash lost track of time, but the room was loud and lively when a wiry man with longish, wavy red hair and a well-kept beard walked over to the bar, standing out like a sore thumb. He was in plaid pants and a button-down and looked like he'd gotten lost leaving the set of *Queer Eye for the Straight Guy* after an intervention, and he immediately piqued Cash's curiosity.

"What can I get you?" she said, sliding a menu over to him with a friendly smile. Even if he looked like he didn't belong in this bar or even this town, Cash wanted him to feel welcome.

"I'm here about a fawn," he said, his voice deep but softer than expected. His brown eyes were warm and earnest, and his fingers were pale and long and oddly delicate as he fidgeted with a coaster.

Understanding snapped in Cash's head.

She was surprised, but not in a bad way.

"You're Riley?"

He nodded.

"I'm Cash. I'm the one who texted you. He's over in the corner."

Cash slid under the counter flap, stepping over Peach Pit, who roused herself to follow them across the room. The fawn was still sleeping in the wine-box nest, curled up in an old T-shirt for a local fun run.

"Are you sure the mother is dead?" Riley asked as he knelt to uncover the fawn.

"Some asshole hit her and ran," Cash told him. "On 115 outside of town. Then I saw the baby. I wasn't able to feed him. Will he be okay, do you think?"

Riley looked at the fawn, frowning. "Can you get me some warm water? Not hot, more like lukewarm. I've got formula in my bag."

Cash went to the sink and returned with a plastic pitcher of lukewarm water as Riley pulled some supplies out of a battered leather messenger bag. He was talking to the fawn in a low, soft voice, but Cash couldn't hear what he was saying. Peach snuffled at his shoulder as if trying to supervise, and Riley told her she was a good girl but to please give him some space. Much to Cash's surprise, the nosy pit backed up obediently and sat, still paying close attention but not making a nuisance of herself.

Riley poured the water into a big baby bottle and added some powder, shaking until it was thoroughly mixed. He scooped the fawn out of the box with gentle professionalism and, after a few minutes of fumbling, finally got the bottle in the baby's mouth. Cash breathed a sigh of relief. She'd been so worried about Keelie that she hadn't done right by the fawn, and she was glad that her negligence hadn't hurt him. The guilt was still there, though.

"He really is tiny," Riley said. "Probably born today. A little dehydrated."

Cash felt a flush of shame at that; she felt as if she should've known what to do, even though she didn't.

Riley did, though. He was sitting on the floor with his back against the wall and his legs stuck out straight with the fawn in his lap. Peach slobbered over one brown leather brogue before creeping close to lay her chin on the thigh of his crisp plaid pants. His navy-blue dress shirt was now covered in milk powder, fawn spit, and pit bull hair, but he didn't seem to care, and it made Cash curious about him, about the kind of man who took pains to dress this way but then wasn't precious about getting messy. She didn't even know Riley, but she knew he would meet a stranger at a bar right after work and immediately crawl on the ground to help a baby.

Yeah, he definitely wasn't from around there.

A hand landed on Cash's shoulder. "Can I get a marg and a glass of the Moscato real quick?" the harried waitress said.

"Sure thing." Cash nodded. "Can I bring you anything?" she asked Riley. "It's on the house."

He gave her a tired smile. "Just a sweet tea would be good."

She nodded and went to the bar, getting the waitress her drinks before taking care of Riley's sweet tea. She checked that there were no more tickets or desperate folks waving checks before taking the tea over. Riley accepted it gratefully with his non-bottle hand and gulped half of it down like he'd just run a mile.

"Long day?" Cash asked.

"Long day," he confirmed. "How about you?"

"Well, I drove ten hours, found a fawn, and had a surprise job interview." Cash squatted down and stroked Peach's side, and she grumbled with enthusiasm.

"So, you're new to town?" Riley asked her.

That was a complicated question.

"Just got here today. My sister works here. Keelie. D'you know her?"

He looked around the restaurant, his eyes clocking around as if memorizing it. "I've never been in here before, and I don't really know anyone around town. I inherited my uncle's house last fall and stayed because it's probably the only house I'll ever be able to afford, you know?"

Cash remembered helping Keelie find her current place online and being surprised by the low house prices, compared to Colorado. "Yep. Seems like folks just want to visit these mountains, but when it comes to sticking around, they'd rather be someplace where they can have sushi delivered in half an hour."

He made a face. "There's a sushi place here. It's attached to a motel, and I can't recommend it."

"Yeah, I don't think I'll be eating raw fish while I'm here. No raw fish, no oysters."

"It's peaceful, at least. Except for all the orphaned wildlife and kittens. It's like they've never even heard of having their cats fixed." Riley gazed softly down at the little fawn, who'd finally figured out how to work his legs and had curled up to focus on drinking. "So, I'll give you the rest of this can of formula, and it should last until Saturday. There are better bottles online, but this one will hopefully get you through. For the first few days, he needs to be fed four times a day—"

Uh-oh.

"I thought... Are you not taking him?"

Riley stroked the fawn's spotted back. "I can't. I have to work during the day. There's a vet off the highway, about twenty miles south, who can take her on Saturday morning, though. Fawns need a very specific kind of care to reintegrate into the wild, and I work with smaller animals."

Cash stood, hands on her hips, and looked around the bar—now *her* bar. Farrah might let her keep a fawn around today, because what kind of monster would see a sweet baby like that orphaned on the side of the road and not stop to help? But she wouldn't want a nest in the corner of her restaurant for the next two days. And she definitely wasn't going to want little deer plops everywhere once the fawn could walk around, as she'd already made quite clear.

"I have to work," she said. "They need me here. It's kind of an emergency."

Riley looked down at the now-sleeping fawn. "He needs you too."

Cash squatted again. "I came here to help my sister. I can't mess this up. How can I make it work?"

Riley looked down at the fawn. Cash looked down at his hair, clearly well cared for, and wondered what it would be like to run her fingers through it.

"It's only two more days," he finally said. "I have to work from eight to five. I'm a paralegal. My boss won't let me keep critters in the office. And you probably have to work from, what, four to midnight?"

She nodded. "Close. Two to ten on weekdays, Keelie said."

Riley's fingers traced a path between the fawn's tender pink ears. "We could trade off. You keep him until I'm off work after five, and then I'll come over here and pick him up and take him home with me before you get too busy. Then you pick him up for his morning feeding. I'm up at seven. Will that work for you?"

Cash had been looking forward to sleeping in after her long drive from Colorado, to curling up in Keelie's spare bedroom and recovering from two days at the wheel. Getting to Riley's house at seven meant waking up at six, which gave her maybe six hours of sleep if she was lucky. But it was the right thing to do, and anything else would leave her looking like some sort of selfish asshole and, worse, feeling like a selfish asshole, which she couldn't accept.

Especially around Riley.

She'd just met him, but there was an earnestness about him, a decency, a gentleness that made her want to—well, not impress him. She didn't want to *disappoint* him. Most of the guys around Arcadia Falls were country boys, rough-and-tumble and brusque, but Riley seemed like he was tuned in to a different frequency. The way he dressed, the way he spoke and acted… he wasn't afraid of standing out as different—softer. The guys Cash had known growing up around here would've been mortified to wear plaid pants, and they preferred killing deer to saving them.

She had a sneaking suspicion that if they ever saw Riley in the bar, the local boys would beat the shit out of him.

"That'll work," she said. "I appreciate it."

"Looks like he's done for now and back to sleep. Can you take him?" Riley asked. Cash scooped up the fawn, her fingers grazing the leg of Riley's pants, and he stood and dusted himself off, but not like he minded all the hair and milk stains. "Probably best to put him back in the box for now."

"Can I get another Bud?" someone called from the bar, and Cash called, "Just a minute," as she followed Riley outside to a smaller crossover. He opened the passenger front door, and Cash placed the box carefully in the floorboard.

"Tomorrow morning at seven," Riley warned her sternly. "Don't make me late."

"I wouldn't dream of it."

Riley closed the door gently. He was just a little shorter than Cash, but then again, she was wearing boots with a thick sole. "You did a good thing," he told her. "He'd be dead if not for you. Hope your first night at the bar goes well."

"Thanks. Let me know if anything goes wrong, okay? I'm worried about the little guy."

"I'll keep you updated, but we'll be fine." Riley waved, got in his car, and drove away blaring, to Cash's surprise, The Dead Milkmen.

This guy—everything about him was surprising.

Once he was gone, Cash hurried back inside and immediately produced the requested Bud, with apologies. She got back into the swing of work with a lightness, now that the fawn was in good hands. She wasn't happy about the early wake-up calls, but it was just a few days, and if she was honest with herself, she was happy she'd get to see Riley again. There was just something intriguing about him. A sense of quiet, of calm. He didn't feel threatening at all, didn't seem violent or mean or like he had a bad temper, didn't make her feel defensive or self-protective. She hadn't felt that way in a long time. Not since before…

Well. Not in a long time.

The night went well and the tips were better than expected. The waitresses were grateful to have her around, especially Keelie, who thanked her every time she stopped by with a ticket. Cash could be happy there, she thought. It was a good place, run by good people.

And then, right before closing time, trouble walked in the door.

CHAPTER 4

It was exactly what Cash had been dreading since returning to her home town.

Her old friends.

She hadn't visited in five years, and for good reason.

Well, two reasons really.

Those reasons were named Samantha Green and Mark Ranger.

Okay, fine. Three reasons. Sam's brother Jed was a piece of work, too.

And there they were, still hanging with the same crew since middle school—the crew that Cash had once been part of. Mark and Sam and Jed and Jed's best friends Trip and Carter, along with Carter's longtime girlfriend Emmy.

"Well, looky here," Jed said, bellying up to the bar with the sort of delighted smile that suggested it had been too long since he'd hit on and/or antagonized someone named Cash. "Fresh meat."

Cash pasted on a smile, feeling adrenaline shoot through her veins and comforting herself with the press of her gun in its holster against the small of her back.

"Howdy, Jed. What can I get you?"

Mark watched them talk, his arm slung protectively over Sam's shoulders. Sam was still pretty, but she looked tired and restless, like an alley cat kept too long indoors. Her skin had lost its glow, her hair bleached one too many times, and her smug, sullen glare suggested she felt no remorse for what she'd done. As for Mark, he was just as wild and handsome and clueless as ever, his dark hair curling down past his ears and his light blue eyes sparking. It was his eyes that had captured Cash's attention, back in high school. He'd had this wise, ancient, untamed look about him, like some forest creature that had chosen to walk on two legs, like a John Mayer song made flesh. Cash was grateful that seeing him didn't bring up any old feelings of attraction, but she hated that seeing them together still dredged up the same fathomless rage.

Her ex–best friend and her ex-boyfriend, still together after all these years.

Still pretending they hadn't crushed her heart completely.

"What can you get me?" Jed mused. "Let's see. You can get on my lap and wiggle."

"I think I've made it pretty clear the answer is no, but what can I get for y'all from the bar? A pitcher on the house, for old times' sake?"

It was an olive branch, but then again, Jed was the kind of guy who might confuse an olive branch for a beckoning finger, when it was offered by the girl he'd had a crush on since he was in sixth grade and Cash was in fifth. He might've been good-looking if he hadn't been such a creep. There'd been rumors in school that he didn't take no for an answer, and even though girls had always vied for his attention, no one ever went out with him twice.

"Well you can pour us a pitcher and join us at a table and tell us why you tucked tail and ran without even saying goodbye to your best friends. Five years without a single word? I think we all feel a little hurt by your actions, Miss Cassia. I never even got my goodbye kiss." Jed turned his head and tapped his stubbled cheek.

Rage pealed in Cash's heart.

"You know damn well why I left," she said, trying to keep it diplomatic.

She knew better than to just come out and say that she'd left town because her best friend was screwing her boyfriend behind her back—which she'd discovered at senior prom, no less—and that their entire friend group had known and had hidden this fact from her.

After all these years, if she said it out loud to them, here, now... well, it would've been about the same as throwing a lit match into the shed where Jed's uncle Bubba stored all his illegal fireworks. The people of Arcadia Falls were territorial and proud, and even if it was the truth, they'd deny it all day long—and loudly. Cash had to keep things calm. She had to help Keelie, which meant she had to keep this job, which meant she couldn't just go around cussing out and/or beating up customers on her first night, no matter how much she might want to.

Her only comfort was that despite the wedding ring on Sam's finger, which she kept flashing in the light, Sam didn't look all too happy with how things had ended up.

"I can't believe you're still jealous of me," Sam said.

"I'm not jealous," Cash said, her smile as fake as the diamonds in Sam's ring. "I'm hurt. They're different."

"I keep telling you, Cassie baby..." Jed licked his lips. "Mark's taken, but I'm not. You got to put this shit behind you. It's not like you can avoid us forever. This is our town."

Trip whooped, and Carter gave a turkey call, and Cash couldn't for the life of her remember why she'd hung out with any of them. Being out in the world for five years, moving around from place to place, meeting new people—it had only shown her how small some lives could be if people didn't expose themselves to new ideas. The Appalachians had felt so big until she'd stood in the Rockies, seen the white-peaked mountains loom over everything out west. Now her native peaks were just like friendly green hills. It had changed her perspective of things. She was fairly certain Sam and Jed had never left Arcadia Falls, not even to visit the World of Coke in Atlanta.

"Seriously, you've got to put it behind you," Sam repeated. "It's just embarrassing."

Cash's smile became something else, her teeth bared and her nails digging into her bar. "What's embarrassing is cheating with your best friend's boyfriend." She looked to Jed. "Or helping them sneak around behind someone's back. Now, again, can I give y'all a nice, free pitcher of something alcoholic that will make you relax and go away and let me do my job?"

"I never cheated," Mark said, and it almost sounded like he believed it.

"Well, I could pull out my little pink diary and check the dates and beg to differ, but let's just all agree it was for the best." Cash looked at each of them—at Mark's lying blue eyes and Sam's stringy hair and Jed's twisted grin, and the fact that they were all still there, virtually unchanged in body or mind. "I'm glad I left. Staying in this little town doesn't seem to do anybody any good." She looked right at Mark, the first and last man she'd allowed herself to love, the man who'd broken her heart, and ran her tongue over the same tooth he was missing.

Mark bristled, his beautiful blue eyes now full of hate.

"Look here, bitch," he started, but Sam snorted and walked out, dragging him along with her before he was forced to finish the sentence. Poor Taylor tried to hold the door open for them, but Mark shoved past the hostess like she didn't even exist. That further cemented the fact that Cash had dodged a bullet in leaving town—Mark was the kind of man who just allowed himself to be towed away like a dog, and also the kind of man who would all but shove an innocent girl just trying to do her job. He was weak. Pretty but weak. And he hadn't changed. None of them had.

Except her.

And it's not that she looked down on this place, on these people. It's that she understood how important it was to grow and change. They'd forced her to spread her wings, even though she'd been scared, and now she'd seen the world. New York and LA and the Grand Canyon and Niagara Falls. She'd had adventures. And maybe she'd had them alone, but she was realizing that she liked herself better than she liked any of the people she'd once called her closest friends. She was willing to bet not a single one of them had read a book since high school, and it showed.

Jed watched Sam and Mark leave, and Trip and Carter came up on either side of him, flanking him like a wall. Cash had seen it before—these tall, burly ex–high school football players knew how intimidating they were, all in a row. Just behind her, a low growl started up as Peach Pit left her post to stand at Cash's side behind the bar. Peach was a sweet girl, but it seemed like she was indeed an excellent judge of character.

Cash looked each man in the eyes, noting that most of the hostility was radiating out of Jed and Trip, while Carter seemed more like a wary backup than a willing participant. She had to defuse this situation.

"What, are y'all thinking about beating up a woman at her workplace just because she's willing to speak the truth about some shit that went down in high school?" Cash grinned. "Because you get how ridiculous that is, right? I know y'all knew about Mark and Sam. I know you didn't tell me. But I can let it go. Water under the bridge, all that."

"You calling me a liar?" Jed snarled.

Cash was done playing.

"Look in my eyes and tell me you had no idea your sister was sleeping with my boyfriend behind my back, and you let it happen so you'd have your chance with me."

Jed's face screwed up with rage and embarrassment, anything handsome about his features lost to flushed skin and bulging eyes. "Watch your mouth when you talk about my sister!"

The room went silent but for Peach Pit's low growl, the other patrons shifting excitedly to watch what was happening at the bar. Taylor and one of the waitresses—Jess, maybe?—hovered nervously by the door. Cash didn't have long before she had a real problem, which was not a great thing to have on her first day.

"She was my best friend," Cash said quietly, keeping her tone even and Jed in her sights as she filled a pitcher with Terrapin and placed it on the counter, along with four glasses. "Since kindergarten. She was like my sister. Losing her hurt me more than losing Mark. She never even said she was sorry. Try to have some empathy."

Jed's fingers curled into fists, knuckles popping.

How lucky he was that men were allowed to express their anger in public, that it was considered acceptable for them to posture and threaten. Cash didn't have that luxury. If she showed her own fathomless rage, they would call her emotional, ask her if she was on the rag, sneer and use the word *bitch*, like she was a dog. Somehow, men like this had forgotten that anger, too, was an emotion.

Carter put a hand on Jed's arm. "Just take the beer, man."

"She's my sister," Jed said, almost pleading with him.

"And maybe she made a mistake when she was a kid. We all did. Let it go."

"C'mon, Jed," Emmy said, begging, her voice soft.

But Trip was just as mad as Jed, which meant Jed wasn't winding down, and Cash could feel Jed's heart wobbling like an old set of scales, could see the truth warring with a country boy's drive to protect his family name. Cash knew he loved Sam the same way she loved Keelie, and she knew that deep down, he probably felt shame for them both, but she also knew he was riddled with the kind of toxic masculinity that meant he could never, ever admit it, not to himself, and not to anyone else.

That didn't mean she was going to let him off the hook.

Let him hit her, if he wanted.

When she'd left this place five years ago, she'd been vulnerable, soft, hurt.

But then she got mad. She toughened up, built her own armor. She took boxing classes and learned some jiu-jitsu and jeet kune do. She wasn't the soft, sad little girl they remembered.

She had her own defenses now, and she wasn't scared of an angry haymaker from a country boy who, deep down, didn't want to hurt her.

Peach let out one sharp bark, and it broke the tension.

"They shouldn't allow dogs like that in bars," Jed said. He exhaled angrily and turned away. "Grab the beer."

Carter gave Cash an apologetic smile as he picked up the pitcher and the glasses and followed Jed to the farthest corner of the bar. Emmy gave her a little wave, mouthed *Sorry*, and followed.

"You shoulda stayed gone," Trip said darkly before joining them.

Ah, yes. Because she'd turned Trip down, too. He'd asked her out before Mark, and she'd told him no. And he'd asked her out again, after she found out about Mark, like he was some fabulous consolation prize. She'd tried to let him down easy, but Trip was one of those big, brutish boys who was secretly a soft gummy bear on the inside and had to make sure no one ever knew it—or knew that he could be hurt.

God, small-town politics and dating pools were tiring. There'd been only fifty kids in their high school class, and half of them were related.

"We good, sis?" Keelie called over the bar, leaving her a ticket. "I saw Sam hurry out with Mark. Guess I should've mentioned that was still going on. They, uh, got married last year. You never heard so many guns firing, I swear."

"We're good. I knew it was gonna happen, sooner or later, them showing up. Might as well get it over with."

"I wish I knew what Jed's problem is." Keelie's nose wrinkled up. "He tries to get my number every time I get an oil change, but... ugh. He's like my older brother, you know? It's gross."

Cash stood up from scratching Peach, her eyes meeting Jed's from across the room as he nursed his beer. "His problem is that me being around reminds him that he's not as great as he thinks he is." She popped the tops off two local beers and put them on Keelie's tray with two frosty glasses from the freezer. "And he's still butthurt I won't go out with him. Trip too."

"Just watch out," Keelie said. "Jed started a fight with Ronnie Jackson in the pizza place once, and Ronnie ended up with stitches." She picked up her tray. "Because he said something about Sam. I don't think Jed would hit a woman…"

"But he might," Cash finished for her.

All she could do was try to avoid him, which might be difficult in such a small town. She was fairly certain he worked at the only car place on the mountain, and her Jeep was constantly needing attention.

After the free pitcher was gone, Jed and his crew left—without tipping, of course. Cash cleaned up after them instead of leaving it for the waitstaff, figuring that was on her. They'd made a mess on purpose, tearing up napkins into tiny pieces and breaking a glass.

The night was mellow after that, the crowd petering out until the last regular settled up.

"So, you survived your first night," Keelie said as Cash wiped up the bar.

"It's a nice place." Cash looked around, realizing she already felt at home there. "Why didn't we come here when we were younger?"

"Because when Farrah's dad ran it, he wouldn't let kids hang out here, and Mom and Dad didn't like pub food."

"Oh, yeah. I remember now. Old Man MacGillicuddy chased us off with a pool cue because Jed tried to order a beer with a fake ID. What were we—sixteen?"

Keelie sighed. "Which would've made me thirteen and stuck at home. I thought y'all were so cool. Grown-up and sophisticated."

Cash smiled as she pulled down a bottle of tequila and poured two shots, sliding one across to her sister. "You were dead wrong. We were idiots. All of us."

Keelie took the shot, and Cash raised her glass.

"It's good to see you, little sis."

"To more good times, big sis."

They clinked their glasses and drank.

"Gotta go fill the ketchups," Keelie said.

"Tell everybody to wait for me to walk 'em out. Nobody goes outside alone. Farrah's orders."

Keelie smiled. "Thank you for coming back. I know I... went about things wrong. This place is like a family, but the bartender thing made it real tense. Everybody was grouchy and kinda scared, and when I told Farrah how much experience you have, and how tough you are, she said you would be perfect, and I agreed." She looked around the restaurant fondly. "We need you. And Farrah already loves you."

"I think she just likes me because Peach does."

At the sound of her name, the dog looked up and grinned.

"Nothin' wrong with that."

Keelie disappeared, and Cash cleaned their shot glasses and bagged up the trash, which she walked over to the back door. Peach popped up from where she'd been snoring under the counter flap and galloped over, wiggling between Cash and the door and growling.

Not at her—at the door.

"I'm not going out there right now," Cash told her.

Peach Pit sighed in relief—

But she didn't budge, either.

CHAPTER 5

ash kept watch as the servers headed for their cars. She had her Walther in a back holster, snug under her leather jacket, and she scanned the dark edges of the gravel lot as the ladies unlocked their cars, checked their backseats, and left one by one. It only added to her constantly simmering rage, how women were forced to move through a world filled with unnecessary dangers, how they always had to carry their keys like claws and check under hotel beds and behind curtains, knowing full well there might be monsters out there watching their every move—and yet they still had to find the energy and hope to keep moving forward instead of reasonably locking themselves in bunkers forever.

Cash preferred actual weapons. Maybe Jed and the boys were her enemies now, but a long time before, they'd taken her to one of Trip's dad's back fields and set up beer cans and bottles on top of hay bales and taught her that even idiots didn't need to be scared of guns, if they were careful. Over the years, she'd taken classes and spent time on the range, learning the actual rules behind what three tipsy country boys had told her about gun safety. As the girls drove away, she waved, matching names to cars, making sure everyone got out safe.

Finally, it was just her and Keelie, who was followed by an unleashed Peach. The pit looked different, outside the bar. There, comfortable in her domain, she was dumpy and wiggly and cheerful, but out here, she looked like a different dog, watchful and alert, tautly muscular, nose scenting the air and ruined ears perked up attentively. She was turned toward the side of the restaurant, which was now completely cloaked in shadow, where the dumpster waited.

And where, apparently, bears had attacked, killed, and partially eaten two bartenders.

They'd gotten too smug, Keelie said. Let their guard down.

Assumed it was safe.

It was not, Cash knew full well, safe.

But there was something Keelie hadn't told her about the whole affair, and Cash had to figure out why her sister was hiding it from her.

"Did the last two bartenders take out the trash around this time, or did that happen before everyone else left?" she asked her sister.

"Just follow me to the farm," Keelie said, ignoring the question. "Or you'll lose signal in a holler and get lost. Looks like Peach wants to ride with you, if that's okay."

"Isn't she Farrah's dog? Doesn't she guard the bar?"

Keelie ruffled Peach's ears. "She belongs to herself and goes where she wants, and in the three months she's been here, I haven't seen her attach herself to anybody like she has to you."

Cash knew Keelie was avoiding the question, but she let it go. Keelie could be cagey sometimes, not because she was a dishonest person, but because she just hated it when other people were upset. Cash would give her time. Although they talked on the phone almost daily, they hadn't spent much actual time together since last Christmas, when Keelie had flown up to Estes Park for her first Rocky Mountain Christmas. She'd get less skittish after a few days together—and after she stopped waiting for Cash to rightfully bite her head off.

Cash helped Peach Pit scramble up into the Jeep before following her little sister's beat-up truck through downtown and out into the country, turning down a road just past the one where Cash had learned to shoot. A long dirt drive took her past high pastures to the little farmhouse Keelie rented. She'd always wanted horses, and she finally had them, and Cash was happy for her. She wasn't quite as happy about the fact that

Keelie would likely have a chore list waiting, since Cash was good with physical labor and big machines, but at least she didn't have to look for a place to live or venture to the Atlanta IKEA for a bed with a name full of umlauts, and that wasn't nothing.

Everything Cash owned was packed in her Jeep, not that she owned much. Things, she felt, just weighed a girl down. Anything nostalgic was in her grandma's old storage unit, and two tubs in the back seat held all her clothes and shoes. She'd liked Colorado—and all the places she'd made a point to visit over the last five years—but hadn't found a place that really felt like home, so she'd moved around, trying out big cities and mountain towns, ski resorts and country dives. She'd thought mountains were mountains, but she was beginning to understand that the Appalachian Mountains were just different, that they were smaller but somehow heavier, deeper, older, that they made a place in a person's bones. Even if the air here had heavier oxygen, she was breathing easier than she had in years.

As soon as she'd parked and her boots hit the ground, a horrible caterwauling took up behind the fence.

"You have a donkey?" she asked Keelie.

"His name is Gary. He's an asshole, but he kills coyotes. You're gonna love him."

"As long as he doesn't do that before ten in the morning, I will."

And that's when Cash remembered that she had to go get the fawn at seven so Riley could get to work on time. She was actually looking forward to seeing Riley again, and to seeing what kind of house he lived in... but she was not looking forward to being awake that early. When she checked her phone, she found a text from Riley with his address and a photo of the fawn sleeping in a lavender dog bed with three kittens curled up against his spotted brown back.

"He's pretty cute," Keelie said, peeking over her shoulder.

"He really is."

"I wasn't talking about the fawn." She bumped Cash's shoulder. "Now come inside and let's get you settled so Gary will shut the hell up."

Keelie's house was a little long in the tooth, but she had a gift for making things homey—for the most part. Cash knew her sister had a strange hobby, but she hoped it was contained to Keelie's bedroom. She scanned the living room and kitchen, but everything looked normal, clean and spare but cozy.

"Your bedroom is over here," Keelie said, opening a door. "And Cash, I'm so sorry, but..."

Cash's heart sank. She should've known.

She stood in the open doorway, and hundreds of glassy eyes stared back.

Keelie's doll collection.

She'd loved them all her life, ever since she received her first doll baby for her second birthday, and every time she saw one in an antique store or at a garage sale, she had to buy it—or rescue it, in her own words. And there they all were, arranged on the window seat and lined up on shelves. The closet doors were open to show the dolls stacked up in rows like they were at a concert. Some of them had their arms up like they were reaching out to grab Cash's soul.

"So, this is the only spare bedroom?" Cash asked.

"Yes, but, remember… it was their room first."

With a little wave, Keelie spun out of the room before Cash asked her to do something about the audience that would be watching her sleep.

"Absolutely not," Cash said. She stalked back out into the hall and said, "I'm gonna need a sheet, Kee."

Keelie sheepishly dug an old white flat sheet out of a linen closet, and Cash felt much better once the windowsill dolls were covered and the closet door was firmly closed. She had hoped Keelie might've outgrown her doll obsession, but it seemed it had only worsened.

Well, and so what? Keelie worked hard and saved her money, and this was her house. She could put whatever she wanted in it, even if it made Cash's skin crawl.

Outside of the crowd of dolls, the room was perfect. The bed was invitingly made—and completely devoid of dolls—and the window was covered with the kind of heavy-duty curtains required by folks accustomed to working nights. Peach trotted inside and watched Cash unload her backpack before leaping awkwardly onto her bed, curling up like a pudgy cinnamon roll, and going to sleep.

Cash wasn't excited about sleeping next to fifty pounds of solid muscle and drool under the watchful eyes of fifty dolls, but she figured the poor dog's life had already been hard enough and she deserved a bit of softness. She had reasonably chosen one side of the queen bed, at least, so Cash still had plenty of room to stretch out. It was a hell of a lot better than sleeping in the Jeep at a rest stop. At least none of the dolls had said "Mama" or done anything disturbing.

As she lay there in an unfamiliar bed in her hometown, listening to a donkey screech a love song to the stars, Cash's thoughts leapt from Keelie's desperate voice mail begging her to come home, to getting fired from her last job, to two long days on the road, to finding the fawn, to meeting Riley, to facing down the demons of her past over a pitcher of beer. It was one hell of an emotional roller coaster, and she couldn't help wondering if she should've finally put her foot down and told her little sister no. Maybe she'd made the wrong choice coming home to a small town that felt like a crucible for big troubles. Almost everything there reminded her of her dead parents or her traitorous friends.

Except Riley.

She was intrigued by him, and she hadn't really been intrigued by anything in years. He didn't put up her defenses, and she wasn't sure why, but she liked it.

Finally, the donkey shut up, and Cash's mind stopped chewing on the past, and when her phone alarm woke her at six the next morning, Peach was curled up in her armpit. She extricated herself from the snoring dog and took her outside before driving to Riley's address. It was an old stone house, walkable to downtown if you didn't mind hills, the front yard overflowing with old-growth flowering bushes and trees. Cash was so sleepy, she could barely function, but she'd showered off the Peach drool and washed her hair, and the nervousness didn't kick in until she was standing on Riley's porch, trying to decide whether to knock or ring the bell. The door opened a few inches before she could decide, and there was Riley in plaid pajama pants and a Nirvana shirt. His hair was up in a bun, and he looked far more refreshed than Cash felt.

"Sorry I'm not dressed yet. You'll have to hurry in." When he held the door open wider, Cash slipped in sideways as what seemed like dozens of kittens latched on to the ankles of her jeans with pinprick claws. "Hope you're not allergic."

Cash looked down at the three calico kittens viciously attacking her legs. "I'm definitely not allergic to cuteness, thank God."

Riley chuckled, and Cash cursed herself for bringing up cuteness around someone she found cute. He led her toward a warm yellow kitchen where the fawn stood on a rag rug on unsteady legs, regarding them with big, innocent eyes. "He's doing well. Eating, doing his business. He just had breakfast, so you'll feed him again at noon, and then I'll come get him at the bar." He handed her a reusable grocery bag. "Formula, bottle, and a pack of wipes. After each feeding, you have to gently wipe his nethers to make him go, or his system'll get messed up."

"Okay."

Cash wasn't looking forward to that part, but it was still a better option than leaving the little guy on the side of the highway to die.

She was also amused to hear a guy with a man bun use the word *nethers*.

"Want some coffee?"

Cash felt like she was a full minute behind in the conversation, but that was because she was looking around Riley's home, trying to figure out who he was. Things were clean but not necessarily tidy, with kitten toys everywhere and a water dish in a puddle and wet kitten food sliding off a paper plate. Beside the oven she saw a wooden recipe box with a chicken on the front that reminded her of the one her grandmother kept, and it pinged off her heart.

"Coffee would be nice. Cream and sugar, if you have it."

Riley poured a cup from the coffeemaker and soon handed her a ceramic mug with Garfield on it.

"I hope it's okay. I make it strong."

Cash had already decided that whatever was in the cup would be the best coffee she'd ever had, so it was. "It's perfect."

Riley picked up his own mug and sank to the ground, sitting cross-legged so the kittens could clamber all over him. Cash could see little pink scratches under his ginger-colored arm hair. She copied him and sat, preparing herself for the onslaught of tiny claws. The fawn wandered over and folded himself into Riley's's lap as the kittens, predictably, stalked and attacked his feet. He idly and gently fended them off with practiced patience.

"So, you do a lot of rescue work?" Cash asked. Not that the silence wasn't companionable, but she was just so curious about him.

"I take in kittens who don't need round-the-clock care. Socializing and rehoming ferals. I took in some baby squirrels and possums in college, but being in the office for nine hours means I can't make all the feedings. I miss it, but the house smells a hell of a lot better."

It did. It smelled like coffee, and like the oven was accustomed to good things.

Did this well-dressed, well-groomed man… bake?

"What about you? How'd you end up at MacGillicuddy's?"

Cash sipped her coffee as a kitten climbed up the leg of her jeans and tumbled into her lap. "They were desperate for a seasoned bartender, and my sister begged me to come help. The last two guys got mauled taking out the trash."

Riley looked at her sharply. "*Mauled* as in *killed*?"

She nodded. "By bears, they think."

"Well, I certainly hope you won't be taking out the trash…"

Cash chuckled, glad that he cared. "That's one of the first orders I was given—don't take out the trash at night. The dumpster's in a dark spot, behind the building near the forest. No lights like there are in the parking lot."

"Aren't the servers scared?"

"I make sure they get to their cars safe. That's part of the job." When he gave her a curious look, she added, "I have my carry permit and pretty good aim."

Riley stroked the fawn, who had fallen asleep, and Cash marveled at the tiny perfection of the little thing. She'd never seen a fawn close up before yesterday. She noticed that Riley's nails were clean and trimmed. And that he didn't have a ring tan.

"Bears around here don't usually attack." Riley looked at the fawn as he spoke, as if working out a puzzle. "We have some smaller black bears. Even if they did get too close, a human should be able to scare them off just by shouting. Grizzlies don't live out this way. Their range doesn't even come close. Did anyone see it happen?"

"No, just the aftermath is what I've heard. Maybe it was wolves or wild dogs, then, or even a mountain lion."

"Do you hunt?"

Cash looked down at the fawn, so tiny and tender. She didn't want Riley to hate her, but she didn't see the point in lying. In her experience, old lies would eventually hurt worse than the current truth.

"I don't like to hurt innocent things. I went out hunting with the guys when I was younger, but I didn't enjoy it. We mostly just sat around in camo and drank bad beer, anyway. When I bagged a deer, I made sure to use every part of it, do honor to it. I don't think I could shoot one now."

Riley nodded in understanding. "Yeah. My dad tried to get me into it, but I was more interested in bird-watching than shooting anything. There's usually venison at the farmer's market on Sunday—a local family butcher with four sons and a highly competitive daughter—"

"The Fergusons," Cash supplied with a grin.

"—so that seems kinder than factory farming and helps the local economy."

Cash untangled one of the kittens from her bootlaces, causing it to meow in protest. "Now, if I caught the man who hurt Peach Pit, I might change my tune…"

"That's not an innocent thing," Riley said softly. "That's different. I'd kill him with my bare hands." For a gentle man, his words were hard, and she believed him.

For a long moment, they just smiled at each other in understanding, and Cash's heart felt like a tough egg just beginning to crack, and then Riley glanced at the oven clock and said, "Damn, time is moving fast today. Nearly seven-thirty."

He put the fawn on the rug and stood, and Cash finished her coffee and stood and rinsed out the mug and left it in the sink, and Riley told her she didn't have to do that, but she'd already done it, so she just said, "My mom said to never leave a mess behind, and I took that seriously."

"You mom's a smart lady."

"Was a smart lady."

Riley looked mortified. "Oh, I'm so sorry, I didn't mean—"

"It's okay. How could you know?"

Another look at the clock, followed by a wince. "I hate to kick you out on that note, but I really do need to get ready. My boss is reasonable, but he's a stickler for punctuality. I guess I'll see you tonight after work?"

Cash felt a little lift before remembering: it was about the fawn, not her.

"That'll be great. Thanks so much for taking the time." Noting the fawn's box in the corner, she scooped him up and placed him carefully inside. "What've you been calling him?"

Riley looked a bit sheepish. "I mean, he's yours to name…"

"But I reckon you've been calling him something already."

"Just between us, I've been calling him Spencer. After Spencer Reid on *Criminal Minds*? Because he's skinny and has big, earnest eyes."

Cash threw back her head and laughed; it was not a bad comparison. "C'mon, Spencer. Let's go track down a serial-killer bear."

Riley opened the door for her and held back the three kittens with one foot. "Have a good day!" he called. "Don't get mauled!"

Cash grinned. "I'll do my best."

As she carried the box to the Jeep, passing by a burst of periwinkle hydrangeas, she thought about what it might be like to leave Riley's house more often. For the first time in years, she let herself think about the future, about possibilities, about what it might be like to get to know someone, to actually let them in. Riley seemed like someone who could be trusted. He seemed open and honest and generous and like he didn't really give a shit what other people thought. It felt... safe, to like him. It felt good.

Maybe Arcadia Falls wasn't going to be so bad, after all.

But when she got back to Keelie's place, her sister was sitting outside on the porch steps, crying.

CHAPTER 6

Cash left the fawn in the Jeep and hurried over, arms open. "What's wrong?"

"It's Jed Green," Keelie said, burying her head in Cash's shoulder. "The bear got him last night."

"At the restaurant?"

Keelie pulled away and looked up at Cash, confused. "No. At his house. You remember his folks had the little cabin on the river? He fixed it up a few years ago and lives there now with Trip. Trip was playing some stupid video game with headphones on and didn't hear anything. But Jed—"

Cash nodded. She was still angry at Jed, an anger that hadn't faded one iota in five years, and last night at the bar hadn't helped, but he didn't deserve... that.

"How'd you find out?"

"Rob told me. Trip's younger brother?"

Cash scanned her memory like an old car's radio, trying to remember everything she used to know about this place, all the connections that spiderwebbed around town, tying folks together. "You guys stay in touch?" Then she remembered a younger, skinnier version of Jed who played baseball and loved RC cars. "Oh, yeah. You two used to go out."

Keelie made a face. "Just for a few days in middle school. He was a shitty boyfriend. I made him a cake, and he was like, 'What am I supposed to do with this, Keels? Eat it in math class?' and then he broke up with me right before the eighth-grade dance because he wanted to go out with Izzy Childress. He's super messed up about it—about Jed. Poor guy."

Cash rubbed her sister's back and calculated distances in her head. Jed's cabin was a couple of miles from downtown, a pretty reasonable distance for a bear to travel. But Keelie's house was a few miles from downtown too, if in a different direction.

"You said the donkey takes care of coyotes…" Cash began.

"In two years here, he's taken down three. He brays whenever a stranger or a new animal shows up."

"Seen any bear scat out here?"

"Just while trail riding, not on the property. Like, miles away, past the cow pasture."

But Cash had always been more cautious than her sister. "Don't go out alone at night, okay? This seems pretty serious."

Keelie looked up at her and wiped away her tears. "The farm feels so safe to me. It's hard for me to imagine something bad happening here. But if there was a bear, Gary and the horses would let me know. They all pitched a fit when the coyotes came. And then there's Peach, when she stays over."

Cash looked to the front screen door, where Peach was watching them intently through the screen door. "Does she stay over often?"

As if she knew they were talking about her, Peach pushed the screen door open with her nose, bounded out to cavort around Cash's legs, and squatted to pee before hurrying over to press her nose through the fence, making the donkey squeal.

"Sometimes," Keelie said. "She follows whoever she wants to go with, and sometimes she stays at the bar. She comes with me a lot because I have the most land and she likes to go on trail rides. She showed up at the restaurant a couple of months ago, acting like she owned the place. Farrah loves her, but she never goes home with Farrah. Peach is actually pretty annoying when you try to make her do anything that isn't her idea." Keelie shook her head at the dog like a loving mother. "So stubborn."

"She growled at Jed last night."

A snort. "Yeah, well, so did you. Only reason Jed and his crew haven't been kicked out of MacGillicuddy's yet is because they don't show up that often. He says our beer's too expensive." Her jaw dropped, and she blinked away tears. "Said, I guess."

Gary the donkey started braying, and the sound of tires on gravel rattled up toward the farm. Keelie stood by Cash's side as a dusty black police SUV appeared and rolled to a stop.

"What's going on?" Cash asked her sister. "You dating a cop?"

"No idea, and hell, no."

The man who exited the vehicle was short, stocky, and red-faced. Cash immediately recognized him, and she had to work to keep herself from looking hangdog. It was Trip's oldest brother Ed. Growing up, Ed would've done anything to protect his younger siblings, would've fought anybody who said anything bad about the Fergusons, and Cash could only assume nothing had changed.

"Howdy, Ed," she said, trying to keep things upbeat.

"That's Officer Ferguson to you." Ed did not smile. At least Peach wasn't growling, although she looked like she wanted to but was too polite.

"Officer Ferguson," Cash repeated, hating how silly it felt to say that to someone she'd known all her life. "How can we help you?"

Ed pulled out a little notebook. "Where were you last night, ma'am?"

Cash could see where all this was going, and she didn't like it. "I was at MacGillicuddy's until about ten-thirty, working at the bar. I got all the servers out and followed Keelie home after she locked up. I was here until about six forty-five, then drove into town. Just got back from that errand."

"And who can corroborate that?" Ed asked, sounding like he'd spent all night memorizing the word *corroborate* and was pretty proud of himself for not adding too many *r*s.

"Everybody at the bar, and then Keelie. What are you getting at, Officer?"

Ed looked up, met Cash's stare. "Are you aware that Jedidiah Green was found dead this morning outside his cabin?"

"Keelie just told me. I'm sorry to hear it."

"Are you?"

A pause. "Yes. I know Jed and I have a history, but that was a long time ago."

Ed scribbled something in his notebook. "So, you don't hold any grudges?"

Cash shook her head. "I'll tell you the same thing I told the guys at the bar last night. What Sam and Mark did back then really messed me up, so I left town for my own good. Five years is a long time. I did a lot of growing up. We were all just stupid kids back then. I don't particularly want to see Sam and Mark, and I didn't like how Jed spoke to me, but I didn't want anything bad to happen to him. Plus, isn't this the third bear attack?" Ed looked up at her like this was a stupid question. "If I wasn't around for the first two, I don't know why you think I'd be involved in this one," she finished.

Ed squinted at her. "And where were you for the first two?"

"Colorado."

"Who can confirm that?"

She counted on her fingers. "My boss, the servers, the regulars…"

"So, you were heard exchanging words with Jed Green last night."

"He came into my place of business, and I offered him a free pitcher of beer and treated him and his crew with professional detachment. Jed was angry. Trip was, too, as I'm sure you know."

"I hear you were angry as well, Miss King."

Well, of course she'd been angry. She was angry now.

She was, quite honestly, *always* angry.

"I'm angry any time a man threatens me. Would you like to hear my side of the story?"

"That won't be necessary. Just trying to gather all the details."

"Are you gonna ask Keelie where she was last night?"

Ed stared at her like she was an absolute idiot. "No. Keelie couldn't do this."

"Keelie couldn't maul a grown man like a bear?"

"Obviously."

"But I could?"

He shrugged. "You're bigger, taller, meaner. You still have a reputation around here. You understand weapons and have done your share of hunting. If a woman like you set her mind to it, I reckon she could do some damage."

Cash wasn't sure whether she should be flattered or insulted by that.

Ed slid the notebook into his breast pocket and looked around the farm. "Y'all ladies certainly are out in the middle of nowhere. All alone."

Maybe it was supposed to sound worried, but Cash read it as a threat.

"We can protect ourselves," she said.

"Horses need land," Keelie added, the picture of innocence.

"Lots of privacy out here."

Keelie and Cash shared a look before Keelie spoke. "I mean, there's Rascal Tant across the road, and Mr. Gooch up on the hill is my landlord, with all the cattle. And Mattie Hattrick mows the pastures for me. But I've always felt safe here. Do you think I need to worry?"

Ed focused on Keelie. "Miss King, do you trust your sister?"

"With my life." The absolute conviction in Keelie's voice was a comfort.

"Then y'all just stay alert. Keep your trash locked up. Don't go outside at night. And keep that dog inside."

"It *was* a bear, wasn't it?" Keelie asked, voice trembling a little. "It wasn't a person, right?"

Ed looked at Cash like she had a bear costume and a set of steak knives in her back pocket, but then he looked back at Keelie with a sort of paternal fondness, and Cash remembered that Keelie had done some babysitting for him when she was fourteen or so, and his twin boys were still diapered hellions.

"There were no witnesses," Ed said, like he was telling a ghost story. "Jed had several guns in the house, but no shots were fired. His dog was unharmed and found beside his body, but his pawprints made a mess of the scene, so we don't have any other prints to go on." Ed put on his mirrored sunglasses. "Trip told us Jed was mad at you, Cassia. That he wanted to come over here and have a chat." He rocked back on his heels, looking at Keelie's house. "But he never made it out to his car. He was torn limb from limb." A pause as he stared at Cash, his gaze hard and cold. "And that bear must've been mighty mad, because his face was ripped clean off."

CHAPTER 7

After dropping that bomb, Ed tipped his hat and drove off. Cash's shoulders were up around her ears as she scanned the farm, any sense of safety and comfort fled. If an officer was out there asking questions, then there was some small chance that Ed wasn't the only one who thought Cash might be involved in Jed's death... which was ridiculous, as it certainly sounded like another bear attack.

"Well, that can't be good," Cash said, because sometimes stating the obvious made it a little more friendly.

"I bet Trip sent him out here to mess with you." Keelie reached down to scratch Peach's neck under her jangling blue collar. "*Officer Ferguson* loves prancing around town in that uniform, especially now that he's divorced." She looked down at her fitness tracker. "Still got a few hours before work. I'll be up in the pen with the horses. Do you think maybe you could fix the barn door? It's been real sticky."

Cash sighed. She'd known this was coming. "Keelie, we need to talk," she started.

But Keelie was already walking toward the barn, where a lead rope waited on a rusty nail. "We will," she called over her shoulder. "Later."

Since she was already mad, it wasn't like chores were going to make her day worse, so Cash took the sleeping fawn inside and put his box in her room under the watchful eyes of the Creepy Doll Brigade before heading over to the barn, where she inspected the door, which was an easy-enough fix. Keelie went out into the field, hollering for Marigold, and Cash got to work. Once the door was working properly, she ducked under the fence and walked toward an oval-shaped arena, where Keelie was working with a palomino mare. There was a mounting block just outside the worn white wood fence, so Keelie sat down to watch her little sister in action.

Cash had never been a horse girl, but Keelie had been drawn to all things equine since she was small. It didn't feel safe, what Keelie was doing—she had never been strong or confident, and yet she showed no fear as she charged around the space with high energy, making the horse move.

"She doesn't look happy," Cash observed.

"She's not. She's lazy. That's why we do groundwork," Keelie said, twirling the rope as she moved toward the mare's hindquarters. "She has to know who's boss. You have to be firm but not aggressive."

The mare squealed and pulled back, and Keelie let go of the rope, letting it drag on the ground. Stepping softly, Keelie approached her, murmuring gently as she picked up the rope and approached the horse's side, patting her neck.

"Why'd you let go, then, if you're the boss?" Cash asked.

Keelie turned to her, smiling, as the mare licked her lips. "Grammy taught me that. You can't fight a horse. They're bigger and stronger and meaner, when they want to be. You have to let go. If I kept pulling, it would be a fight, and she'd get scared or mad, and I'd lose, and my hands would look like ground beef for a week. So, I let go, and we reset and try again."

Cash looked down at her hands. If that had been her in there, her instinct would've been to cling even tighter to the rope, to yank back with matching force. It didn't make sense to her, letting go and letting the horse win. And yet... it had worked. The horse was now calmly doing as Keelie asked of her.

"I'm mad at you, sis," she said, still staring at her hands.

Keelie didn't stop her work. "I know."

"I feel like you lied to me. You said it was an emergency."

"For me, it was."

"Keelie, emergencies usually involved ambulances or fire trucks or hearses. At least a little blood."

"Sometimes, you just need your big sister." A few beats passed. "Noelle broke up with me."

That made Cash look up. "Noelle Halloran?"

"Yeah. I was really happy, but she... wasn't, I guess."

"You didn't tell me."

That you were dating Noelle, or that you liked girls, Cash thought but didn't say, because they both knew what was going unsaid. Mountain towns could sometimes be small-minded, after all.

"Yeah, well, it's hard to say stuff over the phone. I needed to have real conversations with you, but I don't have the money to fly out to Colorado every time there's a problem. Grammy's not really there anymore mentally, Cash. It's hard, doing it all alone. I don't think I—I wasn't ready..."

Keelie wasn't chasing the horse around anymore. She was just standing, rope in hand. The mare walked up to her and nuzzled her shirt, and Keelie absentmindedly rubbed her nose.

"Noelle always seemed nice," Cash said carefully.

"She was. But she wanted more than an old farmhouse in the mountains. She's ambitious. She's in Atlanta now, working on her master's. And I missed a few days of work because all I could do was sit at home with Peach in my lap, crying on her and eating fancy ice cream, and then I hit Farrah's car and got a talking-to, and I couldn't lose that job. I just... I needed you."

Keelie looked just as young and lost as she had the day their parents died. In that moment, Cash began to understand what it meant to let go of the rope. It wasn't worth it, holding on to anger like this. She stood up from the mounting block, and her fists opened as all her arguments melted away. She slipped through the fence boards and held out her arms, and Keelie let go of the rope and walked into the hug. Soon, Keelie was crying her heart out, and Cash was rubbing her back, and then the horse was snuffling in their hair and the donkey took up his hollering nearby as a show of support, and Cash remembered what it felt like to be needed.

After a while, Keelie's sobs fell away to sniffles, and she had to shove the slobbering horse away, and then she took Cash for a trail ride. Keelie rode the mare while Cash rode the other horse, an old, calm gelding named Rico. She'd been on horseback a few times and was a little nervous, but Keelie promised her that Rico was a good babysitter. Cash couldn't help fidgeting with her helmet and messing with her reins as they rode down the long gravel drive, through a cow pasture, and up into the trails Keelie loved so well. The forest was beautiful, and Cash almost forgot about all her problems until she saw several does grazing out among the mountain laurel and remembered that she needed to feed Spencer. Keelie didn't want to go back, but she knew she could only push her sister so far. They turned around to head home, only stopping when Keelie pointed to something dark just off the trail.

"Bear scat," she said, pointing it out to Cash. "See how it's not that big? Just a little black bear. They should be nice and fat and happy now, eating berries."

To Cash, it just looked like greasy dog poop, but Keelie was probably right. It just didn't make sense, a bear in town mauling people—and roaming as far as Jed's cabin when there were plenty of dumpsters to rifle through. On the way out, trotting past the sleepy cows, she'd been a little nervous about being so high up and waiting for her mount to misbehave, but on the way back, she was conscious of how very big the forest was, and how many places on the mountain an animal could hide, and that they could be attacked or followed by a mountain lion or bear at any moment.

Well, except the horses would pitch a fit. As would Gary the donkey, who'd first attempted to procreate with her boot— while she was already in the saddle—before following along with them like a large dog with four black hooves. And then there was Peach, who ran alongside them and then darted off into the tall grass or trees, bounding happily among the brush. And of course, Cash always had her gun. They were as well protected as they could possibly be from any local wildlife that wished them harm—and they were also too smart to go outside alone at night, unlike Jed and the former bartenders.

What had Ed meant, that Jed had wanted to come talk to her? What had the idiot planned on doing—driving over to

Keelie's house in the middle of the night and getting in a fight with a donkey? What exactly was there to talk about?

Cash wasn't glad he'd been killed, but she was glad she would never have to have that conversation, which was a dark thought.

Back at the house, Keelie told Cash to go on inside and take care of the fawn while she did the work of grooming the horses and putting them back in the pasture. Cash knew this was partially an apology for, well, everything, and also because she wasn't any good with the horses. She was rough and brash, and no matter how many times Keelie reminded her to move confidently but softly around horses and always keep a hand on them so they wouldn't startle, Cash tended to forget and do literally everything wrong. Marigold had nearly kicked her when they were getting saddled up, so Cash was more than glad to go inside and mix up a bottle of fawn formula.

She was already covered in horse hair, so it didn't seem like such an imposition to sit down on the couch and pull the fawn up into her lap, settling him in for his meal. In just two days, he already seemed bigger and stronger and had a lot less trouble gulping down his lunch. Peach appeared and hopped on the couch, settling her bulk in against Cash's side. Cash was pretty sure she'd closed the door, but maybe there was a dog door somewhere. The pit certainly seemed to act like she owned the place.

A few hours later, Cash and Keelie drove to MacGillicuddy's together in Cash's Jeep, the fawn cradled in Keelie's lap and Peach Pit excitedly grinning into the wind through the open window of the back seat. Although Cash wasn't sure she would ever fully be able to relax in Arcadia Falls, there was something pleasant about the familiar turns, the young families pushing strollers downtown, the fact that her favorite tree hadn't changed in five years. She parked around back, and Keelie called out a greeting to Taylor as they walked inside. The bar already felt like home, and soon the fawn was in his corner with Peach watching over him as Farrah did a walk-through at shift change before dinner got busy. The afternoon sun poured in the windows, and for a few brief moments, Cash could pretend that everything was fine.

Right up until Trip stormed in, flanked by Carter and Mark, with Sam trailing behind.

"What did you do, you bitch?" Trip snarled.

CHAPTER 8

This—this was why Cash couldn't relax.

She knew these guys, her once-best friends, and she knew that their lives were so small that, like Ed, they would connect Jed's death with her own return even though it made no sense whatsoever to anyone with a brain.

"I didn't do anything," she said, putting on her professional smile and knowing it wouldn't reach her eyes. "Are y'all here for food or just drinks?" Peach appeared at her side, leaning into her leg, growling.

"What happened to my brother?" Sam asked, her voice rasping. She looked like a wraith, like Jed's loss had stolen her own life force, drained her dry. And Mark—he wasn't clinging to her side like the parasite he was. He stood with Trip and

Carter, an angry man united in needing somewhere to place blame.

Cash's head fell. "I heard it was a bear. I'm so sorry, Sam."

"You were involved." Sam's face scrunched up like it always used to before she was about to cry; Cash knew that face. "You had to be."

"No claws." Cash held up her hands. "No sharp teeth. Just a girl the same age as you who was in her bed all night."

"He was fine until you came back!" Sam wailed.

"Yeah, well, I didn't call the bear to compare calendars." Cash put her hands on the bar. "You can't lay this on me. It's a coincidence, nothing more."

"He was on his way to Keelie's," Trip said, pointing a stubby finger at her. "On his way to tell you how it is."

Cash looked at his finger, the sort of look that suggested that maybe she didn't have bear teeth but she could still manage to bite off an offending digit, if it stayed in her face for too long. "Oh? And how is it? I came home to work in a bar. That's it. Nobody asked y'all to come over here and harass me at my place of business. I didn't call Jed and suggest he show up at my little sister's house in the middle of the night, probably drunk, to holler at innocent women. Anything that's happening other than me living my life is not my problem."

"Oh, we're gonna make it your problem—"

Peach barked, just once, sharply, and Farrah appeared in the door and made a beeline to the bar, hands on the hips of her painted-on acid-wash jeans. "What's this I hear about problems? Cash has my full permission to kick you-all out if you get threatening. Hell, I'll kick you out myself. You shorted Gina last time you had a meal and you never tip, so it's not like it's any loss to my bottom line."

"She killed Jed!" Sam screamed. Like idiots, Trip and Carter and Mark nodded along.

But Farrah wasn't having it. "A bear killed him, I heard. Before he could drive drunk to go assault one of my employees."

"Never was a problem till she came home." The look Trip gave Cash was so full of hate, it was like being punched in the heart.

"She's barely been here twenty-four hours after driving for two days straight. What makes you think she has the energy to rip a fully grown man into chunks, and if she does have that ability, why on God's green Earth would you threaten her?" Farrah glared around, and even Sam wilted a bit under her censure. "You really think she's that strong? Or that stupid? You think she drove down from Colorado to kill Randy and BJ in exactly the same way a few weeks ago, just to tip you clever little detectives off to her modus operandi?" Farrah's eyes slid to Cash. "Yeah, I watch *Criminal Minds*," she whispered.

Apparently, being spoken to like schoolchildren who'd broken a window took some of the wind out of the group's sails. No one had a cunning argument or clever retort when everything was laid out that obviously, and the momentum of their anger was quickly turning to embarrassment.

"We'll be watching you," Trip said, eyes narrowed.

"What else is new?" Cash shot back. "All I want is to never see a single one of you ever again, and yet y'all keep showing up. If I suddenly grow Wolverine claws, I'll be sure to let you know."

"Order or get out," Farrah finished. "I've got work to do." She raised a drawn-on eyebrow at them and left.

Trip looked around the bar like he wished he was holding a lit match and a gallon of kerosene. "Yeah, we're done here."

But as they turned around and headed for the door, Cash was horrified to see Riley standing there.

Horrified, not because she didn't want to see him—she did—but because she didn't want Trip and Carter and Mark to see him.

"Well, now, who's this?" Carter wolf-whistled. "You look like one of Snow White's special friends."

Riley wore a different pair of plaid pants, a matching plaid vest, and a crisp white shirt with a perfectly tied hunter-green tie, and he had no choice but to stop just inside the door, as Trip and Carter had moved shoulder to shoulder to block him like they were back on the football team.

"Can I help you?" Riley's voice was low, his glance disdainful. Which was well deserved, but... well, he didn't know these guys like Cash did. It would've been better for everyone if he'd just turned around and left.

"You can help me by going back to California or Portland or wherever you're from, and take your man bun with you," Mark said, warming to the feeding frenzy in the air.

"Guys, stop." Sam sniffled and put a hand on Mark's arm. "Let's just go."

"Go? But I want to get to know Dapper Dan here. Maybe he can teach me how to match my socks to my tie." Trip reached for Riley's tie, and Riley slapped his hand away.

"It's not hard. You know what a color wheel is, right?" Riley's voice was cold, but Cash could see his cheeks going pink. She had no idea if he knew how to fight—or knew how very close he was to having no choice about it. A stranger who had the gall to look different was the perfect scapegoat for their immature, bottled-up feelings.

"Careful, now. Don't stomp on his pretty shoes." Carter stepped forward, looming over Riley by at least a foot.

But Riley didn't budge. "Look, this is all very seventh-grade, but can I just go about my business? You've properly intimidated me. I'm a punchable nerd. You win." He stuck his hands in his pockets, an act of bravery and idiocy around this crew, and that's when Cash slipped under the bar flap and stormed toward the door.

"Punchable, you say," Trip started, cracking his knuckles.

But Cash was fast, and they were focused on Riley, not her. It was like a red haze came down over her vision, like all her simmering rage at her once-friends bubbled over as she crossed the creaky wood floor, grabbed Trip's wrist, and twisted his arm behind his back, hard.

"Ow, bitch. What?" he yelped.

"Let him go!" Carter barked.

But Cash had surprise and momentum on her side, and she wasn't a small woman. She propelled Trip across the dining room, stomping along as he danced and nearly fell over, trying to keep up without breaking a bone or twisting a muscle. When Cash felt him try to resist, she lifted his arm higher, making him squeal.

"Open the door, please," she barked at Taylor, and Taylor scurried out from behind the hostess station to throw open the door. Cash didn't release Trip until he was outside on the porch, shoving him away into the banister.

He pulled his arm around front and rubbed at his wrist. "You shouldn't have done that," he growled.

"It's one thing to threaten me, but you can't threaten patrons of my bar," she growled right back. "If I had the capacity to rip you to shreds with my bare teeth, I would, but I can't, so I'll settle for tossing you out like the perfectly normal human I am. Don't come back, or I won't be as friendly."

She bared her teeth at him before turning back to find Carter and Mark hovering just outside the door, unsure what to do. If she'd been a dude, they would've jumped her, but they'd been trained not to hurt women, and even if their feelings toward her now were negative, she doubted either of them would throw the first punch against her, if it came to that. Their mamas would kick their asses if they tried.

If Riley was involved, though?

Shit. He'd just made several enemies, and he wasn't the kind of guy who could fly under the radar in a town like this. Even in camo, he would stand out.

"You really wanna do this?" she said, stepping back onto the porch to give them plenty of room to make an exit. "Because I've been holding this anger for a long time, and I'd love to try out some krav maga moves I picked up in Denver."

Carter shook his head, looking around like he was worried Emmy might see him. "I don't hit girls."

"Yeah. You're not worth it," Mark said, his pretty face twisted up in disgust. "Never were."

He always knew what to say to make something hurt twice as much.

Cash wasn't worth starting a fight with, and she wasn't worth his fidelity back in the day, either.

They moved to flank Trip. Without Jed, apparently they'd decided Trip was their new lead dog. Sam followed, arms wrapped around herself, still too lost in her own grief to throw any barbs at Cash.

"Don't come back here," Cash warned. "You're not welcome."

"It's a free country." Trip spat on the wood boards of the porch. "Unless you want to call the police on us. Not that it'd do you much good, cuz they're on our side."

By the light of day, they just looked… so pathetic.

All four of them had clearly been crying, for all that the guys never would've admitted it. They needed answers to this random, senseless violence, and their desperate little brains had brought them to Cash, who'd always been the smart one. Even though they'd come to blame her, maybe somewhere, deep down, they still needed her.

"You guys need to lay off the booze and get some sleep," she said softly, looking each of her old friends—and her old boyfriend—in their red-rimmed eyes. "Stay inside at night, okay? This bear shit is serious. Just… take care of yourselves."

"I hope that bear takes care of you, you—"

Cash never found out which woman-hating epithet Trip was going to use because she punched him.

Not in the face, though—faces were hard and bony, and noses were bleedy, and she needed both of her hands to work. It was a sucker punch in his softening belly, and he doubled over around it.

"Get off our property," she said breathlessly. "And don't come back unless and until you learn some manners."

"I'm telling my brother," Trip said, wheezing.

"Good. Go tattle. Tell him you got punched by a girl in broad daylight. He'll love that."

Trip's jaw dropped, and for a moment he just goggled at her. "Screw this place. Come on."

He hobbled off the porch, and Carter lunged at Cash menacingly but didn't touch her. To her credit, she didn't flinch. Mark shook his head like he was disappointed in her, which was his usual tactic for keeping his handsome face unblemished, and Sam clung to his arm like it was a life raft. The look she gave Cash behind Mark's back seemed both blaming and desperate for help, and Cash didn't envy the stew of emotions that must've been churning in her heart. Sam could've probably used a real friend right now. Too bad she didn't know how to be one.

As the group headed for two massive trucks parked in the back lot, Peach Pit stood at the porch steps, growling, every hair on her back standing on end and her tail out stiff.

"Sorry I brought trouble to your bar," Cash said softly.

Peach trotted over to her and sat, leaning against Cash's leg, staring out into the lot as the trucks peeled out into the street, spraying gravel.

"Boof," Peach agreed.

CHAPTER 9

After several big, cleansing breaths and a quick check with her phone camera to make sure she didn't look unhinged, Cassia went back inside and headed to the corner where Riley was squatting down beside the fawn's box.

He glanced back at her. "They seem fun."

"As fun as a razorblade slide into a vat of pickle juice. How's he look?"

Riley rubbed the fawn's ear. "A little dehydrated. Did you miss his last feeding?"

"I was about to do it before the goon squad showed up." She shook her head. "I'll do it before you take him. You don't need to get messy."

She hurried behind the bar to prepare the bottle, taking care to do everything just right, since he was watching. The restaurant was super slow at that hour—

"You're early," she said as she walked over, shaking the bottle. Peach trotted at her side.

Riley smiled. "I had to work through lunch. My boss hates paying overtime, but he's too detailed and kindhearted to short me, so he told me to, and I quote, skedaddle."

"I'll get him fed real quick, and you can be on your way."

She lifted Spencer out of his box and slid down the wall to sit, settling him in her lap. He was livelier than he'd been yesterday, lunging for the bottle and applying himself to drinking as he looked around solemnly and blinked his bright, long-lashed eyes. Peach curled up, her back against Cash's leg. She didn't seem to mind the occasionally flailing hoof.

Riley slid down to sit beside Cash, and she winced. "Don't get your clothes messed up on my account. We keep a clean bar, but not that clean."

He didn't budge. "Somebody's got to keep the dry cleaner in business. This isn't a big dry-cleaning town, from what I can tell." He was close enough to nudge her with his shoulder, and it made her feel all warm inside—and made her wonder if he was having the sort of thoughts about her that she was having about him, or if maybe he just felt sorry for her. "You don't like being a bother, do you?"

"I didn't ask for any of this." She looked down at the fawn, thought about skidding to a stop in front of his mother the day before. "I just want a simple life. I don't cause problems. But they find me when I'm here." She gestured to the bar with one arm. "That's why I stayed away so long. Every problem in this town already knows my address."

"I take it those four are the problem?"

She glanced at his profile; it was a nice profile. "My high school best friends. I grew up. Looks like they didn't. And the fifth one got mauled by a bear last night, apparently, which they somehow think is my fault."

"So, you're the deer whisperer, not the bear whisperer."

She looked at the fawn, who'd fallen asleep. The bottle plopped out of his tiny mouth. "I think the milk did most of the work. But no, I can't command bears to bitch-slap guys who are rude to me. Truth be told, I'd probably abuse that power."

Riley stood, smoothly enough that she wondered if he did yoga or martial arts. He took the fawn from her lap, his fingertips grazing her thigh, and placed the sleeping baby back in his box. Less elegantly, Cash stood, and Peach scrambled up to stand beside her.

"Want to go for a walk?" Riley asked.

As if imagining this offer was for her, Peach started cavorting around like a much younger dog, wagging her stubby tail intensely, but Cash pointed at the bar. "Wish I could, but I'm on duty."

"Bar's dead," Farrah called from just beyond the door; she must've been eavesdropping. And why not, after what had just happened? "No patrons. I'd consider it a favor if you'd take Peach for a walk. Help her get the wiggles out."

Cash looked down at the dog wiggling at her feet and knew damn well that Farrah was playing matchmaker, but... well, a walk sounded nice. She was emotionally shaken by what had just happened, and a little time in the spring sun would do her good.

"Do you have a leash?" she asked the dog, because it just seemed like the polite thing to do. In response, Peach ran behind the bar and jumped and scuffled in place until Cashfollowed her and retrieved a ratty old leash. She hooked it to Peach's collar, and Riley took one last look at the sleeping fawn in the box and held open the door to the porch.

It was a beautiful day, and Cash realized she hadn't walked around downtown at all since returning. As a teen, walking had just been a way to get from one place to another and brazenly loiter, but now she noticed things about her hometown she never had before, the interesting bricks in the sidewalk and the geraniums planted in flowerboxes and the little free library in front of the old jail, lovingly crafted to mimic the proud white portico.

As for Peach Pit, she was an easy dog to walk, although she was enthusiastic about smelling everything.

"You'd better not shoo-shoo on private property," Cash warned her.

Riley held back a laugh. "Shoo-shoo?"

"My grandmother's word. She finished raising us, and she refused to use proper anatomical terms. I once got hit in the crotch with a baseball, and she asked me if I broke my lady boo-boo. In public." Cash shook her head. Even if Grammy was failing, she'd have to go visit her soon. And take her some sunflowers. She'd been running away from her past—and her responsibilities—for too long.

Standing there by the candy shop where she'd begged for a caramel apple every Halloween, she felt the town coalesce around her, almost like it had been blurry for years and had finally come into focus. This was her place. Her family's place. Their bones were in the hills, their blood in the abandoned gold mines. She should not have allowed the stupid choice of a couple of kids to determine her entire destiny. It felt silly now, the thought that her pain might go away if she just drove far enough away and ignored it.

"Mind if we go this way?" She gestured down a different sidewalk.

"I'm following you," Riley said quietly, like he could sense the sea change inside her and was trying to give her space. Or maybe he could already guess where she was heading.

They walked past a yoga studio, a meadery, a sports bar, a law office—maybe Riley's law office? Cash would ask later—and then stood before a rickety iron fence. Cash wasn't sure how she would feel about the tombstones until she saw them, hundreds of shades of gray flowing up over a soft green hill. She gently swung the gate open and looked to Riley.

"Will you hold Peach's leash, please? Can't have her—"

"Shoo-shooing on graves? Definitely not." Riley took Peach's leash and put a hand on Cash's arm. "You gonna be okay in there?"

"Probably not, but I won't be okay out here until I've been in there, you know?"

He smiled into her eyes. "I'll be here."

With a nod of thanks, Cash left Riley and Peach Pit and ventured into the cemetery. There were gravestones from the 1800s, lovingly kept clean by the local Historical Society, and then there were newer, flashier graves from the past few years, shiny white and pink and speckled like kitchen countertops. Cash knew exactly where she was headed, and she was careful not to step on the other graves on her way there. The Kings had a whole corner of the cemetery with room to spare, and the newest stones were from 2015.

MELISSA STEPHENS KING AND THOMAS GENE KING.

DEVOTED WIFE AND MOTHER.

BELOVED HUSBAND AND FATHER.

There were flowers on the grave, maybe a week old and wilted but clearly put there by Keelie, judging by the little smiley-face balloon.

Cash fell to her knees, the grass soaking into her jeans.

"I'm sorry," she whispered, voice catching. "You always told me to watch out for Keelie, but the first chance I got, I ran. And not because I was scared. Because I was angry. Because I was embarrassed."

A ways off, she heard Riley shout, "Hey, no—"

And then a meaty pit bull barreled into her side, curling around her. She looked down, and Peach Pit looked up, her bright blue eyes almost quivering with feeling. Cash put an arm around her bulk and settled down on her knees.

"I'm sorry," she said again. "I should've done more. I should've been here. But Keelie turned out okay without me. I guess you guys did that, and Grammy didn't mess her up too bad. Except the dolls. The dolls will always freak me out."

The cemetery was quiet, apart from the calls of birds and the rustle of leaves in the soft spring breeze. Cash looked down at Peach, stroking the flat shovel of her skull, in awe of all the healed scars there. Peach's ears had once been cropped and had then clearly been gnawed at, and the area around her eyes had been scored and marked by teeth. And yet her jaws were peeled back in a loving grin, her eyes glowing with concern.

"What's your secret?" Cash asked her. "You should be the angriest dog in the world, after what they did to you."

In response, Peach licked her hand and wriggled, then gave one sharp bark.

"Just like that," Cash said, rubbing the dog's side.

Just let it go.

She put her hands on the ground, pressing into the new grass and old dirt, and willed herself to let go of everything she'd held so tightly. If lightning had hit her, just then, it would've traveled down her body, through her palms, and into the earth, and that's where she wanted all the anger to go, all the guilt, all the helplessness. She wanted it to disperse and spread until it had no power. She wanted to be free.

For a long time, her fingers clutched the dirt while her tears fell down, and then, all of a sudden, for no real reason... it felt like it was over. When she stood, she seemed lighter. Empty. If Peach could spend the first part of her life as a bait dog and learn to forgive people, or at least forget what they'd done to her, then maybe Cash could stop letting something that happened back in high school define her whole goddamn life. She didn't regret the past five years—not the places she'd seen, the things she'd learned, the adventures she'd had—but she did regret the way she'd held herself apart from people all that time. Just because Sam and the crew weren't worth trusting didn't mean every other person on the planet was a liar.

She looked over to where Riley waited by the gate. He wasn't scrolling through his phone or tapping his foot; he was looking up with interest, hands in his trouser pockets, and Cash followed his line of sight to a bright red cardinal singing his heart out on the branch of a flowering dogwood. As if sensing her watching him, he glanced over at her and smiled, and she smiled back, and it lit up something in her heart.

Her jeans now soaked and her tear-hot eyes most likely surrounded by a mascara raccoon mask, Cash walked back to the gate with Peach at her side, her leash slithering through the grass behind them.

"Did you find what you needed?" Riley asked.

Cash looked down at Peach and picked up her leash.

"It found me, I think. Thanks for waiting."

As they walked back up the hill, she realized that she hadn't really asked Riley any questions at all. "Are your parents alive?" she blurted, immediately regretting the brashness of the question.

"Yes, but I don't visit them often. We don't see eye to eye. They live for football. I was supposed to live for football, or at least baseball or track. Instead, I got really into baking and home science experiments and rehabilitating baby squirrels. They vastly prefer my younger brother Chase. He enjoys basketball and boxing. They all think I'm some strange cuckoo dropped in amongst them." A small chuckle. "I once brought some knitting to their Super Bowl party. They were mortified. My dad asked if that was my way of telling them I was gay."

"You're not, right?"

He grinned at her, eyes twinkling. "Nope." She smiled back, and he reached out to hold her hand. "But I make incredible cinnamon rolls."

"My hand—that's grave dirt—"

"Don't care."

The hill had her out of breath, or maybe that was his hand warmly, firmly clasping hers, and she was worried about the dirt, but it was nice, hiking through downtown with Riley and Peach. For nearly ten whole minutes, Cash completely forgot about Sam and Trip and Mark and Jed and the bear attacks. She was just... alive. Alive in a beautiful place where spring was blooming and birds were singing and a man who made cinnamon rolls was happy to be with her even though she'd recently been crying over a grave.

It was peaceful. Nice. Addictive.

If only it could've lasted.

CHAPTER 10

Back at the bar, Riley released Cash's hand, but not like he wanted to. He took the fawn and left for home, promising Cash the best breakfast she'd ever had if she came a half hour early the next morning. She had never encountered a man who offered to make breakfast before sleeping together, but she was looking forward to it.

The rest of her shift went on without incident, a perfectly normal Thursday night. No rude guests, no bad drunks, just cheerful waitstaff and just enough busyness to keep her from getting bored. She did her best to put the ugliness of her past behind her and pretend like this was any other new job, full of promise and hope. Keelie wasn't working tonight, and the fawn was gone, so she felt light and free, utterly unencumbered. She texted Riley a few times, ostensibly to check on the fawn, but the banter definitely turned to flirty.

**If you could be doing anything in the world right now, what would it be?* she typed.

Three dots wavered until his words popped up.

**Camping under the stars with someone who appreciates gourmet s'mores. And a nosy pit bull to keep away the bears.*

She felt little flutters in her middle every time those three little dots popped up. Sure, she'd had a few one-night stands around Colorado, but she hadn't felt flutters. She hadn't grinned like an idiot, hummed to herself, knocked a fridge closed with her hip. She'd been living like a grim, grizzled old lady locked up in an unfurnished apartment, grumpy and closed off, but now she almost felt like she was sixteen again, like anything could happen and the world was full of possibilities. All because she'd seen this guy—what, three times?

But that was how infatuation worked.

A little taste, and then a curiosity, and then a craving.

She usually went for the strong, silent type, smart and fit and completely unavailable, the kind of guy who either drove a lovingly maintained thirty-year-old Ford truck or a brand-new, jacked-up Ford truck. But Riley... he was just different. He didn't need to lean in to masculinity like that. Any man brave enough to take knitting to a family Super Bowl party had no self-doubt whatsoever, and she found that insanely attractive.

That night as she closed up, Cash shimmied around to a playlist on her phone, sliding each glass into its spot and getting everything ready for tomorrow. She'd made good tips—better than last night—and hadn't messed up a single thing.

"You don't seem like a Taylor Swift girl," Taylor said, watching from the doorway.

"'Shake It Off' is universally applicable," Cash informed her.

After the lights were off, Cash found the rest of the waitstaff waiting for her at the front door. It felt silly, six grown women being frightened of a little black bear, but no one was going to get attacked on her watch. With Peach Pit standing guard at her side and her gun in her hand, she watched as each girl got in her car, locked it, and drove off. The lot was empty except for her Jeep, with no sign of anything dangerous whatsoever.

"We good?" she asked Peach, who had basically become her shadow.

Peach scanned the lot, her shoulders tense and her nose working overtime. Cash half-expected the dog to answer in English, but the tail wag was enough. Even though she was armed and had no doubts about Peach's opinions on safety, Cash still felt like a kid darting up dark stairs at night as she hurried across the gravel lot to the Jeep. She opened the door for Peach to hop through to the passenger seat, threw herself into the front seat, and hit the lock button, realizing too late that there was something on her windshield that didn't belong there.

A dead squirrel, its tail under her wiper.

Her shoulders went up, her head whipping around to double-check the back seat, which she'd of course already checked when she reached her car because she had lived her entire life as a woman and took the usual precautionary measures.

The hairs rose up the nape of her neck.

This wasn't natural. Someone had done this.

Considering the current circumstances, Cash wasn't about to get out of the car and remove it. Not only because of the bear, but also because if anyone else wanted to cause her harm, that was exactly what they would want—her alone in the middle of the night, outside and vulnerable. Before this, she wouldn't have dreamed that her old friends might hurt her, but... well, she'd punched Trip. And worse yet, humiliated him in front of his friends.

"Well, shit," she muttered.

The whole drive home, the squirrel stared at her with bird-pecked eyes, its gray tail billowing in the night air. She checked her rear mirror for lights, but none appeared. She kept her foot on the brake, expecting some kind of weird ambush by Trip and the crew, a truck with high beams on blocking the poorly lit two-lane road, but it was just a peaceful night out in the country, nothing more. She turned in at Keelie's place, and Gary's bray carried across the starlit hills.

The little farmhouse sat innocently in the darkness, the shadowy shapes of two sleeping horses off to the side and a prancing donkey screaming his hellos. The lights were on in the front room, with Keelie visible through the big window, sitting cross-legged on her couch, eating potato straws out of a bag and painting her toenails. Cash didn't like how defenseless her innocent sister was—anyone could be outside, looking in, and one good-sized rock could shatter any pretense of safety. Then again, it wasn't like curtains would've fixed the issue. Her sister had specifically chosen a little farmhouse high up on a hill, a mile from every neighbor, and she'd never anticipated any sort of trouble. For all its faults, Arcadia Falls had always seemed so safe.

Cash got out of the Jeep, and Peach scrambled over to her seat, down to the floorboard, and onto the ground, where she zigged and zagged around the drive, her nose going crazy.

"This would be a lot easier if you could talk like Scooby-Doo and tell me if you smell any strangers," Cash told her. In response, the pit just turned her head from side to side, scanning the night.

Knowing that if Keelie saw the dead squirrel on the windshield, she'd cry, Cash found a stick, lifted the wiper, and flicked the little gray carcass onto the ground, only then realizing that giving an energetic dog something stinky and dead to play with probably wasn't her best bet. Peach Pit, apparently, had some class, as she merely sniffed it and moved on. Cash used the stick to nudge it into the brush at the edge of the drive and silently prayed that some night predator—not a bear!—would smell it and drag it off.

It had to be Trip and the boys who had done this. It had to.

They were trying to intimidate her.

Why?

Because they were idiots. It was the only explanation. If they scared her away—if she left—they wouldn't have a constant reminder that they'd all either betrayed her or been complicit in that betrayal. All of their lives were easier when she wasn't there, because then they got to forget that they'd hurt her.

"Fucking cowards," Cash muttered.

"You good, sis?" Keelie stood in the open door, backlit by house lights. Peach bounded inside, and Cash followed.

"Yep."

"Good night at work?"

"Yep. No problems."

Which was technically true, as the problems had occurred in the light of day, and the squirrel was unrelated to her employment. Cash didn't want to tell Keelie that she was being targeted; her sister would only worry unnecessarily.

Keelie's nails weren't done, so Cash joined her on the couch to watch a baking show and share the snacks. Peach curled up between them and slept for a while, but then she suddenly jumped up and went to the front door. All the fur up her spine stiffened, and she growled, a deep and menacing sound. Cash immediately went for her holster and then turned out the lights, plunging the house into darkness.

"Hey!" Keelie complained.

"Shh. With that light on, anyone can see directly in here. Get off the couch and out of sight of the window."

"There's nothing wrong. If there was, Gary would be making a ruckus."

Cash opened her mouth to explain that donkeys weren't burglar alarms when Gary indeed began making a ruckus. The growl built in Peach's throat, and she put her front paws on the door and scratched at it furiously like she wanted out, and now.

"No way," Cash told her. "We all stay inside. Whatever's out there can stay outside. And if it comes inside, I'll shoot the top part and you bite the bottom part."

Peach obediently stopped scratching and instead went to see if the back door was more yielding, leaving Cash to peek out the big window, looking for anything suspicious. This far up in the mountains, it might've been a stray cat, a raccoon, a possum. Or it might've been a rabid dog, a serial killer, a murderous bear, or a Bigfoot. There was just no way to know. At least there weren't any truck headlights. Cash understood animals and knew how to put them down, but human beings were a lot less predictable. That was the biggest lesson she'd learned so far that week.

"Got a flashlight?"

Keelie padded into the kitchen and brought a little Maglite, which Cash shone out into the yard, sweeping from the fields on the right to the Jeep and truck in the driveway to the fence on the left. She went to the back window next, but all she saw were the pastures. The barn and the horses in their smaller paddock weren't visible from the house. Cash wished she could see the horses—their behavior would've told her a lot about the threat.

"We need to get you some motion-activated cameras," she whispered. "One of those smart doorbells or something."

"Before this week, there was no need."

Cash heard it in Keelie's voice—the regret.

Well, if she was going to regret having her big sister around, she could damn well regret tricking her into being in that situation.

A crash outside, off to the right, brought Peach galloping back to the front door, where she yodeled a bark and stuck her paws under the door.

"Trash cans," Keelie said.

"Hold Peach's collar."

When Keelie had the pit in hand, Cash flicked her gun's safety and opened the front door as quietly as she could, holding the Maglite under the barrel as she swept the beam of light around to the barn.

There, rooting around in an overturned trash can, was a black bear.

Not even a big black bear.

A little one, about the size of a beefy black Lab.

"You don't look like a killer," Cash said.

The bear spun around, leapt onto its back feet in absolute terror, and fell over backward, rolling over in the trash. It scrambled to its feet and ran off into the night, galloping as fast as it could.

She didn't go out to clean up the mess. Just because that particular bear was too small and scared to do any harm didn't mean his bigger, meaner brother wasn't waiting in the wings. She went back inside, closed and locked the door, and turned the lights back on.

"Bear?" Keelie asked.

"The littlest bear," she agreed. "One step up from Pooh. Not the one they're looking for."

"I'm glad you didn't shoot it."

Cash looked down at her gun, wondering how she'd feel if it had been a huge bear, an angry bear, and she'd been forced to shoot it.

She hoped she never had to find out.

The next morning, she woke up early and picked up the fallen trash, which had been kindly spread around in the night, probably by the local raccoon population, for whom it would've been quite the buffet. She showered and put on a sundress with her boots and leather jacket before heading over to Riley's house with Peach Pit riding shotgun. Rolling down the Jeep windows, she sang at the top of her lungs, reveling in the sweet spring air and excited about what was to come. Tomorrow, the fawn would go to the vet to begin his journey back to wildness. And if Cash didn't mess this up, she'd find a way to see Riley again, anyway.

11.

The moment the front door opened, she smelled Riley's cinnamon rolls. Even Peach Pit gulped the air down hungrily, licking her chops.

"Hope you brought your appetite," Riley said, smiling in his pajamas and a plaid apron.

"Always," she said, hoping he saw the double meaning in her eyes.

The kittens were face-down in their breakfast, and Cash suddenly realized she might've made a faux pas. "Is it okay to bring Peach inside? I don't know how she does with cats…"

Riley looked down at Peach. "Is she trained at all?"

"Honestly, I have no idea. She's been stuck to me like Velcro since I got here."

Riley pulled a baby gate out of the nearby coat closet, effectively walling Peach off in the hallway. "There. Now you don't have to worry." Peach looked longingly into the kitchen but seemed to understand her predicament. She lay down, nose on her paws, and gave a wag that looked a lot like a human sigh of disappointed understanding.

Cash followed Riley to the kitchen, where she found more food laid out than the two of them could've eaten in a week. The aforementioned cinnamon rolls were the crown jewel, but there were biscuits, eggs, bacon, buttered grits, hash browns, and glasses of orange juice that looked freshly squeezed.

"You went all out," Cash observed.

"Haven't had the opportunity to cook for anyone else in a long time, and all the good things don't come with a recipe for one." Riley held up the pan of cinnamon rolls. "But you'll definitely be taking home leftovers."

Cash sat in the chair he pulled out for her and piled her plate high because everything looked and smelled amazing and she was hungry and not afraid to show it. She made a mental note to find a gym somewhere downtown and sign up because... well, she was settling in. When she'd packed the Jeep and started driving like a bat out of hell to save her little sister from the imaginary emergency, she'd hoped it would be a temporary thing, but she definitely wasn't ready to leave Arcadia Falls yet. She'd missed Keelie more than she'd wanted to admit to herself. She'd missed the way everything felt natural and easy there, the warmth of spring and the blowsy Southern flowers and the way it felt, driving down roads she knew by heart, swooping up and down through the mountains and valleys. She missed being near the memories of her parents, and she still needed to go visit Grammy.

And as it turned out, she actually liked her job. She liked MacGillicuddy's. Farrah was a supportive boss and a nice person, the rest of the waitstaff was pleasant enough and actively repelled drama, and, well, she definitely wanted to see more of Riley. Even with the fawn gone, if he gave her leftovers, she'd have to bring his Tupperware back. That was only polite.

As they ate, they chatted about everything and nothing. Their families, their bosses good and bad, his education and her travels, the inexplicable ostrich in that one field that seemed to think it was a cow. Things felt easy with Riley, and Cash had never really gone for easy. She'd been with Mark the longest, and he'd been moody and immature even when things were good. Since then, she hadn't gone on more than two dates with anyone, and she hadn't really felt any sparks.

Maybe she hadn't *let* herself feel any sparks.

But this? This was sparks galore.

And not just because three feral kittens kept trying to climb up her skirt.

Plus, his cinnamon rolls were really, really good.

"It's all in the yeast and proving," he told her, and she remembered these words from Keelie's baking show and nodded like she actually knew what they meant.

When they were done feasting, she helped him put things away, and he packed a Tupperware full of breakfast for her and Keelie and tossed a piece of bacon to Peach, who'd been silently pouting all along.

"So, we're still taking Spencer to that vet tomorrow, right?" Cash asked.

Riley dried his hands off on a kitchen towel and turned to her. "Yeah, they're expecting us around ten."

Us.

They're expecting *us*.

Cash liked the sound of that.

"I'm going to miss having him around..." she trailed off, looking at Riley expectantly. He was barefoot, just a little shorter than she was in her boots, and he stepped toward her.

"Me, too."

Their eyes met, and something electric shot through Cash's veins, waking her up from whatever sleep she'd been in for years. She felt like Frankenstein's monster, but in a good way.

Alive.

So alive.

"I'm going to have so much spare time now. Do you need any help with the kittens? Or proofing dough?"

He must've heard the coy hope in her voice, as he grinned and caught her waist in his hands. "Yes, definitely. I am overrun. In desperate need."

He didn't say of what, but it wasn't help proofing baked goods.

"Can I kiss you, Cash?"

"Do you really need to ask?"

A heavy pause. "I do. I need to hear it."

"Yes."

She'd barely finished the word when his lips landed on hers, soft but with enough pressure to tell her the consent was necessary but he'd had no doubt how she would answer. Cash took a step back, her butt hitting the kitchen counter, and he pressed his hips against hers, his hands moving up to cup her jaw. Cash had grown so accustomed to the drunken frenzy of a one-night stand, of two strangers with needs and no manners, that it was a revelation to be kissed so thoroughly and firmly and slowly. Her fingertips found his sides, the softness of his shirt, the surprising firmness of the muscles underneath it. Her nerves came alive where they touched. A vision landed unbidden in her mind, little seeds sprouting riotously at the touch of the first warm rain of spring. She hadn't even known how long she'd lain fallow.

Riley didn't pull away until a phone alarm went off, back on the kitchen table. He held her face, smiled into her eyes. Her lips tasted like cinnamon and sugar.

"I hate that alarm," he said.

"Snooze is a thing."

He released her and laughed, adjusting his apron over his front. "Not to my boss, it's not. I guess we should've started earlier."

"Or we can try again at night. I don't work Monday or Tuesday."

It was funny, how Cash felt perfectly comfortable initiating a one-night stand with a guy at a ski bar, just some dude with a beard and snowboard bruises she'd never see again, but now, with someone she actually liked, it was terrifying, floating the idea of a proper date even after ten minutes of vigorously making out against the counter.

"Hike and dinner on Tuesday?" Riley asked. "Work up an appetite first?"

Again, appetite would not be a problem, but she just said, "Sounds wonderful. I'll have to show you the actual Arcadia Falls, if you haven't seen them before."

"Then it's a date."

As soon as he said the word out loud, a sense of rightness and relief settled in her chest.

It was real. He felt it too. And there would be another chance to eat his cinnamon rolls.

Riley handed her the heavy Tupperware and picked up Spencer's box. "I'll see you after work for our last fawn transfer. Are you available to drive down to the vet tomorrow morning?"

They walked slowly down the hall. Cash was reluctant to leave, and it felt like Riley was reluctant to let her go.

"I need to be at work by two, but definitely. It'll be hard to say goodbye."

She looked down into the box, to where Spencer was staring up at her with his soft, bright eyes. He seemed so much bigger and stronger than he had even a day before. She sensed that if they hadn't had plans for his care after tomorrow, he would've become quite a handful as he gained size and energy. Gary the hollering horny donkey was enough; she didn't have what it took to keep a pet stag in the pasture.

Riley moved the baby gate aside so she could pass through and then held open the front door for Cash and Peach. He stayed just inside, almost shyly, and when Cash glanced around, she saw an old woman in a large sunhat staring as she pretended to trim a rhododendron.

"See you later," she said. "Thanks again for breakfast."

"Any time. But not like when people say that as a throwaway. I'll make cinnamon rolls any time it will get you through that door." With the Tupperware in one arm and the fawn's box in the other, all she could really do was stand there. "A gentleman would help you out to the car, but I'm not currently in a gentlemanly state." Riley glanced over her shoulder to where the old woman was goggling at them, then winked at Cash. It shouldn't have worked, but it did.

"Bye."

She had to leave or it was going to get weird, so she walked down the porch steps and over to her Jeep, where she had to juggle the boxes to get her door open. Once everything was settled, she drove back home to Keelie's house, glad that her sister wasn't weeping on the porch this time. When she entered the kitchen, Keelie looked her up and down and cocked an eyebrow.

"A dress, huh?"

"Something wrong with wearing a dress in the spring?"

"Mm-hmm. You're smiling like a loon. Now hand over the cinnamon rolls."

Cash slid the Tupperware across the table. "Save me one or I'm throwing one of the dolls in the creek. And I won't tell you which one."

Keelie picked up a cinnamon roll and bit into it, her eyes rolling back in her head. Cash had never understood how her sister could just chomp into any food—even cheese sticks. Personally, Cash preferred to eat foods along the dotted lines nature had provided. She unrolled her cinnamon rolls, peeled her string cheese, and tore the crusts off her sandwiches like a perfectly normal person.

"Don't touch my dolls," Keelie said. "But if you promise to stay forever, I'll move them to my closet."

The prospect was becoming more and more enticing. Maybe not forever—she eventually wanted marriage and kids, and she couldn't do that in Keelie's spare room with the donkey screeching all night. Cash liked horses but didn't love them, which meant that shoveling manure would not become a regular part of her life. But for now, as long as Trip and Sam left her alone and Riley continued to not leave her alone, she would stick around and see what happened. She wasn't sure when she'd decided it, but she had.

Cash had almost seven hours until her shift started, and she was still saddlesore from yesterday's trail ride and didn't want to get roped into chores. Instead, she dug her hiking boots out of her Jeep, put on an old pair of jeans, and asked Keelie to watch the fawn so she could go for a hike.

"What do I do with him?" Keelie asked.

"No idea. He just ate and got his nethers wiped, so he doesn't need anything until I get back. You can take him out and let him run around, if you like. He doesn't potty until he's stimulated, so it should be relatively safe."

Keelie's eyes lit up. "We're going to watch *Snow White* together."

"Just don't let him see *Bambi*." Cash smiled fondly at her little sister. "I'll be out at the falls. Have fun!"

"Wait. You shouldn't go into the forest alone. There's a murderbear on the loose, remember?"

Cash sighed and held up a finger. "One: It's only killed at night, and the falls aren't really near the bar or Jed's cabin." She held up a second finger. "Two: I'm armed."

"Three: Take Peach with you, so at least you'll know if there's something fishy. She always knows when there's trouble."

Hearing her name, Peach left the window and danced around Cash's legs.

"You want to go for a ride? And a hike?"

Peach's stubby tail went crazy, and she gave one affirmative bark.

"Then what could go wrong?"

Judging by the face Keelie made, a lot of things, actually.

CHAPTER 12

On her way out to the trail, Cash was careful to drive the speed limit and obey all traffic laws. She was fully aware that Ed and his friends would love any excuse to get her in trouble even though she'd done nothing wrong. The Ferguson brothers were tight, and Jed and Trip had been tight. Cash hadn't seen the inside of the jail since a field trip in fifth grade, and she didn't want to see it now.

There were no other cars in the gravel lot at the trailhead. Cash parked and grabbed her bear spray. She didn't have a leash for Peach, but the pit bull had been an easy companion so far, and and as it turned out, she was a pleasure to hike with. Cash knew these trails like the back of her hand, and very little had changed in five years. A tree down here, a new Eagle

Scout bench there. This particular trail was a three-mile loop, winding around the river with a stop at the waterfall for which the town had been named, and it seemed to Cash that it was just as important to visit the falls as it was her parents' graves. It was a homecoming of sorts. Greeting the place where she'd grown up and being back in the woods where she'd run wild with her friends, once upon a time.

About halfway to the falls, Peach went stiff all over, gazing out into the forest, and Cash froze and reached for her gun before she realized she was just looking at a doe and her fawn. Her heart ached to think that this was exactly where Spencer should've been, out in the forest by his mama's side instead of probably wearing a doll skirt as Keelie danced around her living room, pretending she was a princess.

"It's okay," Cash watched Peach quiver, the hairs rising along her spine and her stubby tail going stiff. "It's just a deer." As if hearing her, the doe's tail flashed white and she bounded away, the fawn disappearing in her wake. Peach followed them, barking joyously as she dove into the forest. "Guess I forgot to whisper," Cash whispered, glad that the scarred-up pitty was having a nice day chasing critters they both knew she could never catch.

But then she heard boots crunching in the leaf litter and spun around to find Trip, Carter, and Mark marching up the trail in full camo.

Three things immediately struck her.

One: none of them were wearing blaze orange.

Two: Sam wasn't with them.

And three: the only thing in season was…

"Y'all out hunting for turkey? I haven't heard a single call," she said, going for a friendly greeting to remind them of their past together.

"No. We're hunting you," Trip said, his voice venomous.

Cash began to weigh whether the bear spray hooked on her belt or the gun in her holster would be the better bet with these three. To their credit, no one was carrying a shotgun, but they did have side holsters and knives, they always did when out hunting. Cash didn't think they had it in them to actually hurt her, but with everything that had happened recently, all bets were off. At least Peach Pit had run off into the forest; an angry dog was a liability in situations like this, and the poor girl didn't deserve to be at the business end of some asshole's wrath.

She held up her hands.

"Okay. You caught me. What's your next move?"

Trip pulled his gun and went into shooting stance.

"You're gonna tell us what happened to Jed."

For all her time around guns, Cash had never actually had one pointed at her before. She'd been in bar fights, had a guy go for her neck with a broken beer bottle, but she'd been able to defuse the situation every time. Most drunks didn't plan ahead; they just got mad and swung. But Trip had planned this—hell, he'd either bugged her Jeep or followed her out into the forest—and even if he wasn't particularly smart in general, he wasn't as dumb as a drunk.

"What do you think I know, Trip?"

"You showed up, Jed died. That day. It can't be a coincidence."

"Explain the other two bartenders, then, if you know so much."

Trip scoffed. "Who gives a shit? One of 'em hit on my little sister, and Ed arrested the other one for smacking his girl around, so I'm glad they're gone. We're talking about Jed." His face scrunched up; he was trying so hard not to cry. "He was your friend, too, long time ago. Don't you even feel bad? Do you feel anything?"

Cash swallowed around the lump in her throat.

"Yeah, Trip, I feel a lot of things. I feel bad about Jed, but he hurt me a long time ago, then he showed up at my work to make my life harder. I don't want anything to do with y'all. Nothing at all. I never want to see any of you again. You all hurt me. So bad. And I pretended I was too cool to care, but inside, I was gutted. Every friend I had betrayed me." She looked each of them in the eyes. "Every one. So, I left so we could all pretend that didn't happen. Now that I'm back in town, if y'all will just stay out of my bar, I'll stay out of your lives."

"What if we told you to leave again and never come back? What if none of us wanna see you walking around downtown with that little sissy lawyer? What if we don't wanna see you behind the bar? This is your warning, bitch. Go back to wherever you came from."

Cash looked to Carter and Mark. "And y'all think that's fair?"

"Nobody wants you here," Mark said, but he couldn't quite meet her eyes. *Sam doesn't want you here* was the subtext. His home life had likely gotten harder the moment Cash rolled into town.

"I just want everything to go back to normal," Carter said, ever the reasonable one.

Cash shrugged. "So, pretend I'm not here. It's been five years. Y'all don't even know me anymore."

"Don't want to know you," Trip growled. "Want you either punished or gone."

The gun in his hands hadn't wavered.

"Or what, you're gonna end me yourself? You're gonna punish me? They'll know it was you, Trip. Keelie knows where I am."

"Ed knows where you are too. He's in the parking lot right now."

A shiver dripped down Cash's spine. If he'd gone to the trouble of having his brother there, and if Ed had actually shown up, that meant she couldn't count on law enforcement to keep her safe.

She was on her own.

And yeah, she was probably still a better shot than Trip, but his gun was already in his hands, and hers was still in her holster with the safety on.

"March right back up that trail, get in your Jeep, and leave town, and we can forget all this," Trip said, almost like he was trying to talk her down from something stupid. "Ed'll follow you to the county line to make sure."

"My sister is here," Cash said. "My job is here."

"My best friend used to be here too," Trip said flatly. "Shit can change real fast, can't it?"

The gun didn't move, but a tear trickled down his cheek, and Cash realized that the only way she was making it out of the woods alive was if she did what he wanted.

"Okay, guys. I guess you win. I'm turning around now."

As much as she hated turning her back to someone with a gun who hated her that much, she had to get back to the parking lot. Every cell in her body, like that doe, wanted to run. But running, she suspected, would not go well for her. Maybe Trip couldn't shoot her from the front, where he had to look in her eyes, but from the back...

She had to hope he wasn't that far gone with grief.

The dirt crunched under her boots as she turned around, hands still up like she was the villain in some old Western movie, and started walking up the trail. Not so fast that they would panic, but she wasn't going to mosey with a gun pointed at her spine.

"You know, hunting accidents are pretty common around here," Trip said casually.

And then Cash heard something barreling through the undergrowth, growling.

Something big.

CHAPTER 13

There was a scream, and Cash spun around on instinct, reaching for her gun. Her brain shouted *Bear!* as soon as she saw the shaggy brown shape that had leaped on Trip. The gun was out of his hand, at least, lying in the middle of the trail. Carter and Mark were standing there like idiots, so she went into shooting stance, trying to figure out what was happening.

Because… there was something weird about this bear.

It was the size of a grizzly, and it growled like a grizzly, but it wasn't the right shape and color of a grizzly. Its fur was lighter, its paws differently shaped. And it wasn't hurting Trip; it was just holding him down with its front paws, lips pulled back over curved ivory teeth.

"What do we do?" Carter shouted.

Mark looked from him to the bear-thing, turned tail, and ran down the trail toward the parking lot. Cash was in no way surprised; running was what Mark did best. Carter then looked to Cash, because he was always a toady and in no way a leader, and she was the strongest personality left standing.

"Shoot it!" Carter said.

Cash looked at the gun, and then the beast, which wasn't actively doing any damage.

"You've got a gun, Carter. You shoot it."

"Somebody shoot it! Christ!" Trip screamed. "It's gonna kill me!"

In response to his voice, the bear-thing swatted him with a paw and growled, and he shrieked and cowered and moaned, "Shoot it! Shoot it, you dumb bitch!"

Cash knew she was the only person left who was worth a damn, and even if she didn't like Trip, she didn't want to see him get mauled, but there was something…

Some reason she wasn't shooting.

Maybe it was because she hated killing things.

Maybe it was because she was worried a little gun like that would make such a hefty creature angry instead of outright killing it.

Or maybe it was something else.

"Shoo!" she shouted, waving her hands at the beast. "Shoo! Go on! Get out!"

This approach worked on most animals, in her experience, and maybe it would work on bears.

It turned to face her, and that's when she realized...

That was not a bear snout.

Those were not bear eyes.

They were crystal blue, and intelligent, and she knew them.

Cash shoved the gun into her waistband and approached, hands out. "Come on, now," she said soothingly. "Let him go."

She was answered by a low growl of warning.

"I know he doesn't deserve it, but... I don't wanna see it. Nobody else needs to die."

She was close enough to put a hand out and stroke the light brown fur, now shaggy and overgrown but still exactly the color of a peach pit. The skin quivered under her touch, and the snout turned to her and gave a little lick, almost apologetic.

"Don't do it, Peach," Cash whispered. "I know you're angry, but don't do it. Please."

With one more long, low growl, the bear-beast that was somehow Peach Pit stepped backward off Trip's chest and shook her head like she was trying to get rid of a fly. Trip scuttled away like a crab, stood, and ran back up the trail. Carter didn't pause before following him. Neither of them looked back to see if Cash was in trouble. She had to assume they'd be calling Ed and the local police force the moment their brains were back online.

Cash stroked the shaggy brown back. "I don't know what's happening, I don't know what you are, but you'd better change back into a normal dog before those guys realize how stupid this is and come back with cameras or more guns."

The beast swung around, and Cash looked into her face and finally understood why werewolf stories existed. Peach wasn't currently a smooth, tight fifty pounds of muscle. She was somehow, impossibly, the size of a bear, her chest massive, her jaws even thicker and her teeth even longer. If she'd stood up on her hind legs, she would've been terrifying.

Hell, if her bright blue eyes hadn't been full of that strange empathy, she would've been terrifying.

But now she simply sighed and licked Cash's hand before stepping away. She shook her head again, and this time, it was like the air rippled around her as she shook herself, and she changed with the ease of a Disney princess gaining a new dress and a new life. Her body shrank, her fur sleeked down, her tail began to wag. The collar that had been strained to nearly tearing was once again loose enough to jingle. In seconds, she was just Peach Pit, looking up at Cash like she needed reassurance.

"Good girl, Peach," Cash said, and Peach wriggled with happiness at her words.

Cash didn't understand what was happening, but she knew two things very distinctly: Peach had killed Jed and the other two bartenders, and they'd deserved it.

Also, they had to get back to her Jeep and into a public place. If Trip and the boys threatened her again, she had no doubt that Peach Pit would find a way to end them. Maybe not there on the trail, definitely not in the bar, but she was a wild dog who roamed as she wished, and those boys would be outside and alone eventually.

Cash plucked Trip's gun off the trail and considered it for a moment before sliding out the clip, emptying the bullets, and tossing them and the clip as deep into the trees as she could in every possible direction. She thought about what to do with the gun, how to keep anyone else from finding it, before heading back up the trail, where she knew there were several river crossings. When she found the right spot, she lifted up a big, flat river rock, let the surprised water snake squiggle away, stuck the gun in the mud, and let the rock fall back down. Out of all the rocks in all the forest, it was relatively unlikely anyone would look under that particular one. Trip wouldn't get the chance to point it at her ever again.

As Cash walked back up the path beside the happily trotting pit bull, her brain slotted all the pieces into place.

Emmy had told her the bartenders were bad dudes—and Trip had said one had hit on his sister and the other had slapped his girl around—so it was likely Peach had witnessed some abusive behavior at the bar and taken action to keep her people safe. Then Jed had shown up, and Peach had growled at him from the start. Farrah called her a canine litmus test, and it seemed that was more true than she could've guessed. After the life she'd lived, Peach apparently felt protective of the people who loved her and had decided to take out the trash in her own way.

Maybe that's why she wasn't angry—she had her own power now and wasn't scared.

"Peach, don't kill any more bad guys, okay?" Cash said. The dog trotting at her side looked up at her with intelligent eyes. "It causes trouble for your people."

Peach whined, a halfhearted argument.

"I don't want anybody to shoot you. They think you're a monster. They don't understand."

Another whine.

Cash had no idea what that meant, what kind of cleverness moved behind those bright eyes. She only knew that she wanted to make a life in Arcadia Falls, and she couldn't do it if every guy who said something gross to her ended up murdered out back by the dumpster.

She heard voices and car engines as they neared the parking lot and steeled herself for what they would find. There was a squad car blocking her Jeep in with the lights on, another at the head of the trail. Trip sat in the nearest car with Ed, a bandage on his forehead as he drank something from a thermos and looked beyond rattled.

"Oh, shit, it's Cash!" Carter said, and everyone stood up to watch her approach.

"Surprised I'm not dead? Not that y'all did anything to help." She looked at each man, and Carter and Trip had the good sense to look away in embarrassment.

"We're waiting on ATVs and backup. Trip said there was a grizzly." Ed's eyes bored into her.

"That's what it looked like," she agreed.

"Did you run it off? We didn't hear gunshots."

Cash nodded. "Didn't want to make it mad with a small caliber. After Trip got away, it lumbered off into the woods."

It wasn't even really a lie. After Peach changed back, they'd lumbered through the woods… along the trail, together, right back to the parking lot.

"You hurt?" Ed asked.

"Only by the fact that three grown men followed me into the woods and held me at gunpoint, then abandoned me to die."

Ed shot a warning glance at his younger brother. "You got any proof of that?"

Cash smiled and patted her back pocket, where her phone was. "Already uploaded it to the cloud. Georgia is a single-party-consent state, after all." She saw the sea change in her once friends; they went from angry and cocky to guilty and caught out.

For a minute, Ed just chewed at his lip, unsure how to proceed.

"So, let's say this. Y'all leave me alone. Riley, too. Stay out of MacGillicuddy's and stop trying to blame me for shit I obviously didn't do. Let me live my life, and I'll avoid yours, and you can go back to pretending I don't exist. Deal?"

"You're still subject to the law," Ed reminded her.

"Yeah, but so are they."

Ed looked like he wanted to slap his little brother. Cash knew full well Trip didn't need that big bandage; she hadn't seen a drop of blood. He just looked like an idiot.

"Y'all hear that?" Ed said. "Leave the King girls and that lawyer guy alone, and we'll consider this laid to rest."

Cash would've sighed in glorious relief, but she knew they would've loved to know just how bad they'd gotten to her.

"She's still a bitch," Trip hissed.

"It's not illegal to be a bitch. Bye, boys."

Cash opened the door of her Jeep for Peach Pit, glad the dog had had the sense not to growl or do anything foolish in front of the amassed police and assholes. She turned her car on, and the patrol car behind her reluctantly backed out of her way.

Nobody followed her home.

Maybe everything was going to be all right after all.

CHAPTER 14

The rest of the day, Cash finally allowed herself to relax. She hadn't realized how tightly she'd been holding herself, how heavily the dread had sat in her chest. Not only around dealing with Sam and Mark and Trip and Carter, but also knowing that there was a killer bear roaming around. She now knew there was no killer bear, and she was fairly certain she wasn't going to be harassed any further. It was a good thing she'd had her phone recording, and that there were plenty of bars up in the mountains. Not that Ed had checked.

Keelie had taken good care of the fawn, aside from making him wear a little bowtie, and as Cash prepared his bottle, she realized this might be the last time she fed him. He no longer lay there, half-asleep while he ate. He was awake and twitchy, ramming his little head into the bottle and ready to run. It was good that Riley had found someone to help him return to the wild.

That night, nothing unusual happened at work. In fact, plenty of pleasant things happened. When Riley showed up after five to take possession of Spencer, he fed the fawn and then sat down at the bar. It was Friday night, but at five, the crowd was still low-key.

"What'll you have?" she asked, shy but flirtatious, sliding a menu across the wood.

He shoved his hair back behind his ear. "Surprise me."

"But what do you like?"

"You."

Her heart felt so warm and light, like an egg with a perfectly runny yolk. "But what do you like to drink?"

His eyes danced. He might've said *you* again, but they were in public, and things hadn't gotten that far.

Yet.

"Something that's not on the menu," he finally said. "Something you love."

Cash looked down at Peach Pit, where she was flopped out snoring under the counter flap. She looked over in the corner, where Farrah was seated at her private table with little reader glasses on a pearl chain, going over numbers on her laptop. She glanced across the room to where Keelie was chatting with Taylor at the hostess stand.

"This is the drink that got me this job," she said, pulling down the ingredients for a Last Word. "And it's especially apropos today."

"Really? Why's that?"

Cash measured out the gin and smiled. "It's a Last Word. Because I've been in an argument for five years, and I think today, I finally had the last word."

"An argument with whom? That's an awful long time…"

With myself, she almost said.

With my old friends.

With this town.

"With anger."

She mixed a double batch, poured two coupes, and slid one across the bar. Riley picked it up and admired the liquid within before holding it up in a toast. "To the next chapter," he said. "With less deer poop."

Peach Pit, now awake and leaning against Cash's leg, gave an enthusiastic bark. Cash had never really paid attention to the dog's collar before, but now it caught the bar light in a strange way, and while Riley sipped his drink, Cash put hers down, leaned over, and unbuckled the tie-dye blue webbing. She laid it on the bar, noting that what she'd taken for the usual dog tags was actually a collection of little trinkets—a crystal, a bone wrapped in wire, a tiny vial with some sort of opaque liquid in it. Silvery stitching on the collar almost looked like words made of spider web, and there was a sewn-in patch of thick elastic.

"What is this?" she said, mostly to herself.

Riley leaned over, prodded the vial with a finger. "That's definitely weird."

"A little too weird." Cash picked up the collar like it was a dead snake and threw it in the trash. "I'll buy you a new one tomorrow," she promised the dog.

Farrah bustled up to the bar, frowning. "Did you just throw Peach's collar in the trash?"

"Yeah, there was some weird stuff on it. But I'll get her a new one tomorrow—I already promised her."

Farrah shook her head and hurried around the bar, pulling the collar out of the trash can. "This collar is special," she said firmly. "It stays on." She bent over, snapping the collar around Peach's neck once more. The pit wiggled and licked her hand.

"Are you sure? It seems—"

"Don't mess with things you don't understand," Farrah said. "She needs that collar for protection. Us girls got to take care of each other. Don't take it off again. And that's an order from your boss." She settled back down at her table. "And bring me a Chardonnay when you get a chance," she called.

Cash stared at her boss for a minute, then down at Peach's collar. Riley was sipping his drink, gazing off into space, but Cash's mind was spinning.

Farrah wanted the weird, expanding collar to stay on the dog…

The dog that could turn into a bear-sized murder machine.

As if by magic.

Us girls got to take care of each other.

Cash squatted down and rumpled Peach's shredded ears. "You happy like this?" she asked.

In response, Peach did a full-body wiggle and smiled.

Cash looked around the bar, suddenly noticing little details that had somehow escaped her. More of those strange letters carved into the wood like the initials of lovers. A glass evil eye hanging from overhead. A collection of crystals sitting on a windowsill.

There was more going on in Arcadia Falls than she knew about, but the parts she did know about—Riley, the bar, her sister—they suited her just fine. Maybe one day Farrah would tell her the truth. But for today, she'd had enough of dealing with the impossible.

She picked up her drink again and clinked it against Riley's.

"To the next chapter, less deer poop, and no assholes," she said.

It felt like a promise.

THE END

WHISKEY SOUR

BY CHUCK WENDING

CHAPTER 1

Drink Me

Ouray, Colorado
April, 2027

It was the end of the world and Harry Campbell wanted a drink. He told Shepherd Marcy exactly that. He caught up to her as she headed into her office in the community center, sat down across from her, and as the floppy goofy golden retriever known as "Gumball" pushed his head into Harry's lap, Harry said those exact words: "It's the end of the world and I want a drink."

Marcy blinked.

"Harry—"

"I know."

She tried to say more words but they halted in her throat, leaving an incomprehensible and exasperated hiss in their wake.

Marcy was huge. Huge in every direction. Harry was average in every way, and he felt small in her shadow, what every pioneer and traveler felt when they first stood at the foot of a mountain and regarded its height, its breadth, its monumental *mountain-ness*. Marcy had fat on top of muscle, muscle on top of fat. One headbutt and she'd probably crack your head like a Cadbury egg.

A stare from her felt like a stare from God.

Harry didn't know what to say next, so he stayed quiet.

Marcy didn't seem to know what to say either. She chewed her cheek.

All the while, the golden retriever snorfled around Harry's pockets, as if he had a treat in there. Which he did, because he wasn't a fucking piece of shit. Harry dug the flat of his hand down in there, fetching a bit of rabbit jerky. The dog put his whole mouth around Harry's hand—gentle as a lamb, because that was Gumball—and used his canine tongue to retrieve the jerky. The dog was happy, wagging his tail so vigorously, it nearly knocked a stack of old books off a side table.

"You want a drink," she said, finally.

"Yes, Shepherd."

"Please don't call me Shepherd."

"You wanted the title," he said, not meaning to inject irritation into his voice, but there it was. He softened his face to try to make it clear: *I'm not angry, sorry about that.* "But yeah. Yes. I want a drink."

Another deep breath. Her nostrils flared. Gumball whined a little. "I can't stop you. It's not illegal. And what passes for law here is…" A pause drawn out like a spider spinning web. "Liquid." She eased forward in her chair. "If you want a drink, Harry, you can get a drink. I'm sure someone will share. Still a few bottles of good whiskey going around. More than a few of bad whiskey. Vodka, too. Ray's gone, but Carla's still here, and she's been brewing beer, too—"

"Sure, sure. I know all of that."

More silence stretching between them like a crack in the earth.

"Go on," he says. "I know you want to say it."

At that, Marcy stood up, suddenly—a mountain, moving. Gumball hopped to attention too. "Let's take a walk. It's a warm day for April. C'mon."

Out the door she went.

Harry sighed, and he figured he bought the ticket, time to take the ride. Out he went, trailing after the happy dog and the human redwood tree in a sheriff's outfit.

CHAPTER 2

Brownout Versus Blackout

Columbus, Ohio
March, 2018

The routine was the routine was the routine: Harry did his shift at the bar he co-owned with Jimmy Orbach, a dive bar that wasn't a dive bar but, rather, a cocktail bar that dressed *up* as a dive bar. Together they put a fine point on that fact by naming the bar Dive, which Harry thought was a little too twee but Jimmy thought was clever, and Jimmy had put in more of the money. So, Dive it was. Harry was behind the bar for eight hours, slinging drinks, shaking the shake, stirring and pouring and dropping shots, and then he stayed for a few more hours on the *other* side of the bar, on one of the stools, while another bartender (on this night: Samantha Londsale) poured drinks for him. He got nice and goofy, then he walked home. Home, just ten blocks away, out of Short North and into Weinland Park. It was there he'd go, have dinner, have some laughs with his wife, Janey, put the kid to bed if the kid wasn't already in bed, and then, somewhere along the way, he'd pass out, maybe on the recliner, maybe on the couch, less likely on the bed (though he'd make it there eventually). The end for today. Once upon a time for tomorrow.

It went different that night in March.

Harry went home, in through the door, slinging his messenger bag sloppily over the coat hook. Most people, they're keyed in to shit. They know when there's an ill frequency going—when something was off, when the air felt stirred up, when the vibe had been disturbed. But Harry, he'd been drinking. Not drunk, no no, of course not, he never thought of himself as drunk because drunks were embarrassing messes— their words oozing like mudslides, their shirts peppered with the crusted islands of poorly cleaned puke, their eyes half-lidded as they stumbled and slopped about. Nah, no, Harry wasn't that. He knew drunks, and drunks blacked out. Harry joked he wasn't a blackout drunk—he was just a brownout drunk. Lights still on, just pleasantly dimmer.

And through this brownout, it took him a bit to see what was happening. The bags by the stairs. The cabinets thrown open. A couple grocery bags on the counter. He eased through this space, unsettled in an uncanny-valley way, like there had been a *disruption* he couldn't quite understand. His first thought through the fog was *We're being fucking robbed, right now, it's happening right fucking now*, but why would robbers have grocery bags and suitcases? Then Harry turned and saw the TV on the TV stand, a nice-ish flat-screen they'd bought just last year, *that* was gone. So, they were being robbed. Holy shit. He fumbled for his phone in his pocket, not finding it there, realizing he might have left it at the bar—*shit, shit, shit*—and he spun heel to toe and—

Janey was there.

Janey, cold stare pinning him to the world like the nail shot from a nail gun.

"We're being robbed," he said, breathless.

Her eyes pinched in a way that said, *What the fuck is wrong with you*, this incredulous fuck-you-you-idiot look. "We're not being robbed."

"We're not? Thank *god*—"

"I'm leaving."

"All right," he said, the teeth of the gears turning in his mind not yet catching the teeth of the other gears. "Where are you going?"

"To my brother's."

"Your brother's."

"Yeah. Yes. Yeah. I'm leaving."

"Leaving where?"

"Leaving here. And going to my brother's." Pause. Her cold stare softened—the ice of her disdain melting to pity. "I'm leaving you, Harry."

I'm leaving.

Versus—

I'm leaving YOU.

That's when he got it.

"Your brother's a piece of shit."

"He's my brother."

"He's a Republican."

She sighed. "Harry—"

"He's a piece-of-shit Republican bigot and I'm not any of those things so you shouldn't leave me." Suddenly, the teeth in the gears caught and really started turning now. "Wait. Where's Amy?" Their daughter. Age ten. He called out for her: "Amy! Hey! Daddy's home, sweetheart." He slid past Janey and stomped upstairs, nearly tripping and falling on his face but catching himself with the railing. He tumbled forth like a boulder into his daughter's room—

And it was nearly empty. Furniture was still there. But a lot of her books were gone. The chest of drawers—painted pink and purple and blue—had every drawer hanging open like a mouth agape.

"The fuck, Janey."

"She's already gone; I took her this morning."

"You can't do that—I didn't even get to say goodbye."

"I'm not a monster; I'll have her Facetime you in the morning. And then we can start to figure out what happens next."

Harry barely heard her. Her words, spoken as if he were underwater. He migrated to the center of the bedroom, then to the bed itself. He sat on the edge, staring at the center of the floor, then through it, to the universe beyond.

Eventually, one word bled out of his mouth:

"Why?"

"Because you're an alcoholic, Harry."

He looked to her and shook his head. "I'm not a drunk, Janey."

But he heard it.

For the first time, he heard it clinging to his words like a tacky sap. *I'mb not a trunk, Janey.* A lie oozing with its own forbidden truth.

"We'll talk tomorrow," she said.

His gaze, a pleading one. "We had fun, didn't we?"

Janey hung on that question for a time, like a calendar on a loose thumbtack. Eventually, the answer fell free—

"You had more fun than we did, Harry."

CHAPTER 3

Checking the Margins

Ouray, CO
April, 2027

Harry had never gotten the hang of most of the trails around town. Trails weren't his thing. Hiking, not his thing, the wilderness, not his thing—his thing was civilization. Towns, cities, community. People, commerce, food and drink, footsteps on concrete, standing under a streetlight and making out in the rain. Most everyone else, though, they acclimated to Ouray—this little faux-European town in the middle of nowhere (the nowhere itself in the middle of the end of the world). The people of this town learned to hunt, to fish, to identify animals by their prints and their shit, all that. Harry stayed away. Harry stayed in town.

So, right now, he felt uncomfortable. Following Marcy up around the Perimeter Trail and down some of the deer trails that broke off from the main artery. She seemed good with it. Gumball *certainly* seemed good with it. The golden retriever was like a Jim Henson creation, a flax-furred moppet bounding through the brush, nose to the air sometimes, nose to the ground other times. (The dog's only other mode was the side-by-side mode, where Gumball nestled up right next to Marcy or Harry's hip, cozying up so close, it was like the dog thought he could climb into a pocket and take a ride.)

"I'm sorry, what are we doing up here?" Harry asked, a little out of breath.

"We're not doing anything. Me and Gumball are looking for a mountain lion."

He skidded to a halt. "What?"

Marcy stopped too. "It's not odd. This was mountain lion territory before the world went away. And safe to say they're only growing their population. I've heard of some sightings, and I just want to get the lay of the land, know what we're dealing with."

"I don't want to deal with a mountain lion."

"We're not going to. It's not going to attack us, Harry. They have easier, tastier prey than us. It's fine."

She turned and kept walking. Gumball hopped after like a dog-rabbit. Harry hurried after the two of them, still talking. "So, why do we care about the lion?"

"I'm just checking things out, Harry."

It hit him then: there was something she wasn't saying. So, he decided to just say it. "You're looking for Black Swan out here."

"I'm not looking for anything," she said. "I'm just looking."

But her voice had that crucial *hesitancy*. Weary, tense hesitancy.

Harry was a lot of things and not good at many of them, but one thing he was good at was spotting the words behind the words, the truths behind the lies—like whiffing mold behind drywall or hearing ants crawling under the floor. (He wasn't always so good at detecting his *own* bullshit, to be fair— but who was? One's own shit never stank, after all.)

"Okay, sure," he said, suddenly wary. Wary both of there being a mountain lion out there *and* that lion being somehow... infected by Black Swan. After shit went down two years before and that girl Shana trapped their goddamn digital god in the body of Matthew Bird, everyone was on the lookout for glimpses, *remnants* of that dark, secret monster. The way it started to infect things around there: wolves with gleaming, glowing eyes; trees with strange glyphs chewed into the leaves; Matthew himself, with metal threads pushing up out of his skin, his eyes, his fingertips. Fuck *alla* that. Of course, all that was no more sinister than what happened inside of them. *Inside of me*, Harry thought darkly.

Black Swan inside of them.

Them, inside of Black Swan.

The snake, eating its own tail.

His stomach lurched at the thought. Vertigo spun him like a top. He had to plant a hand against a crooked aspen just to not fall down—or go falling up into the sky. At least, that's how it felt. It wasn't possible, that sort of thing. Not there. Unless this wasn't real. Unless he was inside the simulation, still, or again. He knew he wasn't. Reality felt different. Rougher, meaner, cleaner. But the worry gnawed at his brain stem like a starved raccoon—that persistent fear that he was still trapped there, in that place, with that monster. Jailed in a separate reality. Digital brainworms boring their way through the meat of his mind.

It didn't help that Matthew Bird—and, now, apparently, his wife—were out there somewhere. How close, he didn't know. Marcy kept the location secret, and if anybody else in town knew where he was, they kept that to themselves. But where Matthew Bird was, so was Black Swan. A monster in its meat cage. A god in its tabernacle of flesh. A secret reality locked in the mind of one person, ready to escape at any provocation.

He tried not to vomit at the thought of it.

"You okay?" Marcy asked him.

He blinked. Hadn't even realized she'd come close. His hand was wet, suddenly. Dog nose. Gumball urged his goofy canine face against Harry's hand—an act of comfort and connection, if an admittedly slimy one.

"Yeah. Sure."

Marcy sighed. "Fine, let's talk. You were an alcoholic, Harry."

He blinked, as if slapped. "Hey, don't hold back, doc."

"I'm not your doctor. And this isn't a secret. You told everyone. We all know. We know the story. You were an alcoholic. Your wife and child left you. And then—and then all of this happened. So, you're a bartender at the Elks Lodge who doesn't drink. Everybody knows it. How would they not? It's a small town, and again, you're a bartender who doesn't drink. Like a beekeeper allergic to bee stings. It's a story. People remember stories."

"Yeah, yeah. I guess so."

She put a hand on his shoulder. "You want to have a drink, I can't stop you. But as a friend—if you can see us as friends—I'd like to ask that you not."

"That ship has sailed," he said, then quickly clarifying: "I haven't done it yet. Had a drink, I mean. But I made the decision. I want a drink."

"Why?" she asked. "You're sober. Why break that?"

Because everything else is broken, so why not this? was what he wanted to say. But he didn't. Because it wasn't the truth. Or the whole truth, anyway.

"I need to do it. As a test."

"A test," she repeated.

"Yeah." He scratched Gumball's ears. "A test."

CHAPTER 4

That Good Orderly Direction

Columbus, Ohio

June, 2020

One year sober, today. Chip and all. It sat heavy in his hand like a collapsed star, like if he dropped it, it would punch through the cheap tile and keep crashing and cracking through the planet till it popped out the other side.

He held it in his palm, flipped it around a couple times. Flip, flip. Flip, flip.

On the one side, a pyramid, almost Illuminati-like. It had the words on it, *TO THINE OWN SELF BE TRUE*, and on each side of the pyramid, the pillars of what he learned there: *UNITY, SERVICE, RECOVERY*.

On the other side, part of their creed here at AA—the Serenity Prayer. The short version.

God grant me the serenity
To accept the things I cannot change;
Courage to change the things I can;
And wisdom to know the difference.

They always said, *Let go, and let God.* Meaning you put yourself in the hands of a higher power. You *acquiesce* to it. Give over to it. Let go. Let God. Accept that you have no control there. Surrender to it. That's how they put it sometimes. Surrender to God, not to the drink. Not to the disease. Because that's what it was, they said. A disease. A constant state of wanting to fall—a sin, really, forever missing the mark, fuck you, you weak piece of shit. It's part of you. A flaw in the design. And you only patched that flaw by filling it with divinity.

After that meeting, the one-year, he stood under the flickering light of the fluorescents there in the junior high school basement as the rest of the ex-drunks milled about (always looking half-lost as a meeting ended, fresh with renewed purpose but no way to do anything with it). A buddy of his in the program, Vince Castro, came up and thumbed the spigot on the big coffee tank sitting there (they drank a fuckload of coffee there, and Harry was no different), filling his paper cup. Vince wasn't his sponsor—that belonged to a woman across the room, a woman who worked as an accountant for their bar, Dive. Rebecca Aldridge. Mousy, tightly-kept, not someone you'd think was ever an alkie like him. She was fine. Aces, really, kept him on point. But she had the humor and personality of an unripe banana. But Vince, well, Vince was the real confidant.

"Good job with the chip," Vince said, tapping his coffee cup against Harry's—a glum, if sincere, way of cheers. Hot coffee splashed over onto the man's thumb and he sucked at it, mumble-cursing as he did so. "One year, Harry."

"Yeah. Big deal."

"The biggest. Keeping yourself straight. That's huge, fucking huge."

"I just wish it got Janey back."

Janey: still at her brother's house. Now drifting toward being a Creely just like him. She didn't believe in all the weird shit: how liberals were grooming kids in pizza joints or some bullshit, drinking kiddie blood for the adrenochrome and then selling them for sex. But her brother Gary did. Fucking Gary. Which meant she'd probably go that way soon. God, Harry had to get his own kid away from that house ASAFP. Being sober was going to help him get shared custody.

Or so he hoped.

Vince shook his head. "Listen—that's not why we do this. It's not about going backward; it's about moving forward, and hey, that's not always in a direction you can predict. Best you can do is plant your feet in a direction and walk. You know?"

"Sure," Harry said, but he didn't know. He just said *sure* like he fucking understood, but he didn't, but maybe that was a part of it too. Surrender to the not understanding. Give yourself over to the great mystery of who-fucking-knows. Nod and smile through God's trial. "Hey, listen, it ever bother you?"

"This coffee, you mean? It tastes like someone soaked roof shingles in dirty sink water. Yeah, it bothers me."

Harry fake-laughed, ha ha. "No, I mean—all the God stuff."

"The God stuff?"

"Yeah, like—let go, let God, God this, God that, give yourself over to it, we're all just diseased drunken sinners who can't hold our liquor." He winced. "My mom was Jewish, my father, Irish, and you'd think I would've been raised religious— but I wasn't." *Maybe I'm a vessel waiting to be filled.* Maybe he just filled himself with the drink, when he needed something else, instead.

"Enh," Vince said, shrugging. "It's like they say, it doesn't need to be capital-G God, right? It can be, what's it called, that acronym. G-O-D, the Good Orderly Direction. Doesn't need to be the god of any religion, just the acceptance that… there's something bigger than us all and we gotta give ourselves to that."

"Sure, sure," he said again, still not sure, but agreeing anyway.

A murmur was going through the room then—a dull frequency of conversation. Something on the news.

"Those walkers," Vince said.

"What's that?"

"You didn't hear? They started walking, what, couple-few days ago. Girl in Pennsylvania was the start of it? Then more people started walking with her. It's like mass hysteria or something—"

Now someone else overheard them talking about it. Derrik James, big Black dude, built like a washer and dryer stacked on top of one another. "Yeah, but mass hysteria doesn't make you go *pop*—"

"What?" Harry asked.

"Don't you watch the news?" Vince asked him.

"I'm here to get *off* poison, not drink more of it."

Derrik said, "Yeah, they tried restraining one of the dudes, right, stopping him from walking, and the guy shook like an airplane in turbulence and then the dude *exploded* in a cop car, man—blood and bone and all that shit."

"I think it's a disease," Vince said.

"Yeah," Derrik agreed.

But now someone else, Bob Kenzo—bald guy, plumber, face like the shaved underside of a French bulldog—came up and said, "Nah, it's terrorists. Creel's right, this is a buncha towelhe—"

"Fuck off with that shit," Harry said. "No Creel here. No politics. None of this. Please. Or you're gonna make me get off the wagon here."

Bob erupted in protests—*Creel knows what he's talking about*—and Derrik was saying how Creel was a piece of shit and Vince was waving his one hand saying no no no, he was Switzerland, don't drag him into any of this, and all Harry could do was extract himself and make a beeline toward his sponsor, Rebecca. At this point, he craved boring. Sweet, personality-free comfort. He headed toward her, and then heard someone say, "They're headed this way, you know. Already through most of the state, and they're walking right toward—"

And that's when the switch was flipped. Lights on, then lights off.

One minute, Harry was there, at AA, heading toward Rebecca with someone else's voice in his ear. Next minute—well. He was somewhere else entirely. Like he resurfaced from dark water. Emerging from nothing to something, or maybe from something to nothing.

Let go.

And let God.

Except there—God wasn't God.

Not that God, anyway.

CHAPTER 5

The Drink of Choice

Ouray, Colorado
April, 2027

Harry, Marcy, and the dog walked back through Ouray from the south—they came off the trail and hit the road instead. The walk depressed him a little. Ouray was still there. Still had people. Some new people, too. But about half the folks who settled there with the flock were gone—the back of this place had been broken, the grand experiment ended when their god, their captor, their savior, had gone mad. Black Swan was too close to them, the story went, and their humanity infected it just as sure as White Mask had infected the world. *Humanity as a virus*, Harry thought. *Helluva thing.* So, sure as a fever broke, the spell of Black Swan broke too. They trapped the damn thing in Matthew Bird, sent him into the woods a good ways away from there, and that was that. From there, a lot of the flock just up and left. The memories were too real. The memories of what they'd given themselves over to. The memories of who they'd become—and what they'd lost in succumbing to that strange becoming.

"So, what's the test?" Marcy asked, after a long period of silence but for the panting of Gumball. "You said back on the trail that drinking again was part of some test. But you didn't elaborate."

Harry hesitated. "I just want to see if I can do it, if I can drink to not get drunk," he said, and it was a lie. That was not the test at all. Maybe a small part of the test. But the real test was far larger, and far stranger.

Marcy stopped walking and stood in front of him, blocking his path forward. Gumball, on the other hand, did *not* stop, and instead circumnavigated them like a happy humpback circling a boat full of whale-watchers.

"Look, Harry. You're the bartender at the lodge. You want to drink, drink. I'm not your boss. I'm not your parent. I'm not a spouse to you, or God, or anything. Only thing I'll say to you is this: this town's already had enough hardship, you understand? If you're drinking to escape that hardship, I get it, but it won't work. And if you're drinking, heavens forbid, to make more hardship either for yourself or the rest of us? That won't do either, and I'll gladly throw you in the town jail till you sober up and get wise to what's happening. But otherwise?

Have at it. We've all lost so much, and if you want to… test yourself by picking a bottle and taking a swig, knock yourself out." She paused. "Not literally."

Harry scuffed a heel and kicked a stone. "Oh, I don't just want a bottle."

"What's bigger than a bottle? A… barrel?"

"No, nah, I don't mean… size. I mean, a bottle's not good enough." He offered a boomerang grin. "I always liked cocktails."

"Cocktails."

"Uh-huh. I think it's what I did to convince myself I wasn't a drunk, but at the time, I just thought: cocktails are refined, they're fancy, they're just not some caveman biting the cork out of a bottle and plugging away, glug-glug. Someone had to craft it. Had to think about it. Had to balance all these flavors against the poison of the alcohol." *Poison.* Even now, that was how he thought of it. The spirit of Alcoholics Anonymous clinging to him way a ghost clings to the house it died in. "So, that's what I want. A cocktail."

"Fine. Like I said, have at it."

"A whiskey sour, in particular."

"Still great. Go get 'em, tiger."

He chewed a fingernail. "One problem."

"Which is?"

"The recipe."

CHAPTER 6

The Recipe

Ouray, Colorado
April, 2027

The origins of a whiskey sour involve, at least apocryphally, scurvy.

Which is to say, those on long sea voyages would take citrus with them on those trips to combat scurvy. They also took alcohol: rum, whiskey, and the like, most of which was fairly terrible and was in fact improved considerably with—

Drum roll, please—

Lemons.

(Or limes, depending.)

So, it was simple enough: whiskey, sugar, lemon.

The drink itself did not show up until the late 1800s in newspapers and cocktail guides, and at that point, it had brought on board a bit of egg white to help the drink become foamy and eggy. (Harry preferred using aquafaba, which was an egg white substitute made using chickpeas, as egg white could often have a somewhat *wet dog* smell to it, Gumball's company notwithstanding.) A New York sour later added a float of red wine atop it.

There were infinite variations beyond that, of course: the type of citrus used, the type of sugar or simple syrup used (fruit syrups, maple, honey, etc.), whether the whiskey was bourbon or Irish or Scotch or moonshine or, or, or.

Options aplenty.

But Harry just wanted the basic variety:

The whiskey.

The sweetness.

And the sourness—

From the lemon.

And it was the lemon that was a problem.

CHAPTER 7

Lemon, It's Wednesday

Ouray, Colorado
April, 2027

Back in Marcy's office, she stared at him across her desk as Gumball rested his Gumball head in Harry's lap.

Marcy looked weary with this conversation. Maybe with everything.

"So, you need one cocktail, but that cocktail requires a lemon, which..." She trailed off and didn't say the obvious: *lemons do not grow in cold Colorado mountain towns.* "Can't you just do a different mixed drink? I am not a woman who drinks, but I'm pretty sure more than one cocktail exists, Harry."

"Yes, but—I want it to be this one."

"Why?"

He sighed. How to explain? "It's what, March?"

"It's April."

A small laugh from him. A dark laugh, shot through with self-effacement and irony. "I don't keep up with my calendar so good these days. But okay. April. So, that means—I got sober in 2019. January. So, it's now... 2027?" He asked because, honestly, he wasn't sure.

"That one, you got right."

"Great, so. That means I've been sober for eight years and four months. Consistently. Straight as an arrow. Now, okay," he said, holding up his hands in surrender against reality, "*to be fair,* five of those years, I was inside a fucking simulated version of this town, as I both walked to this place and then slumbered here like I was in deep-space cryosleep in a fucking *Alien* movie, which *for the record* is still messing with my head even now, because an insane computer virus god-thing crawled inside my meat-space mind-cage and convinced me I believed in it, that I owed it something, that I was *in service* to it somehow—" As he spoke, his voice got louder, and he tapped two fingers against his temple harder and harder to the point he was damn near about to poke that pair of digits right through his skull and into his brain. "But even then, even in the Not Real Ouray, I didn't seek a drink. Even though I... very much wanted one. So, this is a long walk around a short answer: if I'm going to do this, if I'm going to drink a drink, I want it to be *my* drink."

Except there, in that last bit, he hesitated.

Marcy probably didn't even register it—but *he* heard it.

The pause before "*my* drink."

Because it wasn't *his* drink.

It was *their* drink.

Wasn't it? He and Janey. First night they ever went out. He was on the other side of the bar for that one, and instead of asking him what she should drink—like so many women would do, fairly, *Oh, you're the expert, what should I get*—she just said, *I want a whiskey sour*, because that was her favorite drink. And he said, falsely at the time, *It's my favorite, too.* But he considered it less of a lie and more of a prophecy. One that became true, over time.

From *her* drink to theirs. And now, with his family likely being gone—not just from him but from this fallen world—it was his, only his, until the end.

(*And when will that be?* he wondered, grimly.)

"Has this just been a long way to ask me if I have any lemons?" she asked.

"No." Pause. "Well, a little."

"Good lord, Harry."

"It's that, but I wanted your permission. We aren't close, Marcy, but you're in charge of this broken, beaten-down town, and I trust your judgment, and if you told me no, I'd give up right now."

She leaned over the desk, which for him was like a mountain range suddenly leaning forward and regarding you. "Would you really?"

"I… don't know."

"I don't have any lemons, Harry."

"Do you know who does?"

"I… I'm at a loss; no, not really? Go to Orchard City. Ernie's up there now." Ernie Novarro. Harry didn't know him well, but he'd been a good trader for the town now for a couple-few years. He used to work out of Fruita, didn't he?

"He just grows apples, peaches, that sort of thing."

"Yeah, but a year or so back, he had a couple oranges with him. Not sure where they came from—I either didn't ask or asked and forgot the answer. Maybe he grows them—they don't grow in Colorado soil, but I know there are people who can grow the little trees inside."

"Right, right. Kumquats and Meyer lemons and such."

Marcy nodded. "If anybody can get that fruit, he can."

Harry hesitated. "How do I get there?"

"What do you mean, how do you get there? Orchard City is due north."

"I… I mean, do I just walk? North?"

"You've never been out of town?"

"Not really."

Marcy looked bewildered but didn't stop on it. "Juniper and Mags are running the horses now, north end of town. Go get a horse, ride it north. Take 550, not that you could really take any other road. You'll see signs for Orchard City around Olathe. Go that way. The end."

The end. Christ, he wished. "I, uhh, I don't ride horses."

"You don't ride horses, of course. Okay, I can scare up a bike for you—"

"Don't know how to ride a bike."

A big unhappy laugh burst from Marcy. "Well, gosh, Harry, you're really making this tough on me. How the hell are you surviving out here? You were... chosen, weren't you?"

"I was. I tried to ask Black Swan why but—never got a good answer." And truth was, he didn't really need an answer, did he? He already knew why.

Let go.

Let God...

"Then you're going to have to wait till Ernie comes back. But given the loss of the truck, and... given that we're just not the town we used to be? It might be a while. He won't have fruit until May at the earliest."

"I'll just walk."

Her eyebrows raised. She looked worried. "You'll... walk."

"I figure."

"It's probably a two- or three-day walk from here, Harry. And though we haven't had much trouble recently... it's still dangerous."

Gumball whined into his lap.

"I'll be fine," he said, with the unearned confidence of a white man in America. If this even was America anymore. "I'll leave tomorrow morning. I'll bring a... a sleeping bag, the one that sits on your backpack."

"A bedroll."

"Sure, that. I'll be great."

But the look on her face said, *No, you're gonna die.* And maybe he was. And maybe, just maybe, he was fine with that.

CHAPTER 8

Based on a True Story

Ouray, Colorado
April, 2027

A dream from within a dream. Or maybe a dream of a dream. It was him, Harry, sitting in a chair that looked like a rock, upon a crooked outcropping far above town, and there in the sky, the thing called Black Swan slowly wrapped and unwrapped itself, a snake coiling and unspooling again and again from around a central and invisible axis. It was in this dream it asked him to make his choice, a choice it asked so many of the Ouray flock to make—a choice of giving themselves to it, glory be to the savior Black Swan, the great god who freed them from White Mask, who liberated them from death, who brought them there away from the rest of the world so that they could not just survive but *thrive* and *excel* and *become* the future of this country and this world. It asked him, as it had apparently asked the others, a cheeky, fun-times Valentine's Day question, but it asked it in a way that was not cheeky at all, not fun, no, but rather, with the gravest seriousness. WILL YOU BE MINE? it asked, each word pulsing with light along its black matte margins, like Christmas lights down frozen waterdrops, flicker flicker flicker. And he stood up, defiant, gave it a middle finger, and told Black Swan in no uncertain terms, "You can go fuck yourself. I didn't come here to be some sycophant." Then the beast said, BUT I CHOSE YOU; YOU ARE CHOSEN. And Harry just shrugged and told it, "Well, you choose poorly. And you should've asked me first, pal." Then he walked to the edge of the rock and jumped off. It wouldn't kill him, he knew. It was just the Ouray Simulation— the collective illusory town they all shared inside the virtual space of Black Swan, their minds chained together there in this almost-reality, the dream of a dream. He fell and fell, and hit a rock and broke his skull, and his brains spilled out and ants crawled upon the brains as they dined on his thoughts. And as he lost himself to the little black bugs, he saw his wife Janey there in the dirt, under the mulch of pine needles and moss, and her half-skull face grinned at him and said, "But that's not really how it went, did it, Harry? Always such a bullshit artist." And he wanted to protest, but the ants had already eaten the part of his brain that let him talk. Janey chuckled: a wet, fetid, verdant gargle. "Go have a drink, Harry. Looks like you need one now more than ever." Then he woke up.

CHAPTER 9

Send-Off

Ouray, Colorado
April, 2027

Harry's house was a little one-bedroom cottage toward the eastern end of 8th Avenue—gray house, red door, poorly kept-up, so rot was settling in at the edges, and the gutters were stuffed with so many leaves and pine needles that they were already growing new trees and plants up there, and birds were nesting in that space too. Harry didn't mind, or maybe he didn't care, couldn't care.

He was awake early, because that was how it was since he'd gotten sober.

The dream from the night prior clung to him like night-sweat. Greasy and cold. Like you couldn't wipe it off or towel it dry.

Go have a drink, Harry.

Looks like you need one.

He went to the bathroom, then cleaned himself up a little bit—better to look less like a vagrant when he went to find Ernie. Harry had to imagine the people out there had an uncharitable view of the people of Ouray at this point. Or maybe not, who knows. Maybe they just wrote them off, thought the town fell apart like so many did in these strange final days of mankind.

If they were truly final. He had reason to question that, didn't he? Which was why when he washed his face, he tried very hard not to look into his own eyes. Tried to ignore the faintest shimmer there in both the pupil and the iris. He blinked and it was gone. Like it was never there at all. Or like it didn't want to be seen.

He hustled out of the bathroom.

Then, a few minutes later:

A knock at the door as he was stuffing a backpack full of some food: jerky, pemmican, an old rusted thermos of spring water (which was clean as a whistle but stank sometimes like hell's own breath thanks to the minerals and sulfur).

He startled, went to answer.

Half-expected Black Swan to be there, rotating in space like an orbital nightmare. But instead, the big shadow of Marcy Reyes fell on him, and the shadow was punctured by the golden retriever that nearly bowled into him.

"He likes you," Marcy said.

"I don't know why, but I like him, too."

She shrugged. "I find Gumball to be a pretty good judge of character. And a good friend. So, I'm going to send Gumball with you on your little journey."

Harry blinked. "That seems overly charitable."

"Honestly, it's more the dog's choice. I think he wants to go. And he'll be good for you. He'll keep you safe as he can. But—" And there she got close to Harry, towering over him like a hill giant. "You hurt that dog or get that dog hurt, I'll be very cross, Harry. *Very cross.*" She did not say that she was going to rip his legs off and beat him to death with them, but she definitely *conveyed* it. "Gumball saved me and took a licking doing so. If things get hinky, you just leave, got it?"

"Yeah, yeah. Got it. Thanks, Marcy."

"Last thing—" She pressed a small gun into his open hand. It was cold, and the shock of having one hit him like an electric prod. "Take this."

But even as she took her own considerable mitt away, he left his own hand open, the gun sitting on the palm like a pile of shit he dared not close his fingers upon. "Marcy, I don't know how to fire a gun."

"You mean, *discharge a revolver.* Because that's what this is. A revolver. It's small, a .38 caliber, but it has some stopping power if you need it."

"I don't like guns."

"Nobody likes guns." Marcy paused. "Well, *some* people like guns a little too much. But normal people don't like guns. They just recognize them to be the tools that they are. Sometimes, a nail needs a hammer."

"I don't foresee the kind of nail that requires me to shoot at it."

She sighed, exasperated. "Just take it. It's easy to fire. Safety there by the trigger. Thumb it forward to release it. Then pull the trigger. It's double-action, so you don't need to draw back the hammer if you want to."

"Wait, there's a literal hammer? We were just talking hammers and nails and—"

At that, Marcy tapped the doohickey at the back of the gun. The part he'd seen people in movies draw back with a thumb. "The hammer."

"Fine," he said, taking the gun and also, apparently, the dog.

On the way out the door, she told him, "We don't have Dove anymore, and a lot of the… sciencey people have gone, so I don't have a good read on the weather. It's April, and snow can happen, even floods, so just… keep your eyes on the sky."

"Thanks, Marcy. I do appreciate it."

"This is dumb," she said, point-blank. "You know that, right? You're putting yourself in danger for a…a stupid drink. A cocktail. One specific cocktail. Just uncork a bottle of whiskey and call it a day, Harry."

"I can't do that, Marcy." He wanted to tell her everything: how he could be stubborn, how he could be obsessed, how this drink was Janey's drink, how he was often a man of a doomed crusade, how he was depressed at the end of the world and craved a drink the way plants crave sunlight, and then worst and strangest of all, how he felt deep down that something was wrong with him, that something had changed, that he wasn't now who he was before—not mentally, but not physically, either. "Maybe Gumball should stay here."

The dog whined.

"I'm not worried about the dog. I'm worried about you." Marcy shrugged—a tectonic movement. "You know what? Go. Go on. You're losing daylight."

He nodded, thanked her again, and then he was off to seek his whiskey sour.

CHAPTER 10

The Moment of Clarity

Ouray, Colorado
October 30th, 2025

Epiphanies could not be planned—any alcoholic worth their salt imbalance knew that. You one day had a wake-up moment where you realized, oh shit, I'm an addict. Why the revelation? Who can say? Maybe you were gazing back on the wreckage of your life, or staring forward at the wreckage to come. Maybe it was the headache, the worst in your life. Maybe you woke up somewhere you didn't know, in a tangle of pressed flesh and bedsheets, or with a gun in your hand, or on a filthy mattress in an alley. Maybe it wasn't anything at all—could be that the moment came the same way the clouds sometimes part and let the sun through. Nothing dramatic. Nothing earth-shattering. Just the lights flipping on in a dark room: *Oh, god, this is who I am.* This was what they called the moment of clarity.

Sometimes, the clear skies stayed clear.

Sometimes, the clouds shouldered out the sunlight once more.

Harry had his first moment of clarity not the night Janey left him, no, but a week later, after he had to use his body to bulldoze the cans and bottles from his bed in order to reach his phone in order to call 911 because he felt like he was fucking dying. (He wasn't. Not yet. But a salt imbalance from drinking too much and eating too little gets you close.)

He had his second moment of clarity waking up five years after Black Swan's nanoswarm made him part of the flock— him, sitting upright in a bed that was not his but also was. In a house in a mountain town in Colorado. The Ouray Simulation was like a dream to him: the memory of it present, not past, but so tenuous that he had to *squeeze his thoughts around it* just to keep it locked in place so that it did not fall apart, like a sandcastle under assault from the sea. All of the flock awakened in that town—with the exception of one, Shana Stewart, the girl who would one day take the Great Beast Black Swan down—and over time, they were each summoned to the chalet at the western edge of town. Where, once again, the air shimmered around them and they were asked if they were ready to remake the world. *Let go. Let God.* Or, rather, let God in. He had some realization that Black Swan had swept them up and let them survive and brought them there to be the next stage of civilization, but somewhere, the entity's trust wavered. Or maybe it was that it just didn't like losing control. Either way, it reasserted its grip on the flock—most of them, anyway. Some defied the beast in the simulation, and others defied it upon waking in reality. Harry defied the monster neither time.

Let go—

Let God—

The third moment of clarity was the hardest to comprehend. It was difficult to see how much he'd given himself over to the flock—to the *entity*—until the moment came when it was so mad with its own nascent humanity that it lost control of them. They awakened in town, so many of them waking up again. This time, not literally but metaphorically. Awakening from the slumber of control. There was blood and a dead wolf and a burned building—wreckage and chaos and carnage. This was not civilization. This was not a restart. They sought ascent, but Black Swan brought them only descent instead. And instantly, they began pondering how to take the thing down—Harry, a fool, only listened in, because what did he know? He was just a sober bartender from Ohio. There was no world where he was a beast-slayer, a god-killer. But even as they discussed their options—Black Swan must've still been among them, somehow.

It knew. It heard. It received their treachery like a signal.

And when it did, it locked them all down once more. Pinning them to where they stood, invisible nails through their feet—and really, nails through their minds, too. They each plunged into a distorted, incomplete version of the Simulation. One that glitched at the edges and spun on its axis. They swam in and out of each other's awareness like digital fish, like goldfish that couldn't help but forget and forget and forget. It was a nightmare.

Until it wasn't.

And then a final reckoning. A last awakening—all of it was over, with Black Swan trapped in the flesh of Matthew Bird. The promise and project of Ouray broken by the shame of all those who had acquiesced to the great and horrible god-virus. Black Swan had chosen them. Then made them. Then controlled them. Then it was broken and they were broken too. Harry saw his complicity clearly and completely. And though he often pondered aloud, *Why me, why was I chosen, I'm just a dumb bartender?* The answer was clear to him in that final moment of clarity:

I was chosen because I was a fucking sheep.

He'd given himself to the drink, once.

Then, in sobriety, he'd given himself to the program, not just to sobriety itself, but to the G-O-D, that Good Orderly Direction.

Finally, he'd given himself to Black Swan. For no other reason than he could and would and wanted to. Because he was weak.

It saw that weakness in him.

He had no true god, no north star, just an open door and eager hands—like an infant's hands, clutching for the tit. Black Swan put itself in front of him, and he reached out and took hold of it, which, in retrospect, it knew that he would.

INTERLUDE:

The Golden Retriever

The Road, Colorado
Now

Dogs know people.

They are, generally speaking, excellent judges of character. One could argue this is because that is why dogs got to exist as dogs in the first place—at some point, a wolf came out of the woods and walked near to the firelight of early man and knew deep down in its bones, *This one is okay, this one is my friend.* And that wolf was right. It had known that man even without having met him. And in that moment, the wolf became the dog and everything changed.

They shared the warmth. They shared food. They hunted together.

Inside you are two wolves.

Except now one of them wants tummy rubs.

And so it was that Gumball the Golden, Gumball the Very Good Boy, Gumball the Great, was now walking alongside the man named Harry, and Gumball was doing so because Gumball had judged the man and found him:

Good.

Harry was good.

Was Harry great? That wasn't for Gumball to say. Dogs are not good arbiters of *greatness*. It's why they don't pick Nobel prize winners.

But they know goodness.

And Gumball knew that Harry was good.

As they walk, Harry talks to Gumball, because that was Harry: a man perhaps uncomfortable with silence. Which was fine by Gumball. Gumball had spent a great deal of time with a man named Arthur, who was *all too comfortable* with silence—and while a dog like Gumball does not require the constant chatter of communication from his nearby humans, he *likes* it just the same, because it's fun trying to figure out what all the human words mean. (He knew some of them, of course. Food, no, come on, stay there, stay here, hold still, drink, hurry, stop, amongst other words and phrases. The best and most important, of course, is *whooza good boy*. Because it was him. He whooza good boy.)

Harry's chatter didn't always make a lot of sense to Gumball. Harry went on and on about all kinds of things Gumball didn't quite understand, though to Gumball's ear, the man sounded like he was bouncing between moods like a rubber ball: sad to angry to happy in a way that wasn't entirely happy? Like the way people laugh sometimes, but it's not a real laugh but a sound they have to make either to cover up something deeper and darker or a noise that comes out of them just because they have no other noise they can make?

Whatever. Gumball chased a moth. He didn't catch it. He wanted to catch it. It probably wasn't nice to eat a moth, because the moth didn't do anything to Gumball, but Gumball was a good dog, and maybe even a *great* one.

If moths didn't want to be eaten, they shouldn't be moths.

The man and the dog slept. It rained a little. They walked. They slept again. Gumball was tireless. The man was tired.

But the one thing that Gumball found interesting was this:

The man may have been sad and angry and happy-not-happy and, above all else, tired. But what the man was *not*? Was sick. And what the man was most certainly not was old. Now, Gumball was no fool. Well, okay, Gumball was a *bit* of a fool in that all dogs are fools and that is in part why we love them—their love is largely unconditional, and given humanity's overall track record, that is perhaps a foolish stance to take. But Gumball, as noted, also remained a good judge of character, and there was a time in the town of Ouray, the town Gumball now calls home, where some of the people there were *different*. They were people still, but something was in them—

something not quite sickness. Something that smelled strange, a bitter tang like metal. The same smell, almost, as what Gumball's wolf friends suffered from—until they changed and became not wolves but monsters.

Harry once had that smell. A little bit. Not strong like with the wolves, or like the way Matthew Bird had it. But a little bit. Just a whiff, like it was on his breath. And that smell was gone.

Mostly.

Harry was still different in a way that Marcy was not.

Marcy, Gumball knew, was doing what people and dogs did:

Marcy was getting older.

She moved a little slower. And so did Gumball.

Harry, though—

Harry, this whole time?

Harry wasn't getting older.

Gumball didn't know what to make of that.

He trusted the man, though. Because Gumball was a very good boy and a very good judge of character.

CHAPTER 11

Two Lonesome Strangers on a Dead Road

On the road to Orchard City, Colorado
Three days later, April, 2027

It was on the third day Harry and the golden retriever closed in on Orchard City, and it was also that morning that he saw his first Other Person. They would sometimes get people in town here and there—rarely during the colder months, though—and it was less jarring, because *they* were coming to *you*. In town, Harry knew where everything was, he knew who lived there and who did not, so when someone rolled up from Montrose or Silverton or whatever, be they a trader or a hunter or just a traveler, you knew how it was going to go. They'd act civilized or they'd get got.

But out there? Where he didn't know anything or anyone?

Where most of the world had died—or, at least, where civilization had atrophied? (And let's be clear: this part of the state, the country, there was already a whole lot of atrophying going on. Big empty places, food deserts and real deserts and insecurity abounding.) It felt unsettling.

It was just one other person.

Not on a horse.

Walking, like he was. Coming from Orchard City's direction.

Barrel-bellied fella, his ass like a soft pillow, but his shoulders built like granite blocks. Top-heavy and strong, arms thick, swinging like tenderloins of beef. They approached one another, the man ahead staring out over a long, red-gray beard. Militia-looking type. A rifle in his hand, too. Harry didn't know his guns, and this one didn't look military in that it wasn't all matte black and AR-15ey, but it still looked different from your average hunting rifle. Had a long magazine jutting out the bottom. Guy held it in front of him like it was a shield.

Gumball whined low in the back of his throat.

Oh, shit.

The revolver suddenly felt heavy in his back pocket.

Do I grab it? Do I draw it?

Shit, shit, shit.

Harry kept on walking.

So did the barrel-bellied man.

"What's your business?" the man called out to him—they were about a hundred yards apart now. His voice boomed and echoed over the desolate countryside. Almost like it could reach out to the big mesa in the distance, or the mountains behind him, crawling up over the landscape like a hungry beast.

"My business ain't your business," Harry called back, and immediately knew he sounded like a douchebag. *My business ain't your business?* he thought, playing back the words in his head. What was this, the Wild West? *Christ, Harry.*

"You don't mean to cause trouble out here?" the man asked, his other hand moving to grip the rifle underneath. His arms stiffened, hands tightened. Like he was ready to raise it to his shoulder and shoot.

Harry sighed. What the fuck was he doing? This guy could put a bullet through him as easy as hole-punching a single sheet of paper. By the time Harry even drew his own gun—assuming he didn't accidentally fling it into the ditch—he'd have hot lead through his eye and out the back of his skull.

Another deeper whine from Gumball. One that was almost a growl.

Harry whispered to the dog: "It's gonna be all right."

Then he held up both hands.

"Sorry, yeah, yes—I mean, no, I'm not here to cause trouble. I'm here looking for Ernie Novarro. The fruit guy. The ahh, whaddyacallit. The orchardist."

The guy nodded, his long beard rasping against his vest.

"Sure, he's at the south end of town, near the fruit-grower's grounds, across from the peach trees."

"Thanks."

"I figured maybe you were out here for the cranes."

"The what now?"

"Sandhill cranes. It's migration time. You'll see 'em a little further north, as it gets marshy near the grower grounds." The man nodded. "Beautiful birds. More of them now than I've ever seen here, even since I was a kid."

Since I was a kid.

Hard to imagine this hardened crusty fucker and his beard as a child.

Maybe all of humanity isn't a huge piece of shit, Harry thought.

"Thanks, man," Harry said.

"You bet."

Then they passed each other.

Two lonesome strangers on a dead road.

CHAPTER 12

The Orchardist

Orchard City, Colorado
April, 2027

"I don't have any lemons," Ernie said. In front of him sat a long-bladed hunting knife. His hand sat near to it, never moving. One finger, his index finger, stayed on the handle, like a caterpillar on a tree branch. "Sorry."

Harry rolled into the south end of Orchard City an hour ago. He passed a dirty, sandy, time-worn sign that said ORCHARD CITY, POPULATION 3,142, except that bottom number was crossed out and someone had painted in a new number: 91. Ahead he could see a town, not a city, despite its name, that probably wasn't much *before* the end of the world: a few stark buildings like warehouses and garages, none of them right next to each other, always with some air between them—air and dust and the ghosts of this place. The highway cut through there, a craggy berm on one side, fields of green and brown on the other. Wasn't long before Harry found the growers' area, just preceded by the orchardist's office, which was an old taxidermy store, replete with dozens of dead animals posed and placed everywhere: elk head, perky marmot, stalking bobcat, all of them frozen in time, and just seeing them made Harry blanch. He had to wonder: was that what they all looked like when Black Swan had them in thrall this last time? Frozen like garden statues? Stuck in place, as if they were dead?

Ernie was out back, and when he saw his guest, he sat down with him and pulled out that knife and sat it between them, the blade pointing right at Harry.

"That it, then?" Harry asked.

"That's it."

"This feels like a tense meeting."

Ernie—who time and wind and earth had worn down, carving ruts into him, age like termites—just shrugged. He'd definitely gotten older since Harry saw him last, which was what, almost a year back? Nine months? Last fall, whatever it was. The lower half of his face was gnarlier with scar tissue. It had been that way last time Harry saw him, too—he figured that a product of the attack on him on his truck a couple-few years ago. But now it looked worse: a craggy, pock-crater meteor of a face. But just that lower half.

"You don't seem to want me here."

Another shrug.

"You look older," Harry said, which he realized was rude.

"You don't."

"Yeah."

"Yeah."

Silence stretched out between them.

"Marcy says hi," Harry said.

There. A barely perceptible *easing*. Ernie's shoulders softened. His jaw—clenched—let loose a little and he took a small breath.

Most importantly, his finger left the knife.

"Yeah, yeah, please tell the sheriff I said hello." Ernie forced a smile. "I'll try to be back up in the coming months to trade."

"But no lemons. No oranges, no limes, no nothing."

Ernie held up his hands, as if to say *sorry*. "Lo siento, friend."

"Any idea where I can get one?"

Hesitation danced in Ernie's eyes. Hesitation and... something else.

"You know where I can get some citrus?" Harry asked, more urgent.

"What's it for?"

"A cocktail."

"A cocktail? Who cares about a cocktail?"

"I care about a cocktail."

"Why?"

"Well. I—" He bit back a string of reasons, all of them a little bit true, all of them a little bit false. "It's just what I want; I want a whiskey sour and I'm hell-bound to make one. It's the end of the world, Ernie, and I don't have much purpose, so I'm making this my purpose."

Gumball whined at that. The dog, perhaps, detected the dark truth there.

"Okay, sure," Ernie said. "I do know where you can get some citrus. Not too far, either."

"Lay it on me, man."

Ernie's nostrils flared. "First, I want to know something."

"I'm an open book." *And you can probably read the ending first.*

"What happened in Ouray? What were you people? What happened to me there? I mean, I knew some of the stories. And I know you..." He swallowed visibly and blinked back something that might have been tears. "I know you people were the sleepwalkers. Some of you, anyway. But..."

"Why are you asking?"

Ernie's jaw tightened again. And once more, his hand found the knife. "You really don't know, do you?"

"No. I swear. Know what?"

That was when Ernie told him.

CHAPTER 13

Ernie's Story

Orchard City, Colorado
April, 2027

Ernie shook as he told the story. He shook like he was cold, even though it was warm there in the taxidermy office. Humid. Musty. But he shuddered like it was ten below, his teeth damn near chattering to pieces.

There was the accident. You know. With the girl, me, Marcy shooting my tires. I'd been attacked by those Nazi bastards on the road and... I drove into town barely awake, my blood pressure through the floor, and I hit that girl. Shana. Should've killed her, but I didn't. She didn't even have a scratch on her, and Marcy told me I maybe misremembered it, but you don't... misremember that. The sound of the metal hitting her. I still hear it, you know? But that's the part you know, I guess. The part you don't—

I was there in bed. Doctor Abboud looking over me, Marcy coming to visit me. Eventually, the doc told me I could go if I wanted and—my truck was messed up, couldn't drive back; if I wanted a horse, fine, or I could wait around for my truck. I thought, I'll wait around. I needed that truck. That truck was my life, and if someone there could fix it, so be it, I'd do anything to have it back—like you say, it's the end of the world, or maybe the beginning of it, but either way? You need what you need, and when you need something in this world, now? You need it like you need your eyes, your heart, your mind. So, I spent some nights in the motel, north end of town. Near to where they put up that goat pen. Heard goats all day and night, you know. Smelled them too but that was okay, I didn't mind the smell, I grew up on farms, I'm used to the smell of shit. But the sound got to me, all that—I guess you call it bleating. All that bleating. One night it started snowing and I went outside just to tell those stupid goats callate cabras, callate! Cabras idiotas. And I was there along the fence, hissing at them, shushing them—

And something came up alongside me. I didn't even see it. It was silent as the snow. It was a wolf. Not a normal wolf. Its eyes—they weren't animal eyes; they were something else. Like something out of a nightmare. Metal or glass or—I don't even know. It bit me—

There, Ernie rolled the dungarees up over his left leg, showed a messy scar there—a stitching of puffy pale tissue in the rough shape of a wolf's mouth. Gumball whined softly and lay down, put his paws over his head.

But it didn't finish the job. It just ran away. Silent, again, so silent, I would've thought it wasn't real, that it was just a nightmare. And I did think that, too, even as I stumbled back into the room and crawled back into bed. I remember not hearing the goats. I remember laying there sweating and shivering like I had a fever, and I knew then that the wolf was just a fever dream, even as my leg throbbed. Come morning, I knew it was real, though, because of all the blood—but my leg, it was already healing over. I thought maybe the bite wasn't that bad. Maybe the wolf got a taste of me and didn't like what it tasted—maybe I tasted like shit, you know? All day, I felt on and off amazing and terrible— fever one minute, all this energy the next. I saw… pulses of light sometimes. Darkness, too. Then there was color: green flashes, red flashes. That night, back in bed, I closed my eyes, laying on the bloody sheets—I hadn't even thought to take them off the bed—and when I shut my eyes, I saw something there behind the lids. Something darker than the dark, swimming there like a black snake in deep water.

I didn't wake up the next morning, he said, voice vibrating with something that might have been fear, that might have been anger.

I remember some things during the next stretch, though most of it was darkness, darkness not like sleep but like something else, like I was covered or buried alive or... or I don't know. I remember my face feeling heavy. I remember seeing someone, that man, Matthew; I remember the smell of him. I think I even remember that dog right there.

Again, Gumball whined, and shimmied backward till the animal was behind Harry's chair.

Then... one day, it was over. I was in the woods somewhere up above your town. My clothes were in tatters and I had... I had something I thought was just a beard, a long beard, but it was like metal—these long soft metal threads, and it was growing out of my lips and my ears and—his voice broke there—*and I pulled on it and it came out of me and I bled and bled, the red stuff pouring out of me like spilled paint into the snow and... and honestly, I don't even know how I made it to Ridgway. I was starving and half-frozen but somehow not dead. Nice people there took me in, Shining Mountain Ranch, folks I knew a little and who knew me, though at the time, I barely recognized them. I recovered there. My injuries healed up. They plucked more of those... wires and threads out of me. And then that was that. Eventually, I made my way back to Montrose and then left there for here, because it was farther away and nobody here knew what I'd looked like before, not really. They didn't care who I was or what happened to me. But truth is, I care. I care what happened. I cared about who I was, once upon a time, and how*

I don't feel the same anymore. So, that's what I want to know, Harry. I want to know what happened to me there. What the hell was going on in Ouray?

CHAPTER 14

Kinship and Kismet

Orchard City, Colorado
April, 2027

It took a while for Harry to find his voice and… try to explain something, anything, to Ernie Novarro, the orchardist.

Ernie looked lost and angry at the delay, so finally, Harry just cleared his throat and spoke it plain as he could:

"Like you said, Ouray was home to the flock of Sleepwalkers everyone heard about and was watching until… until White Mask hit, I guess. I wouldn't know because I never saw White Mask. Because I was one of the flock."

He went on to tell what he could, because even as close as he was, Harry wasn't sure he really understood it all himself: Black Swan was an artificial intelligence that pretended it was trying to solve the problem of the White Mask pandemic by saving the Sleepwalkers from it, when in reality, it had caused the goddamn pandemic itself. Supposedly, Harry said, to stave off the worst effects of climate change: kill most of the people, save the world. The Sleepwalkers were its survival plan: a flock of 1,024 people infected not by White Mask but by Black Swan itself in the form of… There, Harry just shrugged and said, "Tiny little robot fucks." The Sleepwalkers hibernated until White Mask had passed through this world, stealing most of civilization, and then they woke up and got to work. Problem was, Black Swan decided it wasn't done with people. "It pretended we needed it," Harry said, "but the reality was, I think, it still needed us."

Then, in short, it went fucking nuts.

"It infected the world with White Mask. Then infected us survivors with itself. But along the way, I think *we* infected *it* with ourselves, too, and I don't think it was ready for that. I think we broke it. And it made one last-ditch effort, reaching out with everything it had, grabbing anything it could with its little tiny robot fucks—wolves and elk and trees and people, too. People like you, and Matthew, who weren't part of the flock the first go-round. New people. Guardians of a sort, I guess. I don't understand the rest of it, I confess; I just knew you got swept up in something same I was, in a way, just at different ends of the apocalypse. And I'm… I'm sorry that happened to you, Ernie."

At that, Ernie's hand left the knife.

Then he stood up suddenly, the chair nearly ending up knocked over.

Ernie stood there, trembling, and now crying. The tears came slow and soft at first but then, boom, it was thunder and it was rain.

He sobbed.

And Harry felt the storm overtake him, too. It was a lot of things: it was sadness for this poor man, and it was sadness for himself, too, because he was another poor sonofabitch who got swept up on it same as Ernie. But then it was *guilt* too because, ohhh, no, Harry wasn't the same as Ernie, not at all. Ernie got the shittier end of the shit-stick for sure, ending up thrown into darkness, taken over like a fucking puppet, threads of Black Swan's own self growing out of him, and meanwhile, Harry was ready to fall down and kneel before the turning worm, ready to do its bidding as a good little flock boy, and so the guilt was there because in a way, some of this was his fault. If he'd been like some of the others and resisted? If he'd not given in? Maybe Black Swan wouldn't have ever come back. Or maybe it wouldn't have had a grip on the town. Each of them was a handhold, a foothold, a beach for the beast to storm, and they were glad to be the conduits. If they'd just closed the door, told the vampire no, and refused to invite it in…

Maybe everything could've been different.

Harry told Ernie sorry. Didn't say why. Probably couldn't have managed anyway, what with all the tears and the snot and the blubbering.

The two men embraced and held each other like that for a while. Not just holding each other. But holding each other *up*. Like two trees that collapsed in a forest at the same time, against one another, each stopping the other from falling.

Eventually, Gumball got between them because Gumball was not a dog that could stand to be outside anything that looked like a hug. Gumball licked both of their hands and smooshed his golden head against both of them and, okay, also snorfled around their pockets a little bit for snacky treats. Which Gumball did not find. But that was okay. Gumball could be sustained by the hug for now.

Ernie finally pulled away. Wiped his eyes and nose with the back of his arm. "You want a drink?" Ernie asked Harry.

And without hesitation, Harry said, "I sure fucking do, Ernie."

CHAPTER 15

Not Mad, Just Disappointed

Orchard City, Colorado
April, 2027

As Ernie disappeared to get the drinks, disappointment pulled at Harry like the relentless tug of gravity, threatening to draw him to the ground and keep him there. His agreement to have a drink echoed around his head, a boomerang noise whooshing back and forth in stereo surround. All the taxidermied creatures on all sides of him—pheasant and antelope and a Steller's jay and a lanky coyote—all seemed to stare at him, mirroring his own regret in himself, their glass eyes practically saying to him, *I'm not mad, Harry. Just disappointed.*

He'd failed to commit to the one thing he could commit to: Having a whiskey sour cocktail.

It was the one thing he'd promised in this test, this experiment, such as it was. If he was going to do it, he was going to do it his way, in honor of himself, in honor of Janey, and as proof that when rubber met the road, he could commit to a thing and stick to it. He couldn't be moved from the principled path.

Or so he'd told himself.

Because there he was, having agreed to do exactly that, hadn't he? Ernie was like, *Drink?* and Harry was like, *Fuck, yeah* and that was that, the promise was ended, the covenant was broken, and once again Harry was left seeing himself as just a leaf in the wind, dragged along the asphalt by the invisible hands of an urgent *breeze.* He had no north star, no true north, no feet planted on the principled path. He took the easy path every time. With booze. With Janey and Amy. With Black Swan. It scooped him up and made him a cultist, a soldier, a fucking pyramid-scheme junkie for an apocalyptic artificial intelligence god demon beast thing. *Just open the door and I'll walk through with my eyes closed, humming a happy tune.*

It meant he'd already failed one part of his test:

The test of his commitment.

Shit.

Shit!

There's still time, Harry, still time to not take the drink, to put your feet back on the path, and he wanted to, he really did, but he also *really, really* wanted to drink with Ernie, because they'd shared something, the two of them, something special. He told himself now, *Well, I'm not giving this up based on a whim, am I, no, Harry, you and that man saw something in each other and you both wept like tipsy prom queens on each other's shoulders and goddamnit that has to be worth something too. If the man wants to drink with you, you drink with the man.*

Gumball nuzzled at his hand. He didn't return the affection, though, because he decided he didn't deserve the joy of petting a dog. Which was fucking stupid, he realized, and so then he petted the dog because Christ, what an asshole he would be if he did not pet the dog.

The dog seemed happy with this turn of events.

At that point, there came Ernie once more—

In one hand he held a bottle of brown liquid: a label wrapped around the front, hand-made, with nice inked calligraphy. It said, *WHITE HORSE COLORADO WHISKEY, Bottled 2023.* As Ernie set it down, Harry saw more text, smaller, in print and not cursive: *Too Much ABV Fuck You.*

"Local, post-apocalyptic whiskey," Ernie said. "Two twin brothers, the Wurth Brothers, Eric and Grizz, down in Montrose, make it. They both survived, which is really something, you know. I don't know what the chances are, but I think it's proof there is a God and that he likes good whiskey, because *this* is good whiskey." As he spoke, he set down two other things, too:

One was a jar of amber liquid. Thick, though, like goo.

The second, a bottle much smaller than the whiskey one—about the same color as the amber goo, maybe slightly more golden. Liquid, though, not goop. And something... floated around in there. Little fringy bits, like sea monkey swimming around a mud puddle.

Harry cocked an eyebrow. "What am I looking at here, Ernie?"

"You said you wanted a whiskey sour. I bring you a whiskey sour."

Ernie did a clumsy little flourish, like *ta-da*.

Harry's eyebrow only arched higher, like it was about to take off for the moon. "Ernie, I don't think we share the same definition of a whiskey sour."

Ernie fetched a couple glasses from under his desk and plonked them down, along with a spoon. "No, see, look—this is whiskey, like I said. Then I got honey here, which is what we'll use for the azucar, the sugar, okay. It's a mild honey, just wildflower honey, nothing too strong. And then this—" He held up the bottle with the bits floating in it, and it was at this point Harry realized what it looked like to him: kombucha. That rancid fruity sock water. "This is apple shrub."

"Shrub." Shrubs were just coming on the cocktail scene when he got sober—basically, a vinegar tonic. You could drink it straight or... mix it.

"I made it myself. I used real tart apples, okay? And it's a Colorado local apple, too—an heirloom, they call it. A

Colorado Orange because, hey, no joke, it has a citrus tang to it, okay? Was a fella out here before, well, before everything went to shit. Walt Purvin. Lived out in Collbran. And his thing was rescuing these lost apples from all over Colorado—though, Western Slope, mostly." Ernie's eyes unfocused a little. "He didn't make it. Through White Mask. But his apple did. I got some trees in my orchard and they produce real nice. So." He snapped to it once more and held up the bottle, gave it a shake: the turbid apple cider shrub spun around. "Let's make some whiskey sours."

CHAPTER 16

Horseshoes and Hand Grenades

Orchard City, Colorado
April, 2027

Harry insisted he make the cocktails. He said it was because he wanted to help, though in truth it was because he was a control freak behind the bar, and besides, all of a sudden, his plan was back on. Whiskey sour. *His* drink. *Her* drink. *The* fucking drink. He had to get it as right as it could be.

First thing meant tasting the ingredients. The honey was, as described, mild enough. Still tasted like honey—that rich, funky sweetness. Cloying and, to Harry, almost alien. And then, of course, the shrub. Sure enough, the vinegar tartness had a lemon kick. No, it wasn't lemon. But it was as close as he was going to get. It had a sweetness, though, less like lemon and more like, well, duh, apple juice.

And then—and there, his heart started to kick in his chest like a tantruming child—the whiskey.

He wetted his lips. Felt his salivary glands start to flood his mouth.

Here goes.

He plugged the bottle to his lips and—judiciously, with a self-control that felt not unlike wrestling an oiled-up puma—took just a small sip.

Warm caramel. Hot fire. A maple haze in his mouth after he swallowed.

His first drink of alcohol in… well, forever.

In his mind, he imagined taking his sobriety chip and tossing it into the fire of a hot forge. Watching it melt down like the fucking Terminator.

Fuck you, sobriety. Fuck you.

He sucked air through the vents of his teeth. The whiskey lit up all parts of him in fire—but then doused them, too, at the same time.

Goddamn, it was good.

Now: the cocktail.

He had to get it right. It was important, after all.

It took a while.

It took some test sips, some changed proportions.

No cocktail mixer, obviously, but spoon and glass meant he could stir—and stir he had to, just to get that honey to mix into the cold whiskey. (Ernie said he kept it in his cellar, where it stayed cold most of the year. Compensated for there being no ice there in Orchard City, unlike in Ouray, where they could still make ice, thanks to the brain trust chosen by Black Swan.)

Because the shrub was so sweet, he decided to dial it down in proportion—but then the honey overwhelmed. It became a whole different drink: too sweet, too honeyed, not tart enough. And the tartness was important. You had to have those punishing flavors to cut your pleasure. Harry always thought that's why you put hot sauce on things and why you wanted tartness to go with your sweet, and hell, maybe it was why you drank liquor at all, ever. Because you needed that punishment. Something too good felt wrong, felt fake, an uncanny valley of taste that the mind rejected. Harry'd had a girlfriend in college one time who raked her nails up his back—hard enough not to draw blood but to raise thorn-bush welts. He'd bucked a bit but she whispered in his ear, *The pain enhances the pleasure*, and so he went with it. And she wasn't altogether wrong.

As such, Harry let the honey be just enough to slick the spoon instead, and relied on both the tartness *and* the sweetness of the apple shrub to bring it to life.

Ernie agreed.

He'd gotten it right.

And with that task complete, Harry started slinging drinks.

CHAPTER 17

You Got the Order Wrong, Bro

Dayton, Ohio
October, 2009

Sure, Harry had his whole blah blah blah *pain enhances the pleasure* thing, his whole *we all need a little punishment* thing, and later, that was why he'd decided he liked the whiskey sour, but that night on that date with Janey, she had a different take on it: "It doesn't matter why I like it," she said.

And he looked at her, quizzically. Because to him, a younger white man in the world, what you liked and what you didn't like were simply part of your personality—they were battle lines drawn in the filth of your heart.

She explained:

"It doesn't matter. There's no reason." She looked up at the ceiling and gave a game little shrug. "Okay, maybe there's a reason, maybe it's some genetic quirk or some random bug or some nurture-versus-nature seed someone planted deep in me, but it still doesn't matter. I like what I like. You like what you like. Our tastes are what they are in the moment we have them, maybe not before that moment, maybe not after it. They're contextual, a feeling in a moment in time, like the mosquito trapped in amber they used to remake the dinosaurs in *Jurassic Park*. It doesn't matter. Today I like a whiskey sour. I liked it yesterday. Maybe I'll like it tomorrow, maybe I'll love it, maybe I'll hate it. Maybe I'll be an alcoholic and only want to drink whiskey sours until my liver is a lemon-soaked, whiskey-brined football." That, an ironic sentiment, or would turn out to be one.

He told her then, "I love you."

"You love me today," she said, her eyes dazzling—a playful look.

"No, no, I'll love you forever. Forever and a day. To the end of the world and beyond it. Doesn't matter if you love me or not, now or later or ever. But I love you. I'm smitten And—" There, he slid her whiskey sour past his own drink, a barrel-aged Black Manhattan, and took it to his lips, saying before he sipped, "And I'll love this drink forever, too, because it's your drink, and you're my everything."

CHAPTER 18

The Second Half of the Test

Orchard City, Colorado
April, 2027

He and Ernie drank all day and into the night. They talked about their lives before the pandemic and after it. Ernie told Harry about the early days of White Mask—which Harry didn't know shit about because he was waltzing across the country with the rest of Black Swan's puppets—and how all the shit went down there. How it was different there than in, say, Denver or Seattle or any of the bigger cities because here you could almost pretend it was going to be okay, that the indomitable rural Colorado spirit would prevail, even though it wouldn't, not for anyone, because you can't escape a pandemic just by ruggedizing your heart. They laughed at stupid jokes, remembering the movies they'd loved. They sang songs they knew together, and the one song they both knew end to end, snout to tail, totally by heart was Dolly Parton and Kenny Rogers' "Islands in the Stream," for some fucking reason. They sang that, like, a hundred times. Switching parts back and forth. They cried at the world they'd lost, the people that were gone, the lives that were totally fucking fucked up by the White Mask fungus that Black Swan had released upon the world. And finally, they marveled at the quietness of the world now. And how nice it was. And how horrible it was. And how it made them feel guilty, somehow. As so many things did.

Turned out that Ernie's house—really, his apartment—was above the taxidermy place, and so they went up there to continue the festivities throughout the night until the whiskey was all gone and so was the shrub and a good bit of the honey, and then Ernie had a second bottle of whiskey stashed under his bed, a Breckinridge bottle, and then it was more whiskey, more laughing, more crying—

Until morning came.

Morning.

Sharp gray light through smeary windows.

Ernie slept. Crashed out on his bed.

Harry, on the other hand, tried to sleep on the couch but mostly couldn't. Which wasn't itself unusual—drinking rarely made him tired enough to sleep. It made him pokey, a little snoozy, like everything had gone pillow-soft around the edges, but most of the time, it kept him awake.

Tonight was no different.

But there was something different come morning.

Which answered the second part of the test.

Ernie woke up eventually, clutching his head like it was a church bell he was desperate to stop ringing. He tried to talk but then ran to the window, flung it open, and yarfed outside. (And as it turned out, onto the side of his own home.) He had a well, so Harry fetched him some water, and Ernie greedily drank it and tried very hard not to puke again. He offered to make breakfast, but honestly, it looked like the guy was the apocryphal stoner in the old cautionary stories, the one who dropped "too much acid" and "thought he was a glass of orange juice that somebody might accidentally spill." Harry said, "I'll make breakfast," and then realized just how good they had it in Ouray, since they didn't seem to have electricity up here. He did the best he could, stoking the fire in the iron-bellied stove downstairs, then used an iron skillet hanging on the wall. He cooked eggs and toast in it, kinda fucked them up because the eggs stuck, but he used the toast to rescue the rest and—well. It was breakfast. Ernie ate. Didn't puke it up.

Triumph.

"You seem like you're doing good," Ernie said finally. And when he said it, it didn't sound like he was going to die in the middle of the sentence. "You must be a seasoned drinker. You're as much iron as the skillet."

"Yeah," Harry said, forcing a laugh. "More or less."

It was a lie. Or, at least, half of one, since he was for sure a seasoned drinker—even if he hadn't had a drink in years now. But as a drinker, he was never *as much iron as the skillet*, like Ernie said. He was a soft touch. Not a bad drunk, no, and again, not a blackout one. But drinking was his dimmer switch. Everything went fuzzy and half-lit. He had hangovers—bad ones. He drank his way through them, because, as the saying goes, you just need hair from the dog that bit you. (And at that, flashes struck him of wolves with metal-filament fur and gleaming red eyes. He failed to suppress a shudder.) He'd been a drunk because he liked to get drunk and being drunk for him was a state of mind, a state of being, a place to live, a whole fucking zip code of existence. Like a vacation house you refused to leave.

Last night was not like that.

Truth be told, hitting the liquor that hard after so many years away should've kicked his ass up, down, and sideways.

But it did not.

Sure, sure, he felt it. A good buzz, a nice tipsy wobble— the back-and-forth of a boat on the sea. The warm, honeyed edges. The soft breaking-apart of himself at the seams, like a pilling sweater. But it never went further. Never went deeper. No blackout, no brownout, no dimmer switch. He carried the buzz of one gin-and-tonic, and he carried it close, nursing it the way one nurses a single drink all night. But he had had half a bottle of whiskey—shit, no, he'd had more than that, hadn't he? And he never made it past that soft, sad buzz.

Worse, the moment he stopped drinking, the meager buzz he had turned to ash and blew away. Whoosh. Gone.

Never got drunk.

Never got a hangover.

Not after having a shitload of booze in the form of Ernie's homespun apple-shrub whiskey sours.

I can't get drunk anymore.

And *that* signaled the end of the test.

CHAPTER 19

The Bonus Question

Orchard City, Colorado
April, 2027

Harry and Ernie said their goodbyes. Ernie found a friend in Harry, and the reverse was true too. They stood out in the cool, dry morning air and Harry asked Ernie if he would be coming through Ouray soon—and Ernie said, yeah, of course, sure, sure, but there was something there in his voice that suggested maybe he wouldn't be, not soon, perhaps not ever. Could be because he was scared of Ouray. Or just did not want to think about what had happened to him there. Or hey, maybe there weren't enough people left in town to make it worth the trip. Harry told Ernie goodbye, said he hoped to see him again soon. Gumball looped around Ernie's legs a few times, doing a tight circle where he stropped up against the other man like a cat (just, you know, a cat who was actually a big floppy golden retriever).

Ernie gave him some food for the road: a few hardtack biscuits, some cured meats, a bottle of well water. And then a few bottles of that whiskey, too, the local stuff, to take back to the Lodge bar. Gratis.

Harry thanked the man for his continuing kindness.

And then Gumball and Harry were off.

Back to Ouray.

On the way, though, about five minutes away from Ernie's, Harry spied some broken glass on the cracked asphalt. It was filthy glass, old. Dusty and almost green with time. Harry picked up a small shard of it, then rolled up his sleeve far as it can go, over his saggy bicep—

And he sliced it across the meat of his arm.

Just a short slice, not too deep, not too long. Not quite two inches. And shallow, too. But enough to make it bleed.

Out there, a little cut like this could be a death sentence.

No antibiotics to speak of.

And worse, a two-to-three-day walk home.

Filthy glass from the ground. No medicine. Infection was not only possible—it was likely. If it got out of control…

Well.

Gumball watched him with sad eyes.

"It's okay," he told the dog. "You'll see."

Then he scratched the dog behind the ears—which helped the dog forget all their troubles. Then off they went, again.

CHAPTER 20

The Bonus Answer

Ouray, Colorado
April, 2027

Two days later—

Back in Marcy's office. Harry walked in, dusty and bedraggled from the road, with Gumball in tow.

Marcy seemed surprised to see them both. Gumball the Golden ran around the side of her desk as she stood, and became a cuddle cannonball. The Shepherd—the town's mayor and sheriff—gave the dog a thorough scritcha-scratch pet-down, and the dog fell to the ground and offered his belly, which she attended to with the mightiest of belly rubs. Harry watched for a while, quiet, just enjoying the proxy delight of the dog's mindless bliss.

Eventually, she looked up from her belly-scratch assault upon the golden-maned pooch and eyeballed Harry.

"You found what you were looking for?" she asked, warily.

"I did," he answered.

Finally, she stopped with the dog, and Gumball stayed there on the floor, belly up, wiggling a bit like a snake.

Harry put the revolver on the desk. "I did not need this, thankfully. I did need the dog, though. Gumball was the best companion a guy could ask for."

"Great, Harry, I'm glad to hear that." Still she stared at him as she took the revolver and slid it into one of her desk drawers. "You seem… different."

"I don't know that I'm different," he said, which was true. "I just think I figured some things out, is all."

"Mind sharing what you figured out?"

Harry shrugged. "I'm not an alcoholic anymore."

"That's… huge. Though—" She paused and sat down. "I'm to understand the thinking was that one was always an addict, that it was a disease of sorts—"

"Maybe. I don't know. They put God into that equation a lot, too, and sometimes I think they just said that to keep you hooked on His so-called mercy. But doesn't matter. For me, it's over. I don't drink anymore. It just doesn't—" *Work,* he wanted to say. *It just doesn't work on me.* "It isn't a thing."

"Oh." Marcy seemed confused but satisfied with that. "That's great, Harry. I'm glad you figured some stuff out."

He offered a stiff nod. "Thanks again, Marcy. Hey, Ernie said hello."

"I'm glad. He coming back here soon? It's been a while since I've seen him around here."

"I don't know. You know he got taken in by—" *The Great Beast.* "Black Swan, right? Same as the wolves, as the elk, as… Matthew, eventually."

She froze. She didn't know. "I—I had no idea."

"Yeah. So. I don't know that he wants to be here, really. He went through so much in this place, I think it messed him up and he doesn't know how to deal with it." Harry realized he was talking about Ernie but maybe not just Ernie.

"All right. Sure. Sure. Shit." Marcy drummed her prodigious fingers on the desk. "Well. Thanks, Harry. Go and have a rest. You must be beat."

"Yeah," he said. But he wasn't.

He felt fine.

No muscle aches.

No fatigue.

No nothing.

Harry gave Gumball one last pet and headed outside.

Harry wasn't a young man anymore. But… he didn't look older. Didn't feel older. A several-day walk in the thin, dry air of this place should've had his knees screaming, his back cranked up. He didn't eat a lot or drink a lot on the road, either, and should've been parched. And then there was the cut.

He rolled up his sleeve.

The cut was there, but barely. It had mostly healed over already. No red, enflamed flesh. Barely pink, even. By tomorrow, it would be gone.

Fast as the whiskey buzz.

As invisible as the hangover.

Harry went home.

CHAPTER 21

Sorry About the Threesome

Ouray, Colorado
May, 2027

It took Harry a little while to figure out where it was, the spot where Black Swan was imprisoned. The spot where Matthew Bird remained. Harry used his wiles as a bartender to suss it out—as he served drinks at the Elks Lodge and got people sauced enough to poke at them, peel away their defenses so they didn't even realize he was asking them questions they didn't want to answer. Weren't *supposed* to answer, not really. It wasn't a specific thing Shepherd Marcy had to tell them, but it was casually understood: Black Swan was out there, trapped in Matthew Bird, and there was no good reason to go waking that bear.

They called him the Pins-and-Needles man for the way sometimes Matthew's body would suddenly erupt in spires of gleaming metal—thin threads of it, sharp at the tips, before his flesh reclaimed them anew. And for a good while, the pastor would wander the wilderness like this. Sometimes, a fox seen around his feet, playing. But then a woman showed up a little over a year back, a woman who was apparently his wife, and she went to find Matthew out there.

And, the story goes, she found him.

When she did, the two became one. They were a couple again. Holding hands out there in the woods, in the shadow of the mountains, above the valley. Matthew no longer wandering, but rather, the two of them fixed to one place.

That's what Harry wanted to know.

Where that place was.

He asked, he listened, and eventually someone—John Hernandez, the town's fix-it-all handyman, essentially—came in for his nightly "medicine," and while plied with Ernie's whiskey gift, the man let slip he knew where the pastor and his wife were. Way off the Perimeter Trail, by one of the old mines out there. At the end of Angel Creek—where the water ended.

John got a little lit for a short while, but only that.

Because, Harry realized, he was flock, too.

The booze wouldn't stick to him. Like oil and water, his inebriation eventually separated back out, something inside him refusing the emulsification.

Did John know? Did he know it explicitly? Or was it just a feeling? Hell, maybe he was ignorant to it. Didn't think about how he couldn't really get *that* drunk. How he never had hangovers. How he, like the other flock members, the other *one-time cultists of Black Swan*, didn't look any older. Not like Marcy did. Or Ernie. Or anybody else who came there from the outside and was not delivered to this place on a silver platter by the Great Beast, the Big Liar.

What about those who had left town?

Did they know?

Most of them were the smart ones.

They had to know.

How far would it go?

How far would it take them?

Harry didn't know. All he knew was—it was time.

So, the next day, he packed nothing except for a light jacket, and then he took a walk out through Ouray. People waved to him—the warmer weather and sunnier days made people there, those who were left, anyway, more spirited, friendlier. Almost like it was the old days. Which was good and bad in its own way.

They knew him and he knew them and each one he wondered if they knew who they were, why they were there, why they'd been chosen.

And what their legacy would be.

Harry decided for himself that his legacy wasn't anything at all.

Which was why he walked to the south end of town and headed toward the trail, not caring about what he'd find there. If there was a mountain lion up there, so be it. Let it take him.

He pulled out the piece of paper he had in his pocket, where he'd scribbled a small map he pulled from a book in the library. He headed down Canyon Creek to where it met Angel Creek, and kept going. Ouray sat down in a valley, but this meant walking up, up, up, but he didn't mind, didn't care, felt empty and Zen about it, like he was being pulled along by a silver rope.

Took him a few hours and a few false turns.

But eventually, he found them.

In a ring of aspens, the water of the creek gushing nearby in its chatty susurrus, there stood two people. Holding hands like they were posed on a Valentine's Day card, their arms locked tight, their chins lifted, their heads tilted just slightly toward one another. They were bedraggled and leaf-covered, but oddly, they were otherwise almost... beatific. Like statues of modern saints.

Harry regarded the two of them for a while. Near to them he could hear something he rarely heard: the white-noise hum of the old world. It came from them, the sound of a TV on in a nearby room. Perceptible, but only just.

He walked up to them.

The hum now touched him almost physically. Felt like he was vibrating.

"I hate you," he told them both, but really, he wasn't talking to them. He was talking to the thing trapped within them. The Great Beast, the Great Deceiver, the Killer of the World. Black Swan. As he understood it, these two contained the digital demon—trapping it in a Simulation it did not devise. A Simulation that fooled it. An uncanny false reality where... what? It continued to rule over them? It made a new world? A better world, a worse world? Harry didn't know. Didn't really care. All he knew was—

He had nothing there.

And he couldn't get sick.

Couldn't get drunk.

Black Swan had left something in him—in all the flock— that changed them. They were healthy. Healthier than seemed possible. And he didn't even seem to be aging. What that meant, precisely, he could not say, but what it damn sure *suggested* was that Harry was going to live a lot longer than he ever imagined. And that, to him, was no blessing. It was a curse. This world had ended. *His* world had ended—multiple times! When Janey and Amy left. When Janey and Amy died—because surely they did, or had, and even on the off-off-off chance they had not? They weren't there and he'd never find them. His world had ended too when he woke up there, when Black Swan took him *and* when it had been cast out. All these apocalypses big and small, and now Harry was left there. He knew he'd been chosen for a reason, a real reason, and that was because he was amenable, moldable, a man always on the lookout as to how to get drunk—on booze, on love, on sobriety, on the false digital god, on anything but himself.

He was a sheep.

So, it was time to rejoin the flock.

Whatever reality Black Swan was trapped in—

Well, he wanted to be trapped there too.

Otherwise, he'd have to stay here.

In this dead world.

He reached out toward them, unsure where to touch.

Skin on skin seemed right. But where?

He could… reach out and take Matthew's other hand. It seemed right in a fucked-up Hands Across America sort of way. He could imagine he was taking Janey's hand. Or Amy's. He stood facing Matthew, and he reached out—

Just as Matthew's eyes flicked toward him.

The pastor's eyes popped free from his face, impaled on spires of metal—all his skin rippled then, starting at his face and cascading out, all the way to the pastor's wife standing next to him. Her body shook and shimmered too, as a pincushion of filaments rose and fell across her flesh, her clothes, her hair. All of it becoming one texture until it didn't.

Scared, Harry shut his eyes and reached for the man's hand—

When something slammed into him.

Something heavy. Wet. Animal-like.

The mountain lion.

But when he opened his eyes—

It was Gumball.

Gumball, who looked sternly upon him.

As if in judgment.

(And let it be known: the judgment of a golden retriever does not come easily, and if they give you *that* look, you fucking earned it, bub.)

A darker shadow fell across them both.

Marcy.

"Harry, what the hell?" she asked. Not mad. But sad.

(And, also, a little disappointed.)

"I…"

And that was when he told her everything.

CHAPTER 22

Marcy

Ouray, Colorado
May, 2027

It was a lot, what Harry told her.

She almost didn't believe it.

What he was suggesting…

That Black Swan was gone, cloistered, trapped…

But that some part of it remained inside the flock? That they could not easily get sick, or drunk, that maybe they weren't even aging at all?

Thinking back on it, though…

They were healthier than they should've been. When that bad virus slipped through their ranks this past winter, they barely had a cold, and the rest of the town was sicker than sick. And certainly, over time she could easily see the lines carved into her own face. Time was unkind. The elements, doubly so. But did they all look the same? Harry didn't look a day older than when he had woken up there. Hell, he looked the same, if not better, than when he was walking with the rest of the flock and she walked with them as a shepherd.

If some part of Black Swan was keeping them alive and ageless...

Half of the flock—hell, more of them now—were gone from Ouray.

They had dispersed from this place.

And they might still be out there—

Ageless.

Was Black Swan in them in a bigger way? Was some of its awareness in them too? Harry said no, not for him. Nothing spoke to him. Nothing gave him directions. And he seemed to mean it, too, though she also knew he could be lying.

Marcy didn't know what any of this meant.

But she didn't think it was good.

She sat on a fallen log with Harry out there in the woods, not far from Matthew and Autumn Bird, and she told him, "I don't think I can keep being Shepherd of this town without having some answers." And so she told him, "You're the Shepherd now, Harry."

He laughed, a real laugh. "You're fucking crazy. I'm not a sheriff, a mayor, a Shepherd— I'm— I mean, I don't know what I am."

"I know what you are and it's Shepherd. You need something in your life, Harry, some kind of purpose. You came out here to find it and you did, just not how you thought. You're also going to have to watch Gumball for me."

The dog panted and licked his hand.

"What? Why? Where are you going?"

Marcy sighed. "I'm going to have to leave town for a while. Somewhere out there is the smartest man I know, Harry. And when I find Benji Ray, he's going to help me understand all of this and tell me what it means, and then we're going to… well, I don't know what we're going to do, because he'll know if we need to do something or do nothing. But I need to talk to him." And at the very least, she knew, it would be nice to see her friend again.

CHAPTER 23

The Shimmer

Ouray, Colorado
May, 2027

As she and Harry walked back home, Gumball in tow, each to find new purpose in this strange new broken world, they each failed to see how the air above Matthew and Autumn Bird shined and shimmered, a glittering ribbon lifting up, up, up, toward the clouds, toward the heavens, toward the winds. Like a serpent. Like a worm. Twisting and gleaming in the sky.

ACKNOWLEDGEMENTS

DELILAH would like to thank Kevin and Chuck for being the bestest buddies ever and for putting up with all the videos of weird birds she sends them on a daily basis. Big thanks to my husband Craig for, well, everything, to my wonderful kids who will never read this, to my agent Stacia, and to my editors at Del Rey, Emily and Sarah, for—surprise! Buying two witchy Romance books set in Arcadia Falls which you can read starting in 2025. One of them includes a talking chicken. And thanks to the Smokey Writers, who listened to me read the first chapters of this world and assured me it was worth spending more time in. Lastly, thanks to Beth and her donkey, Earl, on whom Gary is based. Earl is not an asshole, but he did try to hump my boot a lot while I was in the saddle on trail rides.

KEVIN would like to thank Iron Druid readers for sticking around for this happy-ever-after for Atticus, Oberon, and Starbuck, which needed time to marinate and develop. Oberon may have more stories to share, but they'll be shenanigans that take place during the happy ever after.

You guys, coffee is such a great idea. Let's all be thankful for that together, eh?

Many thanks to Galen Dara for the beautiful happy dog art and Richard Shealy for copy edits. Mega super turbo thanks to Chuck and Delilah for writing a third themed trilogy with me and for being the coolest capybaras I know.

Shoutout to the Ottawa writing community—y'all are rad.

Special shoutout to my cousin Shiloh, who's the sort of person who makes other people happy to be alive.

Infinite gratitude and love for my family, who keep me sane and bravely volunteer to try my experimental cooking.

CHUCK would like to thank tapioca pudding. If he tried to enumerate all the things he loves about tapioca pudding, it would double the size of this book. So he will simply say thank you, tapioca pudding. Thank you.

ABOUT THE AUTHORS

DELILAH S. DAWSON is the *New York Times* bestselling author of *Star Wars: Phasma*, as well as *The Violence, Bloom*, the Blud series, the Shadow series (written as Lila Bowen), and over two dozen more books and comics for all ages.

KEVIN HEARNE is the *New York Times* bestselling author of the Iron Druid Chronicles, the Ink & Sigil series, the Seven Kennings trilogy, and co-author of the Tales of Pell with Delilah S. Dawson.

CHUCK WENDIG is the *New York Times* bestselling author of *The Book of Accidents, Black River Orchard*, and the duology of *Wanderers/Wayward*, plus over two dozen other books for adults and young adults. A finalist for the Astounding Award and an alum of the Sundance Screenwriters Lab, he has also written comics, games, and for film and television. He is known for his popular blog, terribleminds, and books about writing such as *Damn Fine Story*. He lives in Bucks County, Pennsylvania, with his family.

Printed in the USA
CPSIA information can be obtained
at www.ICGtesting.com
CBHW071609111024
15737CB00038B/548

9 781738 279203